The Anonymous Prophet

The Anonymous Prophet

Tim Lezon

ISBN 979-8-9852928-0-0 (Paperback Edition)
ISBN 979-8-9852928-1-7 (Kindle Edition)

Library of Congress Control Number: 2021924002

This is a work of fiction. Any similarities to real persons, living or dead, are coincidental and not intended by the author.

Edited by Steven Cavalieri
Cover image by Tim Lezon

Published by Timothy R. Lezon
tim@timlezon.com

Visit thechildisfatheroftheman.com
and also timlezon.com

For Sanjeevi

Chapter 1

Under ordinary circumstances, Charlie Bishop handled attention gracefully, but as that solitary eyeball stared at him from the corner of the garden, he couldn't help feeling uneasy.

He stood isolated on the stage of his back patio, the sun's spotlight illuminating him through the spring foliage. The remnants of sleep smoldered behind his eyes, and he sought to soothe them with the freshness of the outdoors and the warmth of his mug. He expected to walk out of the house to find the birds and squirrels going about their morning routines. He expected to sip his coffee for a few minutes while enjoying the serenity of the scene, and then to go back into the house and get ready for work. He hadn't expected an audience, or the unnerving gaze of a single eyeball.

He froze for a second, staring at the eye staring at him. Acutely aware of his motionlessness, he felt obligated to only break the extended pause with an action of profound meaning. The longer he thought of what to do, the longer his period of idleness became, and the more pressure he felt to be deeply profound.

This was uncharacteristic of Charlie, who was proud of his ability to abandon self-consciousness when others watched him work in the kitchen. He could masterfully frost a cake under the scrutiny of a high-class customer demanding perfection on a second's notice. He was familiar with the curious glances of other commuters charmed by a man lugging a fifty-pound bag of cake flour across town on a public bus. He knew how to smile and laugh at his own situation, and how to carry on with a stranger. The gaze that he fell under now was not like these jovial looks. This was not the shallow, innocent stare of spectators distracted from the noise of life by a passing oddity: It was the steady stare of a man wrongfully condemned to the gallows. It was cold and foreign and astoundingly unnatural.

He slurped at his mug and glared directly back at that little eye in the grass. "What're *you* looking at?" he muttered in his bravest tenor, hoping his bluff would not be called, and fearing that it would. Charlie could hear the lack of confidence in his own voice. Panic flashed over him as he realized that he was wholly unprepared for any answer except silence. He filled his lungs and listened to the springtime noises. There was no answer, just the chirping of birds.

He stepped off the patio, allowing dew-covered blades of grass to slip between his toes. Walking on the balls of his feet, he angled himself closer to the otherworldly interloper squatting calmly in the corner of the yard. As he came up on its flank, the object of his focus changed unexpectedly.

It moved.

The eye turned to follow him, tracking every move of his approach. He saw it clearly now, open wide in awe or terror, staring directly at his face. He moved his head from side to side, bobbing like a lethargic boxer. The gaze of the solitary eyeball followed.

Now within a few feet of the eye, Charlie squatted and placed his coffee mug on the grass. He reached his hand forward, palm up, as if he were going to pet a strange dog under the chin. Gently, he parted the weeds from in front of the eye, allowing the sunlight to fall directly upon it. The tiny pupil constricted to a pinpoint, and Charlie got his first glimpse of the eyeball's owner in its entirety.

It was a plant – a small weed, just a few inches high. A single spindly stalk rose from a mat of flat leaves at its base. The stalk was dotted with tiny white flowers and, at its pinnacle, a little white eyeball with a blue-green iris.

Charlie bobbed his head again, and the eye obediently followed his motions. For a moment it was pure. Charlie stared at the plant, and it at him, in the morning brightness. The garden sang and bustled with life around them. This was the one pure moment of discovery, when this tiny little magnificent thing that he found was his, and his alone.

He reached into the pajama pocket and pulled out his phone, readying the camera for a video. He shot for about half a minute, making sure to get the entire organism and its response to his motions. Satisfied, he returned the phone to his pocket, picked up his mug, and made his way toward the house. This was a remarkable sight, but further exploration would have to wait: There were cakes to bake.

Chapter 2

Fat BB's bakery had occupied the same store front on Main Street for as long as anyone could remember. Emma Rose Franklin, the town's oldest resident, frequented Fat BB's as a schoolgirl, having been introduced to it by her older siblings some 126 years ago. At the time, Emma – like all the children in town – enjoyed rewarding herself with a mouthwatering Fat BB's apple cake after a long day at school. Plenty had changed since those days: Main Street was no longer the main street, children seldom rode bikes anymore, and all of Emma's elder siblings and school chums had passed. Despite the changes, the bakery that provided Emma sanctuary from the hardships of the schoolyard and the dinner table still stood, and it still served the best cakes in town.

Charlie knew of Emma Franklin, or Miss Emma, as she was affection-ately called by the townspeople, because her endorsement was the pride of Fat BB's. Her photo hung on the wall behind the cash register, above a sign declaring, "You'll have to live a long time to find a better cake!" Taken on her 125th birthday, the photo prominently featured a Fat BB's cake ablaze with candles. Behind the cake, slightly out of focus, sat Miss Emma, straining to peer over the icing, a Galapagos tortoise reaching for a cactus tucked into a high crevice. The glow of the candles reflecting off her over-sized eyeglasses conveyed the enormity of the task ahead of her.

The slamming of the rear screen door announced Charlie's arrival. He tended to get to work at the end of the morning rush, after the office commuters finished gathering pastries to sacrifice at the altars of their early business meetings. He preferred to avoid the business crowd altogether, opting instead to show up a little past nine, when the old folks trickled in. Their crowd was relaxed and either pleasant or easily subdued.

He grabbed a clean apron from the pile and wrapped it around himself as he passed from the kitchen to the store front. At the counter, Ruthie chatted happily with an elderly gentleman who was purchasing a cake.

"A hundred years old!" Ruthie said, "and you're still buying cakes for your wife!"

"That's right!" the old man said with a nod. Pointing a crooked finger at Ruthie, he added, "I've got to keep her on her toes! If I buy her something unexpected, she'll wonder what I'm up to!"

Ruthie looked over at Charlie as he entered. "Hey, Chuck," she said.

"Morning, Ruthie. Remind me to show you something later."

She threw him a provocative look.

"Not that, Ruthie." Charlie flipped through the stack of orders behind the counter. His relationship with Ruthie revolved around mindless innuendo. They worked together for the past seven years, flirting extensively in the early part, and eventually settling into a friendship. They'd even gone on a date once – a punk rock concert with a couple of Ruthie's headbanger friends – but it didn't work out. It was all for the best: Ruthie preferred guys who exhibited a level of badness far exceeding Charlie's capacity. She was also kind of weird. She took the same approach toward boyfriends, hair colors and environmental movements, refusing to settle down with any particular one, but jumping from one to another on a whim. Her free spirit entranced Charlie, but it was impossible for him to keep up. He admired her technique for turning her passions on and off, and he secretly kept his distance in order to save himself from falling in love or out of favor with her.

"Chuck, you know Mr. Wigner?" Ruthie asked, gesturing toward the customer.

"Of course I do," said Charlie. He extended his hand over the counter in greeting. "How are you, Mr. Wigner? What brings you into our bakery this morning?"

The old man's hand shot forth like a serpent and grasped Charlie's with surprising force. "I'm here to purchase a cake."

"It's Mrs. Wigner's 100th birthday next week," Ruthie added, smiling at the ancient man.

"Congratulations," Charlie said. "It's always an honor to bake for a big birthday." Tapping the market of centenarian birthday cakes was one of Charlie's most significant contributions to the bakery's business. Soon after he started at Fat BB's, Charlie introduced a number of elegant cakes specifically for 100th birthdays and 75th wedding anniversaries. When one of these won the State Fair Cake Bake, Fat BB's became the go-to bakery for cakes celebrating anyone with white hair and a cane. The bakery offered a commodity that could never be manufactured cheaper overseas: nostalgia. The super-old loved Fat BB's, their children loved Fat BB's, and so on down the line. As long as humanity celebrated longevity, Fat BB's would provide the cake and sepia-toned memories.

Ruthie hefted a binder filled with photos of the bakery's cakes onto the counter. She flipped the book open and planted the well-chewed nail of her index finger sharply on a photo of a grand three-tiered cake adorned with golden frosting and small white flowers with dark chocolate heads. "This is the one," she said to Mr. Wigner.

Charlie glanced at the book and agreed. "Oh, yeah, that's a nice one."

"A nice one?" Ruthie asked, slapping Charlie on the arm. "That's a beauty, Chuck!" Turning to Mr. Wigner, she explained, "This cake is called *Three Ages of Woman*. Chuck here designed it himself, based on a painting. Isn't that right, Chuck?"

Charlie looked up from his stack of orders to see Mr. Wigner looking intently at him. "Yes," he said, "that's right. It's based on a painting by Klimt. Do you know it?"

The old man shook his head.

"It's a truly magnificent piece. It depicts the progression of a woman's life – from babe, to mother, to – do you think your wife might know the painting? Is she a fan of Klimt?"

Mr. Wigner dismissed the question with a wave of his hand. "We were never into art. Couldn't understand it. But I'm sure that it's a great piece, if it inspired such a good-looking cake."

"It is," Charlie assured. "It's a lovely painting. The palette oozes gold, and the young woman's golden hair is dressed with little white flowers."

"The centers of the little flowers on the cake are made of imported Austrian chocolate," Ruthie said. "Austrian like Klimt himself! It's brilliant, isn't it? Your wife will be thrilled. Now, what kind of cake were you looking for? Chocolate? Angel?"

"Yellow cake," said Mr. Wigner.

"Gold cake is the most Klimt-esque of them all. Excellent choice."

As Ruthie wrote down the details, Charlie spoke to Mr. Wigner. "Now, I have to make the lower two layers rather firm to support the weight of the cake, but the top layer provides a little more freedom. I prefer to make it a little bit soft, so it can be eaten with a spoon…"

His sentence was interrupted by the delicate tinkling of the brass bell above the bakery's Main Street door. Instinctively, he glanced at the entrance. The spring sun shining through the windows masked the entering customer's features in shadow, but Charlie made out the familiar silhouette of a slender lady in a skirt and wide-brimmed hat. His breath stopped as he watched her glide through the threshold of the door in a tip-toe gait.

He knew this woman, or at least knew who she was: Beatrice Martin, who ran Rose's Floral and Gift up the street. Charlie had seen her before and was undeniably, irrevocably, head-over-heels smitten by her. He'd often seen her passing by the bakery window on the way to work, or making deliveries in town, and every time that he saw her he was dumbfounded by her beauty. He would do anything to be able to talk to her, but each time he tried he just made a bumbling fool of himself.

He hid his feelings well – or, at least he believed he did – and admired Beatrice from a distance. The only small complication was that she and Ruthie occasionally partnered up to provide catering and decorations for parties. Much to Charlie's delight and frustration, this arrangement occasionally brought Beatrice into the bakery. His standard solution was to make himself invisible by keeping busy in the kitchen during such visits.

It worked well, as she never seemed to notice him.

"Hi, Bea!" Ruthie called.

"Hi, Ruthie," she answered, "Bad news. We have to change the order for tomorrow. The customer decided that white is too morbid, and he wants everything in red now." She looked at Ruthie, and then at Charlie, who made the mistake of looking back. For an instant their eyes locked. Charlie's equilibrium shifted. All the moisture dried up from his mouth and was re-released from his palms. He shook his head dumbly and looked down, feigning intense concentration on completing Mr. Wigner's order.

"Red?" Ruthie said. "Why can't people make up their minds?"

"I know. I'm struggling to find enough roses for the arrangements. I might have to go with carnations. I wanted to let you know, in case you can change the cake. It'll really look better if everything matches." Her angelic voice rang in Charlie's ears.

Charlie did his best to maintain his ostrich-like invisibility and to not reveal that he was listening to every word she spoke. He intensified his focus on Mr. Wigner's order form, holding the pen in the most under-handedly impressive fashion that he could imagine – in the event that, by some strange cosmic force, she noticed him.

Ruthie sighed. "Well, we haven't started icing it yet, so it shouldn't be a problem to go with red."

"Great. Then I'll see you tomorrow morning. I have to go see if I can find more roses." As she turned to leave, Beatrice waved a hand delicately at Ruthie. As a courtesy, she also waved a weak goodbye toward Charlie, only to find him intently tracing all the letters on Mr. Wigner's order form a third time. She left the bakery, and Charlie – exhausted from the effort of keeping himself invisible – let out his breath. He looked up to see Mr. Wigner staring at the heavily blackened letters of the order form, confused.

"Well, then," Charlie said, "we'll see you and Mrs. Wigner next week! Ruthie here will ring you up." He placed his pen down, slid the completed order form toward Ruthie, and hurried back to the kitchen.

⸺⟡⸺

The bakery's office was a tiny room off the kitchen, cluttered with remnants of days past. Yellowed fliers and newspaper clippings adorned its walls, and a small corner bookcase held an assortment of items collected over the years: the handle from an ancient mixer, a bronzed cake pan, and a handful of trophies, including ones that Charlie won at the State Fair Cake Bake. In the center of the office, under a pile of catalogs and papers, sat a monolithic old wooden desk and a squeaky metal chair covered in green vinyl.

Charlie took a seat and began making a mental list of the day's tasks: placing orders for ingredients, trying a new recipe for rustic whole-grain loaf, finding a new service for washing the aprons. He stared blankly at the desk. What was he doing? How could he not even talk to her? He silently scolded himself for his introversion and lack of initiative. Always sensitive, he took his own scolding to heart and grew ashamed for letting himself down. In the aftermath of this sharp internal exchange of criticism and remorse, an uncomfortable silence fell within his head and he refused to speak another word of it to himself.

Pulling out his phone for consolation, he thumbed through the tiles to the photo album. He opened the shaky video he'd taken in the morning and again watched the little flower turn its eye directly at the camera. He swelled with fondness for this thing, proud to have a marvelous little secret like this, as if the flower had specifically chosen him. Maybe it meant something. Maybe there was some significance to this, beyond a weird little flower in the corner of his yard.

The door opened loudly under Ruthie's simultaneous knock-and-open technique. "Hey, Chuck, was there something weird going on with you and Bea?"

Charlie cleared the screen of his phone and quickly placed it on the desk. "Who?" he asked.

"Bea. The florist. Don't pretend you don't know who she is. You always get goofy when she's around. Chuck. . .do you *like* her?"

"What? No! I mean, I don't even know this. . .what did you say her name was? Bea?"

Ruthie laughed. "Chuck, we gotta play poker sometime. I'll buy myself a new car."

"Shut up, Ruthie."

"No, really, Chuck. You should come over to my house for a game Saturday night. I'll make sure not to invite ol' Whats-Her-Face from the flower shop, or you two might knock each other's teeth out."

"Ruthie, did you come in here for any particular reason?"

"Yeah, Chuck, you said you wanted to show me something."

"Yes!" Charlie's eyes darted around the piles of papers on the desk, landing on a trade magazine. "This!" he said, picking up the magazine and showing its cover to Ruthie.

"*Trends in Small Business Baking Quarterly*?"

Charlie looked at the cover. It proudly displayed a pompous-looking soufflé. He pointed to the caption, written in bold green letters, and read it aloud to Ruthie: "Soufflé Days!"

"Soufflé Days? Chuck, you've gotta be…"

"It was BB's idea," said Charlie, referring to the bakery's owner. He knew Ruthie's take on BB and figured that the whole idea would have less appeal to her if it came from the top. "He wants to offer something new, something that the other bakeries around here don't have. He wants us to do it so well that no one will be able to touch us. I told him I can't do it, but maybe you could, and I'd talk to you about it. I understand if you think it's a dumb idea…"

Ruthie's face lit up. "Omigod, Chuck! This is perfect!"

"It is?" Her sudden enthusiasm was a problem. He'd hoped she would protest, they'd have a heated exchange, he'd capitulate, and neither would ever mention Soufflé Days again. The strategy seemed foolproof. He couldn't find the flaw in his thinking.

"Totally! I've been telling you that our customers are too old. I mean, I love them – don't get me wrong – but nobody who's young wants to come in here and buy a cake."

"Thanks, Ruthie."

"You know what I mean, Chuck," she continued. "The cakes are good and everything, but they're what you get when you go to Grandma's house, you know? Nobody's gonna, like, hang out and eat

Fat BB's cakes and chill, you know?"

Ah, there's the flaw: Charlie hadn't fully considered the extent to which pure random thought influenced Ruthie's worldview. Working with her was like counting cards: Statistically, you might be able to influence the long-term trend with some careful thought and planning, but in the short term it's all up to chance.

Ruthie went on, "But if you get a soufflé, that's cool! People will buy soufflés! Real people, not workaholics and geezers. They'll buy them for dinner parties – or wait! We can have a soufflé that goes with grilled food – like a barbecue soufflé! So people can have them at their cookouts! Or a savory soufflé that goes with craft beer! Or maybe we should start selling gourmet coffee..."

"Ruthie!" Charlie interrupted. "Why don't you write down your thoughts on it? Come up with a list of things that you think we should try – no gourmet coffee – and we can discuss it tomorrow."

"Yeah, good! But tomorrow I've got that party to cater."

"Fine," Charlie said, "Then we'll talk on Monday." He waved Ruthie out of the office. In the back of his mind, he added *Kill Soufflé Days* to his to-do list. He straightened himself up, took a deep breath, and got to work.

Chapter 3

The sun still floated above the rooftops when Charlie returned home at the end of the day. The muggy afternoon carried a hint of a breeze, and his bike ride home from the bakery was alternately scorching and refreshing: Uphill was punishment, but the wind rewarded him sweetly as he coasted downhill. He pulled into the alley and placed his bike in the garage before detouring through the garden on his way to the house.

Charlie crept over to the corner of the yard where the little plant grew, as if approaching a bunny petrified in the grass. The plant stared at him unflinching, like a gunslinger on a dusty road a high noon. It looked dry from the day's heat now, and he wondered whether it was thirsty. He opened his bottle and squirted some water at the base of the plant. He squirted some into his mouth and stared at the plant, observing its every detail.

Aside from the eyeball, there was nothing particularly noteworthy about the plant. From its base, a clump of oval-shaped leaves spread out star-like in all directions parallel to the ground, pushing neighboring plants aside and preventing competitors from germinating nearby. Three long stalks shot up from the center of the leaf-star. Two were adorned with diminutive white flowers; the third and tallest stalk was topped with the very human-looking eyeball. In the afternoon sun, it took on a deeper blue shade than it had in the morning.

Charlie pulled out his phone to take another video. To set up the shot, he cleared some of the weeds from around the plant by yanking them up at the roots. As he reached for a particularly menacing bit of crabgrass adjacent to the plant, his fingertips brushed the underside of the plant's leaves. To his surprise, the eyeball quickly jerked away from him, its stalk angling to the ground, and the eye staring directly at him.

Strange, he thought. He reached out a finger directly at the eyeball, just to see whether it would move more.

Nothing.

He pulled his hand back, and then shot it forward quickly at the eyeball.

Nothing.

While he was in the midst of repeating this gesture several times in quick succession, his phone buzzed. It was Ruthie. "Chuck," she said, "I was thinking about your soufflé thing."

Charlie cringed. "Yes, Ruthie?" He didn't want to have this conversation now.

"Everything has to be locally sourced, right? I mean, if we're going to sell soufflés, then they have to be, like, uber-cool. I was thinking that we could try all different kinds of flavors, and even traditional things, like cheese. My friend has goats, and they make their own cheese..."

"Ruthie, this is great," Charlie lied. "Can we talk about this later?"

"Yeah. Chuck, listen. I was thinking about this. We have sources for everything but the eggs, right? So where we getting all those eggs, locally sourced?"

"Ruthie, I'm hanging up."

"No, Chuck –"

Charlie ended the call and went back to staring at the plant. He repeated his finger-flick bluff a couple more times, to test whether the plant would flinch. Then he touched it. He reached right out and poked it in the center of its little eyeball. Just a gentle tap, just to see what would happen.

The eye shut. The sepal leaves shot forward from behind the eyeball and closed it tightly.

Charlie jumped back. He turned on his phone and took several snapshots of the plant in its retracted, tightly-closed state. He immediately felt guilty for the affront and hoped that he hadn't ruined this nascent friendship, or harmed the plant itself. He feared the little plant would die, and he'd be left with nothing but a story and a 30-second video. Like a predator pursuing prey that suddenly feigns death, he lost interest in the flower once it adopted a truly vegetative state.

His stomach rumbled. *Eggs*, he thought. *Ruthie, you're unbelievable.* He grabbed his stuff and headed inside.

—◦◦◦◦◦◦—

There's something about a nice fried egg, cheese and tomato sandwich that really calms the nerves. Charlie's particular technique evolved over the years, starting from the pure necessity of feeding himself breakfast on Saturday mornings as a child and growing into a task that was simple enough to perform reflexively, yet gave surprisingly tasty results. He started with a slice of buttered toast topped with tomato and a sunny-side up egg. The bread varied according to the bakery's offerings – today it was a whole-grain wheat. He splashed a bit of Tabasco sauce over the egg and covered this with freshly ground black pepper and a slice of cheese – preferably American. A few minutes in the broiler melted everything together. Although the contents tended to slide out from the sandwich, the mixture of egg yolk and hot sauce encased the lips in a delectably sticky crust that stung ever so slightly. For dinner, Charlie noshed on two such sandwiches while scrolling through page after page of plant websites on his tablet. He browsed with his little finger, meticulously holding it away from his sandwich.

As he read through a page about carnivorous plants, his phone rang. "Hey, Chuck, listen," said Ruthie from the other end, "you know that farm off Route 108 past Meadeville?"

"No, Ruthie."

"Really?" She sounded genuinely disappointed that he didn't know what she was talking about. "You know, if you're on the way to the state park, you pass a bunch of windmills, and then there's that farm that sells all the free-range and grass-fed stuff? You know it?"

"No, Ruthie."

"Yes, you do. Anyway, they've got a lot of chicks that are dirt cheap, and me and Clyde have been talking about diversifying our poultry portfolio. Actually, he wants to get a goat, but I said that we should stick with poultry, at least until we get our farming groove going. Do you think that's a good idea?"

"Yes, Ruthie."

"Really?" Her disbelief was clear. "You don't like Clyde, do you?"

"Clyde's fine," he said. The truth was that Charlie couldn't stand Clyde. He struggled to recall anyone as vapid, yet somehow Clyde seemed to get by swimmingly. He was one of those guys who thrived on mediocrity, hugging the middle of the road with all the enthusiasm of a marathon runner making record time. Clyde had nowhere to go in life, and he was already there. Charlie admired and despised him for it. "Ruthie, what's the point?"

"Calm down, Chuck. I just want to know: When are we doing Soufflé Days?"

Charlie pushed exasperation. "I don't know, Ruthie. When do you want to do it?"

"Next month?"

"Sure. Go ahead. Make it happen." Charlie hung up the phone and went back to his browsing, eventually landing on the web site of Logan Biotechnologies, a local company. He read with interest how Dr. Phineas Snodgrass, a former professor at nearby State University, founded the company a decade ago. Its flagship product was *Apitoxincredizole*, an anesthetic based on bee venom. The website prominently featured images of happy people, ostensibly free from the multitude of worries and pains that plagued the lives of regular folks like Charlie.

When he tapped on the tab that urged *Contact Us*, he was presented with a form for sending suggestions and inquiries via the website. He entered his email address, and in the blank space provided for text, he entered:

Found: A plant with an eye. Is it yours?

He sent his message into cyberspace and remained hunched over the tablet at his table, dirty plate nearby, until sleep got the better of him.

Humm-mmm-mmah! Humm-mmm-mmah!

Charlie's phone grunted and pushed itself across the nightstand, basking his bedroom in the soft glow of its touch display.

Humm-mmm-mmah! Humm-mmm-mmah!

He grabbed the phone and looked at its face. Ruthie's profile picture smiled back at him. He cleared his throat. "Hello?"

"Chuck! Sorry if I woke you. You know those guys? At the farm? With the chickens? They make their own booze!"

Loud talking and laughter filled the background on Ruthie's end. Charlie looked at the old clock radio next to his bed. It was midnight. "Ruthie, don't you have to work tomorrow?"

"Their own booze, Chuck!" Ruthie continued. "I wonder if we can use it in cake. You know, like rum cake?"

"I don't know, Ruthie. Listen, it's late, and I need to sleep. Can we talk in the morning?"

"Don't be such a grump. This is why you don't have a girlfriend."

"Because I don't like it when people wake me up in the middle of the night with stupid questions?"

"Yeah, exactly that. You know, you need to relax and get out more. I can set you up with a friend."

"No, thanks, Ruthie. Last time we tried that I got stood up at the movies."

"You mean Jessica? Yeah, she's kind of a bitch, anyway. But seriously, Chuck, I can set you up with someone nice. Like Bea."

Silence.

"Chuck?" Ruthie asked.

"Ruthie, go to bed." Charlie hung up.

Humm-mmm-mmah! Humm-mmm-mmah!

Charlie grabbed the phone, glimpsed Ruthie's face on the screen and answered. "Goddammit, Ruthie, that's enough! Stop calling!"

"Chuck," Ruthie said, "I need you to cover for me."

"What? Ruthie? Knock it off!"

"Chuck, listen." she sounded anxious. "I've been arrested. You're the one call that I have."

Charlie sat up in bed. "What?" He was still mad at Ruthie. In fact, he was more mad at Ruthie that she possibly managed to get herself arrested, and even more so that she'd do it on a work night.

"It's a long story, and I don't have much time, but these *dickhead cops*," these last words she shouted away from the phone, seemingly to get the attention of someone on her end of the line, "won't let me leave the station tonight. Something about being too drunk and possibly stealing more turkeys. I convinced them to let me call you."

"Ruthie, do you need bail or... wait, did you say turkeys?"

"Long story, Chuck."

"Do you need me to come and pick you up?"

"No, we've got Clyde's truck. I'll just hang out in this shithole for the night. But there's one thing that you can do for me, Chuck...I'm supposed to cater a party tomorrow. Can you do it?"

Charlie clenched his teeth. "Dammit, Ruthie..."

"Come on, Chuck. It would mean so much to me. And I'll do anything – whatever you want. I'll owe you. You *have* to do it. Come on, Chuck..."

"Fine," he said, mostly just to get her to shut up.

"Great, Chuck, thanks. The info's at work. I've gotta go. Sergeant Dickhead is giving me the stink eye." Ruthie seemed to pull the phone from her mouth before screaming the last lines that Charlie heard before the call was dropped: "Keep your goddamn jockeys on, you mustachioed freak! I'll get off when I'm goddamn good and – "

Click.

Charlie checked the clock. Three AM. He could still get a few hours' sleep before heading to the surprise catering job.

Chapter 4

Charlie rode his bike slowly the next morning to keep the dirt off his clean, white shirt. His hands numbed against the bike's grips as the breeze swept over them. Evidence of the emerging spring peppered the lawns with purples and pinks – creeping phlox in mulched beds welcomed the eyes and led them up to azaleas blooming next to houses. Early buds peeked out from the foliage of lilac bushes, here and there blessing the breeze with their fragrance. The closed caps of dandelions perched on their stalks speckled about the lawns, poised to open to the day's full sun. The flowers and wet asphalt smelled of winter's finality.

Charlie's usual route into town took him past an old church on top of a hill. On the lawn in front of the church stood a white sign with removable black letters. Today the sign read:

KNOWLEDGE IS A FOUR-LETTER WORD

but the baker gave it little thought. Throughout the night he sparred with various ideas of how to approach Beatrice, imagining the details of their meeting. Each conversation he pictured with her started smoothly and ended in his humiliation. He grew increasingly nervous as the nighttime darkness gave way to the first light of day, and dawn offered no consolation.

By the time Charlie arrived at Fat BB's, Sierra had already baked and frosted the day's cake. She was one of the *cupcakes*, as Ruthie and Charlie affectionately referred to the group of coeds who worked the counter. The bakery's owner demonstrated a penchant for hiring buxom females within a year of turning twenty, nearly all of whom studied at the university in neighboring Bloomvale. It was part of the small-town charm.

Per Ruthie's last-minute instructions, Sierra colored the icing red. Other desserts – mini eclairs, fruit tarts, lemon squares – were stacked neatly on covered trays, and Ruthie's artisan dinner rolls occupied others. Everything was in order, despite Ruthie's absence. Charlie relaxed slightly. He walked from the kitchen into the store front to find Pearl, another *cupcake*, tending to a half dozen elderly customers. As he double-checked the order in Ruthie's catering book, a group of customers honed in on him and slowly flocked to the counter behind which he stood.

"Excuse me, can I get this bear claw?" asked Mrs. Hilbert, pointing toward a display case. She was a delightful old woman when she wanted to be, but a cutthroat when it came to obtaining pastries.

"No! I'm next!" said Mr. Ewald, waving his ticket in the air. "Don't give her that bear claw! She didn't take her ticket!"

"Ticket?" asked Mrs. Hilbert, impersonating a confused person, "It was right here in my hand a moment ago. Oh, dear! I must've misplaced it."

"I'm sorry Mrs. Hilbert," said Charlie, "but you know the rules." He pulled the next ticket from the roll and handed it to her. "Now don't lose this one, and maybe I'll be able to find you another bear claw in the back when it's your turn." Exchanges like these drew Charlie to the bakery life. The innocuous tactics of the elderly vying for sweets provided him with hope that all of humanity's struggles could someday boil down to an argument that could be solved by pastries. Eased by this thought, he called the next number on the electric *Now Serving* display and tended to customers until it was time to leave for the party.

Charlie followed the GPS directions past farms and forests, until he arrived at a small gravel road that wound into the woods. This he traveled up for half a mile to a clearing holding a white-trimmed wooden house. A few open-sided tents sheltered an arrangement of folding tables and chairs on the lawn, and several vans and pickup trucks sat on the driveway near the garage. A man in a green Rose's shirt unloaded floral arrangements from the van at the end of the row. Charlie parked next to it on the grass. "Is it OK for me to park here?"

The man shrugged. He only understood flowers.

Charlie asked again, vigorously waving his finger at the van and in the general vicinity of the other vehicles. "Is it OK for me to park here?"

The gestures seemed to work. "Si, si! Aqui es bueno!" The man smiled and tipped the basket he held.

"Thanks!" said Charlie, then added, "Gracias!" He took pride in his ability to successfully communicate.

The man smiled and nodded. "You welcome."

Charlie returned the smile and asked, "Do you know where I should go with the cake?"

The man, who'd thought his management responsibilities ended when he correctly interpreted and answered Charlie's first question, shrugged. He peered over the tops of the vans for somebody who might save him from this moron's interrogation. As Charlie prepared to ask the question a second time (but while waving his hands), the man raised his own hand high above his head and waved it vigorously. "Señorita!" he bellowed.

Beatrice marched out of the house's back door, directly toward Charlie. "Freddy!" she called, "What are you doing? I told you to bring those flowers inside!"

The man complied, grabbing two large pots of flowers from the back of the van and bolting for the house before Charlie could ask another question. The baker assessed the situation. He'd been ditched on the driveway, between two vans, and face-to-face with the quickly approaching girl of his dreams. Devoid of ammunition for a proper first impression, he launched the line he had already queued up: "Do you know where I should go with this cake?" As he said this, he gestured toward the van and made a cake shape in the air with his hands. The gestures appeared much crisper in his head.

Beatrice stopped a few paces in front of him and stared at his hands, wondering why he pretended to grasp the buttocks of a plump and invisible ballerina. "What cake?"

Charlie shoved his hands in his pockets. "The one in the van," he said. "I'm from Fat BB's. I'm filling in for Ruthie."

Beatrice flashed the same glow of understanding that the flower-carrying man displayed earlier. "Oh! Hi! Chuck, right?"

"Charlie, actually. And you're...Bea?" He knew very well who she was.

"Beatrice," she said, extending her hand.

Charlie shook it, noting its firm yet silky texture, like angel cake. He felt guilty for besmirching this gentle creature with his dirty hoof. It was a little bit naughty.

"It's nice to meet you. So where's Ruthie?"

"She got arrested for stealing turkeys," said Charlie, relieved that the introductions were over.

"You're kidding, right?"

"No. It's kind of a long story."

"Well, it's good to meet you," she said. "Come with me. We'll find out where everything should go."

Like a happy puppy, Charlie followed Beatrice into the house.

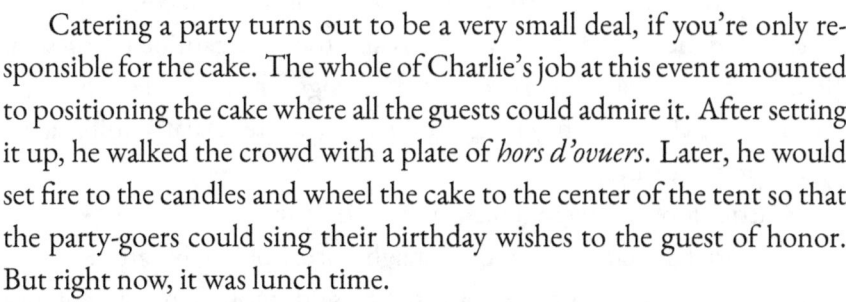

Catering a party turns out to be a very small deal, if you're only responsible for the cake. The whole of Charlie's job at this event amounted to positioning the cake where all the guests could admire it. After setting it up, he walked the crowd with a plate of *hors d'ovuers*. Later, he would set fire to the candles and wheel the cake to the center of the tent so that the party-goers could sing their birthday wishes to the guest of honor. But right now, it was lunch time.

Charlie possessed a plateful of leftover appetizers and a total lack of conversation topics. Beatrice, who'd sent her crew home, remained at the party to help pass the *hors d'oveurs*. The two ate in the kitchen, he in a chair along the wall, his plate balanced on his lap, and she perched on a stool at the kitchen's island, scrolling through pages on her phone using a combination pen/stylus that read *Oh's Kendo*. Charlie ate slowly and in silence, keenly aware that the end of his time alone with Beatrice crept closer with each bite. He picked through the contents of his plate: bits of cheese, raw vegetables with hummus, assorted pastries, fried calamari.

This last item particularly interested him. Although delicious, Charlie knew, squid far from the smartest of the cephalopods. That honor belonged to the octopus, which was followed in intelligence by the cuttlefish, the nautilus, and then the humble squid.

Charlie had developed an extensive knowledge of such matters by dedicating a significant portion of his idle time to meticulously contemplating the Relative Intelligence of Things. During those brief moments when it was not inundated with information spewed from various electronic devices, his mind drifted toward a careful analysis of which species of frozen fish, for example, had the highest IQ. The habit began innocuously in his childhood and stuck with him ever since. He carried distinct memories of early comparative studies on the brain power of various invertebrates huddled under rocks in his back yard: Centipedes, of course, were among the highest scorers, with idiot wood lice taking up the rear.

Although he'd largely outgrown it, the contemplation of intelligence still comforted Charlie in times of boredom and frustration. Unfortunately, his expertise translated poorly to social settings: More than once, he'd found himself at the uncomfortable ending of a conversation that he inadvertently steered toward this obscure passion. Now, contemplating his calamari, he considered his options and took the cautious approach. "Poodles are one of the smarter breed of dogs," he said. "People think they're dumb because they look stupid, but they're actually quite clever by accepted measures."

Beatrice looked up from her phone and squinted.

He stared directly back with a straight face, holding his ground.

"I'm more of a cat person myself," she said, proudly holding up her phone to show him a photo of a black cat with a white chin.

"Cute," he said, straightening up.

"She's Lulu. She lives at Rose's."

Charlie waited for her to offer additional details. He didn't know what kinds of questions cat people like to get about their cats. It seemed like a great chance to show off a little, so he said, "Cats are pretty smart, too."

"Uh-huh," Beatrice replied. "So what happened to Ruthie?"

Nobody ever wanted to talk about the things that most interested Charlie. It didn't matter to him now: He was having a conversation with Beatrice, and he felt he'd be all right. "She got caught stealing turkeys from a farm in Meadeville. Knowing Ruthie, they were probably some exotic breed that she wanted to add to her collection."

"Her collection?"

"Yeah, Ruthie has chickens. In fact, she's got something of a record of poultry-related run-ins with the law. One day the police show up at her house, telling her that she's over the village chicken limit – turns out you can only have six or so. Ruthie argued that the chickens weren't hers, but were Creatures of God, free to come and go as they pleased. She argued that people feed birds in their yards all the time, and nobody ever complains. She called it anti-chicken discrimination. She said that if they were bluebirds or hummingbirds, nobody would care. But if you throw out chicken food and a bunch of chickens come to your yard, everybody hates it. She made a big noise about it. The charges were eventually dropped, but the laws have been changed since the incident."

Beatrice laughed. "The chicken incident! She never told me about that!"

"There's a lot to Ruthie that she doesn't let on to," Charlie said, "and probably a lot that nobody really wants to know."

"She's a real free spirit."

"Free spirit? That's an understatement. Ruthie's spirit and mind are so free, they wandered off and never came back. She's clinically insane."

"I wouldn't say that."

"That she's crazy? Isn't it obvious? You've seen the kinds of stunts that Ruthie pulls. She's loony."

"No," said Beatrice, "I mean that if I were you, I wouldn't say things like *insane* and *crazy* and *loony* when I'm talking to someone I hardly know, and about whose life and experiences I know nothing." She had the tone of a schoolteacher scolding one child for making fun of another.

Charlie stared at the floor, acknowledging his insensitivity. If Ruthie had been reliable, he wouldn't be here right now, having this conversation. He looked at his plate, but had no appetite for veggies and hummus or calamari – that goddamn troublemaking calamari. "I'm sorry if I offended you," he said, mentally kicking himself. This was familiar territory for him, as he'd often managed to get himself into perfect situations and, without any outside assistance, completely bungle them. What had started off as a great first impression was quickly turning into a disaster.

Then he did something entirely unplanned. He pulled his phone out from his pocket, swiped to the video of the plant, and offered it to Beatrice. "Here," he said. "I have something to show you."

Still frowning, Beatrice looked at the phone and then at Charlie.

"I haven't shared this with anyone," he added, trying to convey the grandeur of the gesture.

She reached out and plucked the phone from his fingers. As she watched the video, her scowl softened to a look of confusion, then bewilderment, then awe. Her eyes widened. "What is it?" she asked. "I've never seen a plant like this before in my life." Her eyes were fixed to the phone's screen as she looped repeatedly through the video.

"It's growing in my back yard. I just found it there. I have no idea of how it got there, or what it is."

"Wow! It's probably something from Logan Biotech."

"That's what I thought. Do you think it could be? I emailed them, but I haven't heard back."

"I should show this to my friend Bill, he'll know for sure. He's in grad school for plant biology. He knows everything about plants. He used to work for one of my growers, and then went to school for it. If anyone can tell you about this, it's Bill. Do you mind if I send this to him?"

Charlie's heart pounded. He hadn't considered that she might want to share his innocent little plant with some guy. "Why don't you come by so you can see it in person?" he asked, hoping to avoid the video going viral.

"Great idea! I'll text Bill, and we'll swing by your place."

Charlie smiled. He'd have to clean the house.

When Charlie returned from the party, Ruthie was already behind the counter at Fat BB's, half listening to a conversation among three regular customers who were sitting at the lone table in the front corner.

"Your sister?" Mr. Sommerfeld asked. "Isn't she in Tampa? I thought she was in Tampa."

"Nah, she ain't in Tampa," said Mr. Cooper. "She's the one who used to work for the seamstress."

"The seamstress on Locust Street?"

"No, right here on the corner – not the Chinawoman, but the original seamstress. Who was there back when the IGA was across the street..."

"You mean the one the mayor owned? That wasn't the IGA."

"Not the mayor, the fire chief, what's his name? Wallace?"

"No, Casper. Mayor Casper..."

"Yeah, Wallace Casper. He was the fire chief..."

"He was the mayor."

"He was both," said Mrs. Sommerfeld. "He was the fire chief back when they had the volunteer fire department. Then when they got the full-timers, he ran for mayor because he didn't like the union."

"Right," said Mr. Cooper. "Wallace Casper. He was a fine man. His wife was an Indian."

"Yeah, that's right," said Mr. Sommerfeld. "He owned the Woolworth's."

"That wasn't a Woolworth's. It was the IGA."

"It was both."

"How could it be both?"

"First it was a Woolworth's, and then it was the IGA."

"That's right. So what about it?"

"You remember the seamstress shop across the street from that?"

"The Chinese woman?"

"No, before that."

"Yeah?"

"My sister used to work there."

"The one who moved to Tampa?"

Charlie positioned himself at the counter next to Ruthie. "Well, look who's here!" he said. "Did you learn any new tricks in the can?"

"Bend over and I'll show you."

"You're such a gem. So what happened last night?"

Ruthie relayed her tale, embellishing the exciting parts and diminishing the boring bits, as storytellers are apt to do. She explained how Clyde came across a beautiful antique theremin on an internet trade site, but when they drove out to Meadeville to make the swap, they found the theremin completely unlike its on-line description. Clyde called the deal off, and Ruthie suggested they stop by a nearby farm that sold fresh produce. One thing led to another, and they wound up having dinner with the farmer, Jacques, and some *agritourisme* guests at the farm. When Jacques emerged with quart jars of clear liquid, Ruthie and Clyde learned the pleasures of indulging in spirits that were both organic and local, or *orgaloco*. Ruthie initiated a discussion on the proper selection of eggs for a soufflé, and after a few rounds decided to liberate some turkeys from the barn of the theremin seller. Unfortunately, she was caught in the act. "It was a great experience. You should try it sometime," she told Charlie. "So what about you? Did everything go well today?"

"Yeah, it was pretty fun, actually. I wouldn't mind doing it again, if you need the help."

"Oh, really? So now you've caught the catering bug! This wouldn't have anything to do with Ms. Martin, would it?"

"Who? No! It was just nice to get out, see how the other side lives, you know…"

"Uh-huh," said Ruthie, inspecting her fingernails. "Well, I'm glad that I didn't spend the night in jail in vain. At least you and Bea got to spend some quality time together."

"Shut up, Ruthie."

"I love you, too, Chuck," Ruthie said. "Anyway – since you asked – I could use your help for a party, three weeks from today: The big Chan shindig. He was just in here this morning – I nearly missed him. You're going to have to talk to him yourself to get the details, but this guy has a tall order, for sure."

CHAPTER 5

The sweaty guy pulled into Charlie's driveway on an alloy bicycle with shocks on the frame and clips on the pedals. He was a generally hairy fellow, sporting a shaggy beard and a mop of greasy hair that fell to his shoulders. He pulled off his helmet and draped his hair over his ears. "Hey, man, you got some kind of a mutant plant in your yard?"

"You must be Bill," said Charlie, introducing himself. He'd been waiting on the porch for Beatrice to arrive, and he hadn't expected Bill to show up solo. He didn't deal much with graduate students, but he always suspected that they knew too much about one thing and dangerously little about everything else.

"You work at Fat BB's, right?" asked Bill. "Oh, man, I love that place! I used to work for a greenhouse that supplied flowers to Rose's. Sometimes my boss'd stop by your bakery after deliveries and pick up a half dozen apple cakes. Oh, man! Those things are tasty as shit!"

Apple cakes, for the uninitiated, contain absolutely no apple products. They are small, nearly spherical cakes covered in semi-firm frosting that is deliberately colored to resemble the sun-kissed skin of an apple. They are, exactly as Bill assessed, tasty as shit.

"It's one of our specialties," said Charlie.

"Hey, lemmee ask ya," said Bill, scratching the back of his head, "how come they're only apples? Why not other fruit, like bananas or grapes?"

"It's basically a cupcake. We'd need a special baking pan to make them banana-shaped."

Bill thought about it. "Yeah, but if they're just cupcakes, you could make the same thing and just change the icing, right? Like, instead of apples, you could make cakes that look like oranges, or baseballs, or light bulbs."

"Why would we make a cake that looks like a light bulb?"

"I don't know. Maybe for inventors or something."

Charlie considered this answer and wondered how well he'd do in graduate school. Compared to light bulb cakes, Soufflé Days glistened like a Nobel Prize winning gem. Before he could reply to Bill, an old pickup truck rumbled up the street. Behind the wheel sat Beatrice, singing along with some mindless pop tune pouring out of the open windows. She pulled to the curb in front of Charlie's house, killed the engine, and hopped out, closing the truck's door with a slam that echoed through the neighborhood.

After saying their hellos, Charlie invited his guests to see the plant. The trio walked in a large arc across the yard, Charlie at the lead. He stopped ten steps from the plant and pointed. The others' eyes followed the imaginary ray from Charlie's fingertip to a small white sphere in the grass. "Right there," he said. "Approach it slowly."

Bill immediately lumbered toward the plant. After a few paces, it turned smoothly toward him and fixed its gaze upon his face. Beatrice gasped and looked back at Charlie, who remained motionless. The baker smiled in reassurance.

"Oh man!" Bill said. "That's so cool!" He approached the little plant without further hesitation, crouching down to inspect it. "It's *Arabidopsis*. And a big one."

Charlie and Beatrice huddled around Bill, observing him observing the plant. As with bakers, it's not every day that one gets to watch scientists at work. "You know what this is?" Charlie asked.

"Yeah, I know her. *Arabidopsis thaliana*."

"Allie Anna?"

"*Thaliana*. This is a model plant species. Anyone who took an introductory plant genetics class would know this little girl."

"Ah, I see," Charlie nodded. "Introductory plant genetics. I was registered for that in culinary school, but it conflicted with my quantum physics class. Does *Arabidopsis* usually have an eye?"

"Naw, man. It's just a plant! But it's been studied for years. It's like the fruit fly, or the mouse. Scientists all over the world know about *Arabidopsis*, and there're a ton of lab experiments dedicated to her. The first plant genome that was sequenced was *Arabidopsis*. There are entire conferences dedicated to the species. I mean, like, thousands of scientists converging on a convention center just to talk about lines of *Arabidopsis*, traits of *Arabidopsis*, what different mutations do to *Arabidopsis*..." He pulled out his phone and photographed the plant, continuing his speech as he shot. "If there's one plant that scientists know everything about, it's *Arabidopsis*. They trade its seeds and create hybrids and all kinds of mutants. But I have never, *ever* seen an eye on one. I mean, you can change the size and shape of the petals or leaves, and you might even be able to express some animal trait in *Arabidopsis*, but an entire eye? Man! That is *nuts!*"

He removed his wallet from his pocket and withdrew his driver's license, which he propped vertically in the grass next to the plant. "I need this for perspective," he explained. He took a few more photos and then pulled a plastic sandwich bag from his back pocket. Smiling, he waved the bag at Beatrice. Before Charlie knew what he was doing, Bill turned the bag inside-out over his hand and plucked a leaf off the plant.

The eye shut and the stem recoiled.

"What are you doing?" Charlie yelled.

"Oh, man! That is so cool!" Bill said. He folded the bag neatly around the leaf. "I need a sample." He continued prodding and molesting the plant.

"What are you doing?" Charlie asked again, standing over the hairy grad student like a boxer taunting his opponent. "Get the hell out of here!"

Beatrice intervened: "Bill, do you think you have to get that to the lab tonight? Don't you have to freeze it or something?"

"Yeah, I probably should," Bill said. He pocketed his ID and stood up, oblivious to Charlie's emotion. "I'll take it back to the lab, and show it to my professor tomorrow. She'll probably want to at least run it through the sequencer and find out what's unique about it…compare it to known animal genes, stuff like that. We'll just run a whole battery of tests to see where this beauty came from. It should take a couple of weeks before we have preliminary data. I'll let you know." He slapped Charlie on the shoulder. Atta boy.

Charlie nodded his head, bewildered. Did this dude just torture his plant in the name of science?

"This," Bill said, shaking the bag gently, "This is going to be my PhD, man." He strapped on his bike helmet and marched toward the front of the house.

Charlie crouched next to the still-recoiled plant, his hand over his mouth. "Do you think he can help?" he asked Beatrice. "Or is he just going to kill it?"

"Bill's a good guy. I think he'll be able to find something." She squatted next to him. "It was only a leaf that he pulled off. We prune plants all the time. It'll survive."

Without a word, Charlie pointed at the plant's tightly closed eye. Just at the seam where the two lids met, a tiny drop of clear liquid formed. It slid down the curve of the eye and along the plant's stem, leaving a threadlike trail behind it. The plant wept.

The two stared in silence for a few moments before Charlie spoke: "Have you ever had the feeling that suddenly, for some reason, the universe decides to like you? Like, suddenly it shows you some intense beauty that you never thought could exist? That's how I feel lately – like there's something wonderful in the world that I didn't know about, and I get to experience it all for myself. And I'm afraid that something's going to come along and kill it, so I really have to protect this, you know? I have to protect this." He looked her in her wide, sympathetic eyes. "You must think I'm an idiot."

"No, Charlie, I think you're perfectly reasonable." She smiled at him softly. "You're a remarkable person. Most people I know would just cut this down with the lawnmower, or pour some poison on it. But you *care*, Charlie. I think that's sweet." She patted him on the back. "I think it's sweet that you want to protect your baby."

"Can I make a request?" he asked. "Can you not tell anyone else about this? Just for a little while I'd like to keep it secret, before the rest of the world hears about it and ruins everything."

"Sure, it'll be our little secret."

"Do you think Bill will tell anyone? I mean besides the professor?"

"I'll ask him not to."

"Thanks. Once we find out more about it, either it'll be a big deal that the whole world knows about, or it'll be nothing at all. If it turns out to be nothing, I don't want to make a big deal to begin with."

"But in the meantime," Beatrice said, "you and I can have fun speculating on the origin story. Where do you think it came from? Mars? Do you think it's a creature from outer space?"

Charlie relaxed a little. "I think it was developed by an adversarial foreign government, so they can track our every move."

"So they put it in *your* back yard?"

"You don't know what state secrets I'm in on."

"Right. Ivan the eye-flower. From Russia!" Beatrice laughed. "I don't believe that you think it's a spy; you wouldn't be so nice to it."

"But I'm nice to everybody. Everybody needs love – even creepy Russian spy plants."

Chapter 6

The wind cooled Charlie's face as he coasted down the country highway, steering his bike along the wide shoulder, giving the cars ample room to pass. The mid-day sun shone on the valley that engulfed him in a symphony of green and brown. He sped past fields of wildflowers and farms pinstriped with the beginnings of this year's crops, just sticking their noses out of the soil.

Charlie was on a mission of science to State University, in the neighboring town of Bloomvale. A few days earlier he received an email from Bill:

> Hey Charlie,
>
> We did a preliminary analysis of the sample that you so generously provided, and we'll be discussing it in a lab meeting on Tuesday. The lab's principal investigator, Prof. Amelia Wigglesworth (cc'd here), asked me to invite you to join us for a discussion about our findings and future directions of the project. The meeting will be held in room 3356 of the Noonan Life Science Complex. We hope you will be able to attend.
>
> Best,
> Bill

The opportunity thrilled him, as he'd struggled for years with dreams of becoming a scientist, before he realized that he was more of an artist. The baking was something of a compromise – a mixture of chemistry and sculpture. He called in a favor from Ruthie, who still owed him for cater-ing the party, and headed out of town after lunch. Passing the church, he read its sign:

THE PROOF IS IN THE PUDDING. THE
THEOREM IS THE SPOON.

Now, navigating the hills of the highway, he pondered what Bill and Pro-fessor Wigglesworth found in the pudding of his little plant.

After Bill unceremoniously ripped one of its leaves from its frame, Charlie paid even closer attention to the little weed. He checked the wound for signs of infection, even though he really didn't know what to look for. Bill pulled the leaf off cleanly, not leaving any part attached to the plant. Feeling scientific after Bill's visit, Charlie initiated his own line of horticultural research, studying the plant's behavior. He found it most easily noticed him when he wore black, and least easily noticed him when he wore green. Its attention was held longest by loud Hawaiian shirts, and it seemed particularly fascinated by dancing.

As Charlie arrived at Bloomvale, the pulchritude of the wide-open valley gave way to the syrupy charm of the college town. Young people permeated the place like a cloud of gnats riding skateboards and chasing Frisbees. The rhythmic intonations of a drum circle beckoned from the distance. The baker passed cafés with outdoor seating crowded with stu-dents pretending to be studious. He delighted in the circus around him: A bunch of dudes kicking a foot bag, a mob of angry girls yelling angrily about the issue that angered them most, a group of retirees enjoying ice cream on a break from classes.

He rode toward the quad, remembering when he himself studied art here and lived in a dorm with some weirdo roommate. At the time he offset the cost by working at Fat BB's, an experience that eventually con-vinced him to leave the university and enroll in culinary school. He al-most never looked back since.

Charlie swerved onto the grass to avoid plowing over a group of stu-dents sitting in a circle right in the middle of the sidewalk. Looming be-fore him, at the far end of the quad, was the Noonan Life Sciences Com-plex, a network of blue-tinted glass buildings joined together by elevated pedestrian walkways. He headed to the main building, its huge central atrium radiating the vibe of modern science. False-colored cryo-electron microscopy images of pollen, viral capsids and other tiny specimens hung from the red brick walls, and here and there a desk or white board betrayed the presence of nerds. Staircases at each end of the atrium wound their way up all five stories. The baker ascended the far staircase to the third floor and walked in a loop, until he reached a set of glass double door that read *Suite 3300 PLANT GENETICS*.

A woman at the reception desk greeted him with a friendly smile. "Dr. Wigglesworth is having a lab meeting," she told him, "but she's expecting you." She provided him with a bottle of water from the office refrigerator and led him down the hall to the conference room.

Inside was dark, the only light coming from the large projector screen at the room's far end. A young man stood in front of the screen, presenting a slide with a bulleted list titled *Summary*. About twenty people sat at rows of desks facing the screen. A few turned their heads toward the door as Charlie entered. He took a seat in the rear and listened as the woman in the front row interrogated the presenter.

"This last bullet point," she said, "*BSL19 negatively regulates TRA75 through CTD-CTD interactions*. Is that really what you found?"

"Yes," answered the presenter. "This is the result from our last paper, remember?"

"Of course I remember. I was the senior author on that paper. But did you emphasize that during your talk? That point didn't really seem to come across."

"That's what the whole third part of my talk was about."

"I see," said the woman, "but I don't think that was clear."

Charlie assumed that the woman asking questions was Professor Wigglesworth. He recognized Bill sitting among the crowd, giving exasperated looks to a laptop computer on the table in front of him. The computer – in typical computer fashion – seemed not to mind. A young lady sitting near the front of the room spoke: "Maybe he can say that he elucidated the mechanism of TRA75 regulation through the BSL19 pathway…"

"What's that, Julie?" Professor Wigglesworth asked.

"He can say that he elucidated the mechanism."

"Yes," said the professor, "what a great way to put it! Did you hear that, John? Julie suggested that you specifically say that you…how did you put it, Julie?"

"Elucidate the mechanism."

"Elucidate the mechanism, yes! You elucidated the mechanism through which BSL19 negatively regulates TRA75. I think that really conveys what you did, and this cannot be emphasized enough. You should make the point during your talk that you elucidated this mechanism; otherwise, your committee members may think that it had already been elucidated, which it hadn't, correct?"

The student stared at his professor blankly.

The professor continued. "It is important that you point out that this mechanism was previously obfuscated and that it is only now elucidated."

"Also," said Julie, "have you accounted for stochastic effects?"

"Stochastic effects?" The student at the lectern wrinkled his brow.

"Like random effects. Noise."

"Yes," agreed the professor. "You must account for stochastic effects. Too many people neglect stochastic effects, and I didn't hear you mention them once in your presentation. When is your thesis defense again?"

"In two weeks."

"Two weeks? And this is what you have? This is not good. You can't go in front of your committee with this. You'll never pass your defense! You really need to work on this, but I think that it will take quite a long time to go over everything, and I don't want to waste any more of everyone's time."

The defeated student closed his presentation and removed his laptop from the lectern. The professor took a deep breath, exhaled, and clapped her hands together. Smiling, she turned to face the audience. "We have a special treat today!" she said, looking each lab member in the eye while maintaining her smile. The lab members knew better than to offer comments. "Some of you may know that Bill and Julie have been working on a *secret* project."

A few of the students nodded knowingly, to mask the fact that they had absolutely no idea what she was talking about. Others refrained from nodding, to show that they were obedient students who kept to themselves and didn't stick their noses where they did not belong. Neither response impressed the professor.

"This project," she continued, "is something that is outside my usual area of research, but about a month ago Bill approached me with it, and since then he and Julie have made remarkable progress. So today they're going to tell us about what they found so far, and we have a very special guest, Charlie Bishop, who provided Bill with a remarkable sample. Mr. Bishop, why don't you come take a seat in the front? Why don't you introduce yourself? Come!"

The entire room turned and stared at Charlie, who walked to the front of the room and faced the audience. "Thank you, Professor," he stammered. "Hi everybody. My name is Charlie Bishop, and I'm the head baker at Fat BB's in Milton."

A murmur scintillated across the room.

"What is this?" Dr. Wigglesworth asked her lab. "You know this place? What is this place?"

"Oh my god!" exclaimed one student. "Fat BB's! I *love* their apple cakes! They're *sooo* good!"

"Fat BB's," Dr. Wigglesworth said, relishing the way the words felt leaving her mouth and entering her ears. "It's an interesting name for a bakery. I've never heard of this place. Do you know it, Julie?"

"Yes," said Julie. "It's a bakery in Milton. They make really good cakes."

"And you bake these cakes, Charlie?"

"Yes."

"Well, you've already made quite an impression on the group. It's too bad that you didn't bring any samples," said the professor. "You didn't bring samples, did you?"

"No."

"No, I thought not. But I will try this place, Fat BB's. And maybe

I will bring samples to a lab meeting. But that's not why you're here, to bring us samples. You're here for science, because we're scientists."

"Yes," said Charlie. "I found an interesting plant, and a friend of mine directed me to Bill, so I think he can tell the story."

Bill proceeded to the lectern and plugged the cable into his laptop computer, which promptly crashed. "I hate the internet," he told the crowd, "you can never find what you're looking for in that place. My laptop's been on the fritz for weeks, so I ordered a new power cord online. It arrived today, but it's the cord for the Takyi 9000A laptop, not the Takyi 9000. Stupid thing doesn't fit. But I have a backup plan." He pulled from his pocket a flash drive advertising Tiegue's Quarry (motto: *Rock It!*), inserted it into the lectern laptop, and began his presentation. His introductory slide had the title *Phenotype Analysis of Arabidopsis Mollyanna.*"

"*Arabidopsis mollyanna?*" Professor Wigglesworth asked. "What is this, *mollyanna?*"

"I named it after my girlfriend," said Bill, scratching his neck. "Her name is Molly. And her middle name is Anne. So – you know – *mollyana*, like *thaliana…*"

"But your title implies that this is a new species," said the professor. "Has it met the requirements for a species? Do you even know what those requirements are?"

"I kind of meant this as a joke."

"Oh, I see. A joke. Very clever. Are you going to talk about science today?"

"A few weeks ago," Bill explained, "I received a text from a friend telling me about a unique sample that happened to be growing in Charlie's yard. When I went to inspect it, I found this." He showed a picture of the plant with his ID next to it. Whispers trickled through the crowd. "Obviously, this is *Arabidopsis thaliana*, or so one would think from a visual inspection. The one anomalous physical feature is the presence of what appears to be a mammalian eye in place of flowers atop the stem. It's otherwise morphologically identical to the wild type. Given its position and coloration, the eye has the outward appearance of a malformed flower; the petioles act as eyelids and the petals as the white part of the eye."

"Sclera," Dr. Wigglesworth interrupted. "That's what the white part of the eye is called."

"Right," said Bill. "The petals are like the sclera. Upon closer inspection, it seems that this isn't the case. It exhibits unusual behavior patterns, including motion and sensitivity to light. When I took a sample of a rosette leaf, the eye closed and the stem turned away from me." Bill showed a picture of the plant with the eye closed and the stem bent away from the camera. "Truly, this is an unusual plant. I brought the sample to the lab for genomic analysis."

He handed off to Julie, who launched into a presentation filled with colorful graphs and odd-sounding words. She explained that microscopic inspection revealed neuron-like cells in the leaf, and that the plant's DNA was *Arabidopsis thaliana*, with thousands of human genes distributed among its chromosomes. She regurgitated a bewildering array of scientific jargon that everybody but the baker accepted intuitively. "Then we analyzed codon frequency," she said, "and found that codons for cysteine and methionine were enriched."

"Enriched like flour?" asked Charlie. He had no idea what they were talking about.

"Flowers? No, it wasn't just the flowers that showed enrichment. The cysteine and methionine codon frequency was high throughout the DNA."

"Huh."

"Julie," Professor Wigglesworth said, "maybe you should explain the underlying ideas to our guest."

"Of course. What I mean, Mr. Bishop, is that the cysteine and methionine codon frequencies were enriched in this plant. Cysteine and methionine occurred more often than expected."

Charlie nodded cluelessly.

Amelia raised her hand. "Julie, stop. I cannot watch this go on. If you don't know how to explain something to a fifth-grader, you'll never be able to make a living as a scientist." She turned to Charlie. "What my student is trying to tell you is that the plant's DNA is different than expected. You see, DNA contains the instructions on how to make an organism. It's like…like a cookbook." She smiled at herself, tickled with the cleverness of the analogy she'd created.

"Sure," said Charlie, "a cookbook."

The professor continued, "Each recipe in this cookbook is called a *gene.* Just as a cookbook is a collection of recipes, DNA is a collection of genes. The dishes that the DNA recipes tell us how to make are called *proteins.* Each gene is a recipe for its own protein."

"I see," and he really did. This was something he could understand.

"Proteins are all made of common ingredients called *amino acids,* like the cysteine and methionine that Julie mentioned. Each gene tells us which amino acids go into a specific protein, and in which order. It's just like when you're baking, you might first mix eggs with butter, and then add flour. There are certain quantities of each ingredient, and a certain order in which they should be added."

Charlie nodded. Science was easy!

"Now suppose I gave you a cookbook, but I erased all the names of the dishes. How would you know whether a certain recipe was for an entrée or a dessert?"

"I'd just look at the ingredients."

"Exactly! Are you sure you're not a scientist? You'd look at the ingredients. This is precisely what Julie did. She looked at all the ingredients of all of the recipes in the cookbook that is your plant's DNA, and she found that some ingredients appear too often."

"Like everything had too much salt," Charlie said. He couldn't believe this is all these scientists did.

"Yes, exactly!" Amelia said. She looked over her team. "See everyone? You can explain molecular biology to even a baker if you just know how to put it into simple terms."

Julie interjected, "We also found a short sequence that appeared multiple times on each chromosome. The probability of this happening randomly is almost zero."

"Julie, please put that in terms of the recipe, so our guest can understand," said Amelia.

"Oh! It's like finding the same part of a recipe scattered throughout the cookbook. Like, 'boil smoked trout in buttermilk,' appearing over and over." Julie shrugged, "Or something like that. I don't know. I'm not much of a cook."

"No, that's good," said Bill, "because it's a really weird sequence. The amino acids – uh, ingredients – here are phenylalanine, threonine, histadine, glutamic acid, methionine, alanine, asparagine. Using one-letter amino acid abbreviations, this reduces to *F-T-H-E-M-A-N*."

Raucous laughter filled the room.

"What does this mean?" Dr. Wigglesworth asked, silencing the students immediately.

"Well, it looks like *F the man*," Bill explained.

"Yes, and who is F? Is that the man's name?"

"You know, like, *F the man*!" Bill pumped a hairy fist in mock anger.

"What?" Dr. Wigglesworth looked at Julie, who looked at Bill.

"*Fuck the man*!" a voice called from the back of the room.

Dr. Wigglesworth turned. "Who was that? That type of language is very inappropriate in a lab meeting!"

"But that's what it means," said Bill, trying to save his fellow student from certain ejection from the lab.

"It means…Oh! Oh! *F the man* means *that*? Why would that be in the plant? Who would put such a thing in a plant?"

The students looked around nervously.

"Charlie," said the professor, "have you ever heard of this company, Logan Biotechnologies?"

"Of course. I rode by it today on my way to the university."

"Do you know what kind of research goes on there?"

"They develop drugs, right? Isn't their motto, *Making the World Better…with Drugs*?"

"Yes, that's them. But they are extensively invested in human-nonhuman interactions. They pour a ton of money into things just like this: engineering other organisms to interact more favorably with human biochemistry, developing chimeric domesticated animals, expressing human genes in other organisms. Your little plant is right in line with their research, and they are right in your back yard."

"Really? They're doing all that?"

"Yes, and that's what worries me. If Logan Biotech learns about this plant, they'll just claim it as their own and turn it into something horrific. We at the university have the opportunity to do pure science, to understand the nature of life. I'd hate to see some company come in and interfere with that."

"But what if they invented it?"

"That's an even more troubling possibility," professed the professor. "How can we trust anyone who suddenly springs something like this on the world? Where are the assurances that this organism is safe? It has to be studied objectively. The very existence of this plant needs to be peer-reviewed."

"I see."

"Then you agree to let my lab continue research on this plant?"

"Sure. That's why I brought it to you."

"Good!" Professor Wigglesworth stood. "Thank you very much for coming by, Charlie. I'm very happy to be working with you, and I think that we'll be able to do some very interesting science together."

"Thanks, Professor. I'm very excited about this, too." Charlie sincerely admired her.

"Please call me Amelia. Not even my students call me Professor. Although perhaps they should."

"Fine, *Amelia*."

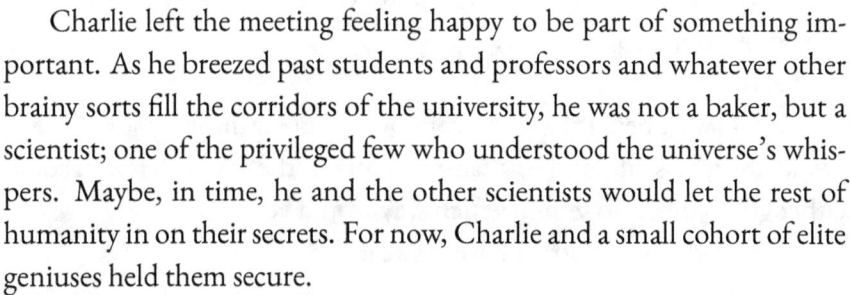

Charlie left the meeting feeling happy to be part of something important. As he breezed past students and professors and whatever other brainy sorts fill the corridors of the university, he was not a baker, but a scientist; one of the privileged few who understood the universe's whispers. Maybe, in time, he and the other scientists would let the rest of humanity in on their secrets. For now, Charlie and a small cohort of elite geniuses held them secure.

He walked his bike proudly across the quad, stopping every now and again to survey the buildings and quiz himself on their names and purposes. Charlie oddly missed the university, and for a moment he wondered why he'd left in the first place. Although he never liked going to class, he wasn't a *bad* student. He always completed his assignments, and he worked hard enough to get by. He knew at the time that it wasn't for him, but right now, as he was strolling across campus, he couldn't remember what drove him to that conclusion.

As the baker neared the far end of the quad, he spotted a grubby-looking man rummaging through a garbage can. In a well-practiced maneuver, he cast a spell of invisibility over himself. He spotted an everyday object in the distance – a branch on a tree – and focused intently on it, giving the rest of the universe the illusion that he was so immersed in deep thought and contemplation that he was oblivious to all activity around him.

The tactic failed. As he was passing the trash can on the far side of the sidewalk, the man walked from it directly toward Charlie. "Do you have any cans, or bottles?" he asked.

"No, sorry," Charlie answered reflexively with a shake of his head. He tore his eyes from the branch long enough to survey the ragged man.

He could have been a tenured professor. He had wild hair and an unkempt beard, and wore a moth-eaten tweed jacket. He was barefoot. "You have an empty bottle in your hand," the man said.

Charlie looked down at his hand. Between his last two fingers he grasped the empty water bottle that the receptionist gave him. Embarrassed, he handed it to the man. "I'm sorry," he said. "I was just thinking about something."

"Was it about whether you would go uphill or downhill if being chased by your doppelgänger?"

"Pardon?"

"If you were being chased by your own doppelgänger – your own evil twin," the man said, "and you came to a fork in the road where you could either go uphill or downhill, which way would you turn?"

"That's the only bottle I have. I swear."

"Forget the bottle and think about it: If you go uphill and sprint, you might gain some distance, but the doppelgänger might pace himself and catch up after you tire out. If you go downhill, you can get a lead on him and hide, but if he's your double he'll know where you're planning to go. It's about knowing your limits."

Wishing to end the line of questioning, Charlie said, "I'd run uphill."

"Wise choice," said the bum, shaking the empty plastic bottle toward Charlie. "You look like the kind of fellow who might trip over his own feet running downhill."

"What about you, man?"

"The only time I ever encounter doppelgängers, I'm the one doing the chasing."

Charlie nodded and continued walking his bike.

"Wait!" called the man. "Did you just come out of one of these buildings?"

"Noonan Life Sciences Complex." So much for the quick getaway.

"Be careful. *Thankless foul science cowards cause doom.*"

"If you say so."

"I don't say so. Shakespeare says so." He handed Charlie a small pamphlet. "Thank you for your donation."

CHAPTER 7

Charlie never canceled Soufflé Days, partially because he felt guilty about Ruthie's arrest, but mostly because he feared her retribution. His worries were unfounded: Unpredictable though Ruthie was, she always compensated for her lapses in judgment with sweet actions of kindness. It was one of her most endearing features.

Soufflé Days turned out to be a muse to Ruthie. She spent late nights at the bakery creating new varieties of soufflé and perfecting old ones – experimenting with flavors and consistencies, with methods of mixing and storing. Eventually she found a niche of delicious-yet-unusual flavors, each more intriguing than the next: chocolate tangerine, white truffle habanero, garam masala. She made hundreds and consumed dozens of soufflés. As she learned the process, she taught the *cupcakes* how to make them, tapping their feeble little brains for ideas on flavors and textures. After a month of whipping eggs, testing flavors, adjusting oven temperatures, and tiptoeing around the kitchen, she was just one dress rehearsal shy of prime time. Ruthie decided to throw a soufflé party at her house. This excited Charlie for at least two reasons: First, it gave him something to do on a Friday night; second, it meant he wouldn't have to cook for a change.

Before leaving for the party, Charlie pulled up the Logan Biotech web site. Annoyed that the company never responded to his emails, he entered another message into the *Contact Us* portal:

This plant sees all,
Big and small,
Because, y'all,
It's got an eyeball!

He sent this to the *Research* team, hoping it would grab the attention of some scientist who knew what he meant.

———— ⚭ ————

The sun was completing its languid descent to the horizon as Charlie pedaled across town. Passing the old church, he read the sign:

NOTHING THAT HAPPENS, HAPPENS FOR A REASON

Ruthie lived in the old part of town, a neighborhood of brick houses tucked into a little hill and surrounded by tall elms and gnarled oaks. This very neighborhood was home to some of Milton's most longstanding residents. It was a quaint nook, where couples walked hand-in-hand along the sidewalks and families sat in chairs on their porches, listening to the *dat!dat!dat! chikka-chikka-chikka-chikka!* of their lawn sprinklers. The din of the party, audible from a good block away, marred the neighborhood's serenity. All the house's lights were on, and an outdoor stereo played background to the loud conversation and laughter erupting from the back yard.

Charlie stashed his bike behind some bushes and approached the front porch, decorated with homemade mobiles of soda cans and broken glass. When he stepped through the front door, the crisp stillness of the outdoors ceded to the homey warmth of the living room, filled with aromas of baked goods and smoked herbs. A jam band laid down a relaxing beat over the decades-old sound system, and the room glowed softly from holiday lights strung along the ceiling. A large dog barked loudly, startling Charlie.

"Zeus! Quiet!" somebody yelled from the couch in the center of the room. It was Red, one of Ruthie's housemates. He was an alright guy –

generally good-natured and thoughtful. He certainly wasn't the dipshit Clyde was. He and another dude who Charlie didn't recognize were sitting on the sofa, aggressively pounding on video game controllers with their thumbs. Red paused the game and turned to look over his shoulder at the visitor. "Hey, Charlie!" he said, then returned swiftly to blowing open zombie skulls on the TV. Why dwell?

"What's up, Red? Fellas?" Charlie waved toward the other occupants slouched around the room. They nodded at the newcomer. Zeus cautiously walked over to Charlie, who made friends by scratching him under the chin. "Hey, Zeus!" he said.

"Hey, Zeus! Christos! Heaha!" a stranger on the floor giggled.

"What's up, Dude?" Charlie said, observing standard stoner etiquette by greeting the stranger with the honorific *Dude*, which expresses either approval (as in *Dude! That was some good weed!*) or disapproval (as in *Dude! That was some shitty weed!*). "Anyone want a beer?" he held up a six pack. "They may be a little shaken up from the ride, but they're probably still cold."

"Yeah, I'll take one," called Red, thumbs furiously working the controller as his digital avatar dispatched zombie after zombie, preferably with graphic blood-spattering head-shots. The others stared at the television dumbly.

Charlie pulled a beer from the pack shimmied the bottle into a small open area on the table's surface between a stolen ashtray adorned with the logo for Finley's Pub and a large red bong.

"You want a hit?" asked Red, motioning to the bong. "It's orgaloco."

Charlie inspected the contents of the pipe. "Is Ruthie around?"

"She's out back with everyone else. Dude, you gotta try the soufflés."

"That's the plan."

"Dude, those soufflés are so *good!* I had one of the sriracha ones...man! That's awesome! Are you gonna sell those at the bakery?"

"I think so."

"Dude, you *gotta*, man. Those things are awesome."

"I'll be the judge of that." Charlie walked to the kitchen, where Pearl worked the oven.

"Hi Charlie?" she said cheerily. Like many of the *cupcakes*, Pearl had a penchant for upspeak. Most of her sentences sounded like questions, and Charlie was never quite sure how to converse with her. He learned to count to three after she spoke, to make sure that she was finished.

"Hi, Pearl. I was told that I have to try one of the sriracha soufflés."

"Oh yeah? Everybody loved those! But I made a batch? Like, twenty minutes ago? And they're gone! I'm sorry! I think maybe later? I'll make some more? Do you want to try a Thai coconut in the meantime?"

Charlie waited to make sure it was really a question and then said sure, he'd love one. The soufflé was still warm, not quite hot. It shook delicately on his fork before its spongy delicious sweetness rolled over his tongue. The taste was exquisite: a hint of lemongrass mingled with some unusual flavor – maybe tamarind? Charlie had dabbled with soufflés in the past, but Ruthie created a new art form. "Wow, Pearl, these are great."

"Thanks! But I can't take all the credit! Ruthie? Like, totally made this all happen! She put together all the recipes and everything? Like, she wanted to use ostrich eggs? Isn't that awesome?"

One... two... three...

"Yeah, she's great. You all did a great job."

"Thanks! Do you want some grog? It's like this punch? Made with some liquor? That the guys from the chicken farm make?"

One... two... three...

"I think I'll pass."

"That's probably a good idea. I think this stuff is really strong? There's a cooler in back, if you want to put your beer in? The fridge is really full, because we've been cooking."

"Right." He exited the kitchen to the large wooden deck. Just off-set from center stood an old picnic table stolen from Crenshaw Park, the carvings on its surface testifying to the eternal love of high school sweethearts from decades past.

Charlie placed his beer in the ice chest and surveyed the crowd, his eyes landing on a slim figure standing on the lawn by a corner of the deck. Although her back was to him, he knew immediately that it was Beatrice. Illuminated by the glow of a nearby tiki torch, she possessed the air and beauty of a tropical flower in its native jungle, at once completely out of place and right at home. She stubbornly defied the party's implicit jersey-and-denim dress code with a green floral-print dress that hugged her contours gently, revealing a mellifluous transition of waist into hips. A few glistening locks of her hair spiraled down to her shoulder, their faint shadows dancing along the slope of her neck with the flickering of the torch. Past her, Charlie could see her conversation partner, Ruthie.

Ruthie waved at Charlie and called. Beatrice turned, her dark eyes sparkling in the light of the torch. When she recognized Charlie, her smile blinded him. Charlie took a deep breath and made his way across the deck, paying close attention to how the soles of his feet rolled over the boards as he approached.

"Stupendous coconuts, Ruthie!" he called. "They jiggle so lusciously!"

"Why, thanks, sexy! You can jiggle my luscious coconuts all you like!"

"Hi, Charlie," said Beatrice. Her voice was like springtime.

"Hello, Beatrice. Sorry for being crass just now; Ruthie brings out the worst in me."

"That's all right: She brings out the worst in me, too," Beatrice purred. "So, how's your aunt? Any news from the doctor?"

"My aunt?" Charlie had no clue what she was talking about. His mother's sister Mildred, in Sheboygan, had no medical problems of which he was aware. Perhaps she had high blood pressure, on account of her weight, so it was all the stranger that Beatrice should refer to her as *little.*

"Yes, Charlie! Your aunt! She had a problem with her *eye*, so she was getting evaluated by the doctor…"

"What, an optometrist?" How the hell did Beatrice even know his aunt? Did she have connections in Sheboygan?

"Your *aunt*, the Allie Anna." Beatrice pointed to her eye.

"Allie Anna?" Charlie's aunt's name was quite definitely Mildred.

"The Allie Anna. With the *eye*." Beatrice grew impatient with Charlie's obliqueness.

"Oh!" said Charlie, finally getting it. "My *aunt*! Allie Anna!"

"Yes, *the* Allie Anna. How is she?"

"I'll tell you later," Charlie nodded conspicuously toward Ruthie.

"Hey!" said Ruthie, faking a kick to Charlie's shin. "Well, ha ha ha! So you two have your cute little secrets. Ruthie goes off to jail, and you make inside jokes. Aren't you guys just so cool?"

"Oh, poor Ruthie!" Beatrice said in mock sympathy. She gave Ruthie a hug. "Don't feel bad. We still love you. Don't we, Charlie?"

"I love you mostly for your coconuts," Charlie replied.

Ruthie attempted to step on his foot, but he pulled away too quickly. "Whatever," she said, "Does anyone want a refill? I'm going to bring around some more soufflés."

"Excellent!" said Beatrice, "That'll give us a chance to talk about our..." she put her arm around Charlie's shoulder and pulled him close, filling his nostrils with her perfume. "*Secrets!*" she whispered with a squint of her eyes and a slight bob of her head that Charlie found incredibly alluring. Beatrice giggled.

Ruthie rolled her eyes and walked up the porch stairs through the crowd, leaving the baker and florist alone by the light of the tiki lamp.

"So?" said Beatrice.

"So!" said Charlie.

"So, what did the professor say?"

"She said that the plant is poisonous and anyone who's been within twenty feet of it will need to get a series of injections in the stomach."

"She did not say that!" Beatrice shoved Charlie gently, and he felt it in his innards like a child on a swing who'd just been launched skyward. "What did she really say?"

"She said that she doesn't know what it is," Charlie confessed. "She's still testing it. She sounded really intrigued by it. They found a weird message hidden in its DNA."

"A message? What kind of message? What did it say?"

"*F THE MAN.*"

"*F THE MAN*? What does that mean?"

"You sound just like the professor," Charlie said. "You don't know what *F the man* means? What, did you grow up in a convent?"

"No, I mean why is it in the plant's DNA?"

"I don't know, but can you believe it? It seems my little Aunt Allie Anna has some problems with authority."

"*The* Allie Anna," said Beatrice. "I'm so glad you finally caught on to that. I was trying to find a way to bring it up without having to explain everything to Ruthie."

"It was very clever, and I half suspected that you'd already told Ruthie about the plant."

"I'm hurt. I told you that I wouldn't tell anyone."

"I know, but who keeps their word anymore? I guess I don't expect it."

"Neither do I. My mother taught me at an early age that boys lie. In fact, right before you came we were talking about…a person who tells lies. But I can keep a secret."

"And I appreciate that. I assume that you took your mom's advice and were therefore never hurt by lying men."

"Not men; boys. And no, I didn't take her advice. I was a young girl who knew everything. And besides, she was…" Beatrice looked off to the side. "Can we talk about something else?"

"Sure," said Charlie. He'd talk about anything with her. "What do you think of the soufflés? I only had the chance to try the Thai coconut so far, but I'm hoping to try one of the sriracha ones. The guys inside highly recommended them, although taking culinary advice from a bunch of stoned dudes is probably about as wise as taking charm lessons from a crocodile. Or any lessons, for that matter; crocodiles are pretty dumb, even for reptiles…"

Beatrice stopped him. "I think the soufflés are outstanding. My girl Ruthie's done a great job. Hey, are you catering the party tomorrow? It would be great if you came along."

"I have to," said Charlie. "The cake is ridiculous. Just wait 'til you see the thing. I have to assemble it on the spot."

Ruthie returned and set a tray full of soufflés on a nearby stump. She lifted a pair of tiny plastic cups from it, offering them to Beatrice and Charlie. "Have a shot with me," she implored.

Beatrice took a cup and sniffed it. "What is it?"

"It's grog. Basically moonshine and powdered drink mix. We got the booze from Jacques at the farm. Have a taste." Turning to Charlie, she taunted, "Chuck, don't you want to do a shot with Bea and me?"

Charlie grabbed a cup and raised it in a toast. "Ruthie, you pulled off one heck of a soufflé party. I have to admit that you far exceeded my expectations. I'm recommending to BB that we go ahead with Soufflé Days as soon as possible – and you know that BB always listens to me. Congratulations on a job well done! To Ruthie, and soufflés!"

"And *F the man*," Beatrice added, glancing at Charlie.

"Yeah! Fuck the man!" belted Ruthie, downing her shot. "Chuck, you're the best!" she enveloped him in a great hug.

"I know," said Charlie. He hoped Beatrice was taking notes.

———————————————

The typical late-night debauchery and revelry ensued. Charlie, filled with the spirit of the party, found himself having an absurd amount of fun. In his experience, fun was meted out like stale candy from an elderly neighbor's glass dish. Now, he was immersed in a vat of it, frolicking and splashing about without a care. Blowing bubbles of fun. Doing cannonballs into it. He was in tune with the universe, and for the first time in a long while was moving along with it instead of struggling against it.

The same was true for Ruthie, who was just as alive as ever, but less scattered. The soufflés focused her and softened her; they extracted some glimmering purity from deep beneath her tumultuous crust. Whereas Charlie usually fought against the pounding breakers of life, Ruthie always moved across them at top speed, a cutter tacking through the swells. This party relaxed her sails – not entirely, but just enough so that she moved harmoniously with the wind and the waves, not straining for speed, but sailing more swiftly nonetheless.

And Beatrice was also relaxed. The evening subdued whatever anguish hid behind her dark eyes. She indulged in the summer night just like Charlie and Ruthie and the others, forgetting the pain and enjoying the moment and the soufflés of life.

On went the night until Charlie and Beatrice found themselves seated on lawn chairs around a fire pit, talking and laughing with the other guests. Clyde lectured the group on the proper procedure for claiming and preserving the meat of a deer, should one's car strike it in the middle of the night on a deserted highway. Ruthie interrupted him with a pensive sigh. "James is here," she said.

On the porch stood James Techenap, boyfriend to Beatrice Martin. He was a big man, James, and rather a pasty fellow. In contrast to the chiseled stud that one might expect to win the affections of the exquisite florist, James wore the puffy face of a privileged boy who enjoyed sweets. He proudly sported jeans, white sneakers, and a purple polo shirt from which his paunch protruded. He adopted a very cop-like stance as he surveyed the yard, arms akimbo – not too stern, but definitely looking…concerned. Old James wanted to make sure that this place passed the muster and that everything was on the up-and-up. Yessiree, James was here to see to it. No shenanigans around James, and – most of all – none of the resident riff-raff were to corrupt his lovely Beatrice.

Oh, Brother.

James moseyed on over to the fire and stood right next to Beatrice, hands parked on hips. Looking from face to face around the fire, he laughed quietly, as if he'd just told a horrendously funny joke and was awaiting comments from the audience. Nobody else got it. They all stared at him.

The fire popped and spit its smoldering red saliva onto the grass.

"So, we're all around the fire pit, huh?" he said, continuing to nod and grin. "Everybody looks real comfortable! You're all comfortable?"

Still, nobody got it.

He looked down at Beatrice. "Hey, babe, how's the party?"

Beatrice looked up and smiled. "Hi, James!" she said sweetly, if not a bit tiredly. "I thought you'd be at the auction."

"There was nothing good. I texted you when I left Schutzburg."

"I haven't been checking my phone. Pull up a chair."

"Take mine," said Charlie, standing up. Perhaps it was the moonshine taking effect, but he wasn't bothered by James. He was happy just to be there, in good company, enjoying a summer's night. He had some far-out plant to call his own, and he'd broken the ice with a lady he couldn't approach for years. So what if her boyfriend showed up?

James looked him up and down quizzically.

"Charlie Bishop," said Charlie, extending his hand with a smile.

James grasped Charlie's hand too tightly and gave it a shake. "Thanks," he said, "but I think we're about to get going. What do you think, babe?"

Beatrice objected quietly, and then she and James shared a hushed exchange in which she protested leaving, because she was having a good time, and he protested staying, because he was not.

Charlie produced a glass jar filled with clear liquid. Dispensing some into two tiny red cups, he extended one toward James. "James, try some moonshine."

James paused his conversation long enough to look suspiciously at the cup that Charlie held forth. "Nah. That stuff'll kill ya."

"That's exactly what I thought. Then I tried some." He turned to Clyde. "Clyde, you been drinking this moonshine?"

"Yup."

"You dead?"

"Nope."

"You blind?"

"Nope."

"C'mon James! The two great things about this party are Ruthie's soufflés and the moonshine. We'll get you some soufflés in a second. First, have a drink and enjoy the fire."

James, not about to be accused of not being fun, reluctantly took the seat next to Beatrice. It *was* a nice fire, after all.

Charlie turned a log on end next to him and sat. Surely there must be some redeeming quality about this guy – something that Beatrice saw. He decided to find out what it was. "Did I hear you say that you were in Schutzburg today?" Charlie asked, sipping from the red cup. "I have cousins there."

"That place is a dump," James answered. "I only went there for business."

"James is an entrepreneur," Beatrice announced. "A pretty successful one, too."

Ah, so that was it. "James," said Charlie, "you're a businessman?"

James went on to describe his small antiques business. A twisted modern-day Robin Hood, he bought from the dead and sold to the rich. He frequented estate sales, where he collected the leftovers from lives recently lost. These he cleaned up and sold on internet auction sites or at flea markets. He regularly drove a hundred miles or more in search of some collectible to complete a set, boosting its resale value. When he finished, he asked Charlie, "And what do you do?"

"I'm a professional karaoke singer."

"For real?"

Clyde burst out laughing from across the fire.

"No," said Charlie, "I'm a manager at Fat BB's."

"I love their apple cakes," said James. "I mean, my parents' friend won third place at the State Cake Bake a couple years back, so I have high standards. You got any pie birds?"

"Pie birds?" Charlie remembered James' baker friend as a mediocre cook with a crumbly chocolate cake.

"Pie birds," repeated James. "Little ceramic birds that you put in the middle of pies to vent the steam while they bake. Like that rhyme, *Four and twenty black birds.*"

"Hey, that's where Fat BB's got its name! When the bakery first opened, it was called *Four and Twenty Black Birds.* They called it that for decades, but then it got expensive to print out all th' letters, so they abbreviated it to *F.A.T.B.B.'s.*" The baker swigged grog directly from the glass jar.

"So there's no fat guy named BB?" James believed since childhood that such a character existed.

"Sorry. No pie birds, either."

"That's too bad. I've been looking everywhere for the red and yellow 1937 Johnstone pie bird to complete a set that'll be worth thousands."

"S'impressive," slurred Charlie, his cheeks growing numb. "Who knew that grave robbing could be so lucrative?"

"What's your problem, dude?" asked James. He did not mean *dude* in a nice way.

"I see what you like in this guy," Charlie said to Beatrice. "Wanna do another shot?" He turned to James. "She dida shot wi' me earlier." His tongue was as nimble as a python digesting a goat.

Ruthie stood. "Chuck!" she said, "let's go get some soufflés." She grabbed Charlie by the arm and pulled him to his feet. He managed to down another swig from the jar before she marched him away from the fire's light into the darkness of the yard. As she led him across the grass, Ruthie scolded Charlie for his bad behavior. "What the hell do you think you'll accomplish by telling James that Beatrice was having fun without him?"

"I's just makin' conversation." Charlie struggled to pronounce the words. Standing up quickly must've caused his mouth to shrink.

"Chuck, I'm totally in your corner here, but making an ass of yourself isn't helping." She dragged him into the kitchen, where she started pulling soufflés from the fridge.

Charlie sat down hard on a chair against the wall, a load of broken concrete falling from a dump truck. He squinted in the bright yellow light of the indoors. The room was tilting slowly. "But, Ruthie," he said, "you said yourself that she doesn't have a boyfrien'!"

"She *doesn't*," said Ruthie. "She *shouldn't*. It's complicated. James is on his way out."

"But when? I'm so much better for her than that dick."

"You are, Chuck. *In vino, veritas*. But what're you gonna to do? Fight him?"

"I've got far too much class for 'at, dear." Charlie stood up. By constantly moving he could steady the planet. "I might challenge 'im to a duel, though."

"Is that what that was? You challenging him to a drinking duel?"

"Damn right!" Charlie walked carefully to the counter. He grabbed a used cup, spilled some grog into it and drank deeply. He belched his approval and prepared his next sentence.

Just as he was about to pontificate on his many virtues, Charlie bore witness to a remarkable occurrence. Ruthie, who was previously standing directly in front of him, slowly drifted upward. He blinked his eyes, instantly bringing her back to her proper location at eye level, but then she floated up again, like a child's balloon. No sooner had Charlie found that he could stabilize Ruthie's position with precisely timed blinks than her twin appeared. Charlie saw not one, but two Ruthies, standing side-by-side, slightly overlapping. He could eliminate one by closing an eye, but this also threw off his balance. He needed air.

"Chuck, you should sit down," Ruthie said. Charlie stumbled out of the kitchen toward the living room. He vaguely sensed the stoners staring at the TV, and he thought he heard a giggle as he bounced between couch and wall like a spinning pinball. He groped his way to the front door and crookedly meandered through it into the night.

CHAPTER 8

Charlie was shitfaced.

In the past he'd been drunk – hammered even – but tonight he was well beyond standard run-of-the-mill three-sheets-to-the-wind. *Buzzed* was too far behind him to see, even with binoculars. He passed the more innocuous, and even the mid-level, euphemisms miles ago. Only words that conjure images of violence and destruction applied to his present state. *Destroyed* could work, as could *plastered*, *plowed*, and *wasted*. Shit-faced fit best, as Charlie couldn't see straight without contorting his mug into an otherworldly grimace, and even then the horizon continuously drifted into the sky.

He lurched down Ruthie's driveway to the sidewalk and then turned in the direction that seemed more interesting. The neighborhood was dark, save the occasional pockets of yellow light provided by streetlamps. Charlie ambled along the sidewalk, veering to and fro, occasionally stepping on the soft grass. He staved off nausea by sporadically spitting the thick saliva that coated his tongue. As he wandered, he repeatedly re-lived the events of the evening, from saying hello to Beatrice and Ruthie, to their conversations and laughs, to winding up in a cozy spot next to Beatrice mesmerized by the fire. And then James swooped in and crashed it all.

Charlie spat.

"How coul' she like 'at guy?" He filled the night air with angry muttering, knowing but not caring that he'd receive no answer. It felt good to say these things, to hear his voice. The quiet utterance relieved some of the screaming within his head.

His wandering brought him down a hill to an unfamiliar portion of the neighborhood – a cozy little street with small houses tucked in amongst the bushes and trees like little birds' nests in a great hedge. The sidewalk and street lights came to an end after several blocks, but the street continued into the darkness, hugged by trees on both sides.

Intrigued by the sight of the gray pavement disappearing into the blackness, Charlie continued along the road. He was palpably alone, and the slight panic of being isolated in a strange environment helped to straighten his stagger. Moonlight illuminated his path, although he wouldn't dare look up to view its source, lest he set the earth spinning violently on some axis through his ears. His spitting and cursing ceased with the sidewalk, and he now walked in silence, awakened slightly by the cool, damp air of the forest surrounding the road.

After minutes that seemed like hours, the trees fell away, revealing a few wispy clouds bright against the dark night sky. As the canopy opened overhead, the regular pattern of a wrought iron fence became apparent on one side of the road, contrasted against a silvery field of cut grass illuminated by moonlight. Large blocks cast ebony shadows along the field at regular intervals. This was the edge of Milton's old cemetery, about which the locals spun arabesque tales.

Charlie reached the broken cemetery gate and walked in, following the path that meandered into the headstones. He slowed and picked his way through the grave markers, sensing the sanctity of the place in the stillness. Most of the stones were well-worn, their engravings dulled from exposure to a century's worth of weather. Here and there one was immediately legible, angled just so that its inscription laid bare and black against the stone's white reflection. These graves held the remains of folk who lived harsh lives, plagued by infant mortality and infectious diseases. Charlie decided to find the oldest grave. The task focused his thoughts and distracted him from his drunkenness.

In the heart of the cemetery, he grew weary and rested against a headstone. He thought of what he was doing, why he was there, whether he was wasting his time. He decided that Beatrice should know what she was putting him through. Surely, he thought, if she knew how much pain she was causing him, she'd do something to make it stop.

He pulled his phone from his pocket and looked down to see two phones in his hand. They were floating upward. Charlie jabbed at the screen in vain, and a photo of his plant popped prominently to the foreground. Two plants, floating slowly upward. His thoughts of Beatrice blended with curious emotions for this little green entity that replaced his misery with joy. He flipped lovingly through his photos of the plant, recognizing the miracle of its existence. As he was submitting to a sense of the sacred, something stirred off to his side.

Charlie turned. About twenty yards ahead, a dark figure was walking directly toward him. Knowing that only two types of beings frequent cemeteries at night, Charlie concluded that he was subject to an imminent encounter with either a ghost or a madman.

"Beautiful evening, isn't it, friend?" the figure said in the strong, weathered voice of an aging stage actor.

"Isss very pleasant," said Charlie quietly, so as not to disturb the serenity of the night.

"I myself like to walk through here on evenings like this," said the specter. "It clears the mind, and there's nobody around to disturb – well, usually no one, alive anyway. I have to say that it's rarely that I encounter somebody walking through this place alone. What brings you here?"

"I'm a sp'lunk'r. Thought I saw a cave come 'is way."

"Mmm-hmmm."

It was at this point that Charlie realized he was speaking with a living person: Ghosts have a better sense of humor. "Do y'often hang out in cem'tries?" he asked the man.

"Do *you* often hang out in cemeteries?"

Well, I asked you first, thought Charlie. He closed an eye to eliminate one copy of the man standing before him. In the moonlight, he made out a beard, a gray suit and bare feet. "Hey, wai'a minnit! You're th' can man from the quad! I me'choo th'other day! I go'chor religiture!" Charlie searched through his pockets for the pamphlet he'd received on the university lawn. "I mussssa lefffit a'home."

"You're drunk."

"Ahh! You go' me!"

"Shut up," said the man. "I've been around this town and this cemetery enough to know that you're not just some drunk wandering around. You're alone and miserable. I'm guessing that you tied one on at a party because some lady – or man – didn't pay enough attention to you."

"Dude, does 'is happen allot? I mean, you psycho-an'lyze guys inna cem'try?" Charlie wondered whether this was how people got involved in cults.

"No, this doesn't happen a lot. Your situation is pretty obvious, though, don't you think?"

"S'o'vious t'me! Maybe's o'vious t'you too!" Charlie knew there was no way to turn invisible now. His whole life was visible to this man in front of him, and he was too intoxicated to hide any of it. "I dunno why women love ass'oles s'much, d'you? I'm a nice guy – I me'*now* I'm drunk, bu' I'm a nice guy. Why 'osen't she see me like 'at? Why she hang out with that dude instead? 'Cause he *rich*?"

"Ah, yes," said the man, stroking his beard. "The object of your affection has her eye on a man of means. T'is an ancient tragedy."

"But I got som'thin' he don't! A plant withan eye onnit!"

"A plant with an eye on it," repeated the man, "sounds special, indeed. I'm going to help you. First, you are suffering from unrequited love. To this I say: Get over it. If she doesn't love you, she's not going to start just because you're always around. Take my advice and cut your losses. You're a fool if you keep chasing after that skirt."

"Sh's'no' a skirt! She's very nice! She's not lea'ing me on – she 'us does't know. I'm'a tell her how I feel!"

"How's that? Drunk?"

Charlie laughed in a way that caused a gob of foamy saliva to spurt onto his chin.

"That can be a problem, Romeo. Here." The man extended his hand, palm up, to reveal a small white pill.

"What's 'is? Drugs?"

"It's science. Well, not quite science. It's Nature. Fungi and what-not. It'll sober you up."

Charlie stared at the pill.

"Trust me," said the man.

Charlie grabbed the pill and swallowed it.

The man smiled and handed him a bottle of water. "Walk with me to the gate. The pill that you just ingested is a cure for drunkenness that I concocted some years ago. Unfortunately, it never got FDA approval: The company abandoned it because of concerns with marketability – strictly financial stuff. Scientifically, it's a gem."

Charlie's ears rang at a level that distracted him from the stranger's narrative. His mouth became a salt mine, and he greedily gulped water from the bottle the man handed him.

"The pill starts to take effect immediately," the man explained, "as you've no doubt noticed. It contains a number of natural compounds that reverse the effects of alcohol and catalyze its breakdown in the blood."

Charlie's heart was pounding and he felt the rumblings of an enor-mous headache building behind his eyes. "You gave me drugs," he said.

"Well, yes, technically. But don't act like it's that bad. It's not an illicit drug of the type that's been used harmlessly for thousands of years but is banned by governments. It was developed in a laboratory by scientists with PhD's and white lab coats, and it's completely non-addictive. Like I said, it's all-natural, mostly – it comes from yeast. But you have to listen to me, because its effects are going to intensify and I don't want you to panic."

It may have been too late for this, as Charlie already felt anxious. Ket-tle drums beat in his brain. He poured water down his throat.

"The drug speeds up the process of growing sober," said the man. "Instead of passing out, sleeping for ten hours and waking up with a throbbing head, this pill does it all within a half hour. You are experi-encing the onset of an abbreviated and intensified hangover. Soon you'll be sober as a judge, most likely with an insatiable craving for greasy food. Before that you'll experience headache, ringing in the ears, sensitivity to light, nausea, possible emesis, maybe diarrhea. My best advice is to sit down and breathe deeply. If you're not completely sober in a half hour, take a second dose. Now, as much as I'd love to stay and watch your misery, I bid you adieu. It's late. Did you understand all that I said?"

Charlie nodded his pounding head.

"Good," said the stranger. He placed another pill in Charlie's hand and walked off into the night.

Charlie sat down on the grass near the cemetery gate and took slow, deep breaths that eased the pain a little bit. He squeezed his head with his fists to relieve some of the throbbing from within. Eyes closed, he rocked himself slowly on the grass, barely able to hear himself moan over the fire siren in his ears. He was desperately thirsty, but had drained the water bottle soon after receiving it. His eyes hurt. His temples hurt. His forehead hurt. His saliva tasted like Brussels sprouts. He continued breathing deeply, practicing the Lamaze of hangovers.

The breathing helped. With each exhale, some of the pain left his head. He kept it up for several minutes until he noticed that, with each inhale, the rumbling in his stomach intensified. He had a primordial hankering for eggs Florentine with a side of buttered whole wheat toast, but one of Ruthie's soufflés would substitute nicely. Energized by appetite, he stood up, pocketed the extra pill that he still clenched tightly in his hand, and walked soberly out of the cemetery.

⸺◦◦⸺

At that same moment, a server two hundred miles away spat a series of electronic zeros and ones through one of its ports and into the void of the internet. Almost instantaneously, this series of zeros and ones arrived at a machine that routed the little electric package toward a specific region of the internet. On went the little package from router to router until, just a fraction of a millisecond after departing its home, it arrived at a computer sitting on a bench in a biology laboratory at State University.

This computer had been expecting the package and, to be quite honest, was a little annoyed that it was taking the package so long to arrive –

as if it were stopping along the way to talk to all the other packages-in-transit that it met. This, the computer reasoned, was typical behavior of a data package.

The data package, on the other hand, couldn't care less what the computer thought. It was rather nihilistic, as data packages tend to be.

Upon the package's arrival, the computer was too elated to be upset and foretook all the usual pleasantries and how-do-you-dos and immediately set to processing the data by converting the series of zeros and ones into a continuously varying electrical current that it sent through wires attached to a device port. The original nihilistic series of zeros and ones was completely lost during this process, just as it had expected. Its analog manifestation was amplified and successively converted, via coiled wire, magnet and paper drum, to a magnetic field, mechanical vibration and audible sound to the effect of "Ooh, Baby! Oooh yeah, Baby! Yeah yeah Baby!"

The two grad students who occupied the laboratory that housed the computer vaguely understood the complexities of this process, but more or less ignored it as long as their streaming music played uninterrupted. The vestigial remnants of the data package that had traveled so far to meet them echoed softly through the laboratory in the form of another song in a random shuffle.

"Do you know where you're going when you graduate?" asked Bill. He was sitting at the very computer that had just destroyed the well-traveled package and pumped its eidolon into the atmosphere.

Julie was sitting behind him at another workstation in the lab. A significant portion of their interactions took place back-to-back, as their workstations were mere feet from each other and facing in opposite directions. Over the years they learned to respect each other's privacy and not turn around unless something of true importance demanded it.

"Not yet. Amelia hasn't even read my manuscript, and I really need to have that published before I'm considered seriously for a job. Why can't she just hurry up? I've already missed a few great chances."

"I don't know why you're so desperate to stay in science. We're sitting on a goldmine here, with this plant."

"So you're planning to go into the plant business?"

"No. Freelance lab tech. I've got mad bench skills. Plus, I'm in on the ground floor of this breakthrough…Whoa, what's this?"

Keyed by the *whoa*, which indicated something of enough importance to justify turning, Julie swiveled her chair around and peered over her lab-mate's shoulder. Bill had been running a secondary analysis on the plant's DNA sequence. He highlighted a sequence of letters on his computer screen. It read *THECHILDISFATHER*.

"The Childis father?" said Julie. "Like Professor Childis? Where did this come from?"

"He's Professor Child*ress*, not Childis," Bill said. "This is an analysis of repeated amino acid sequences in the genome. I did the same thing before, when we found *F THE MAN*, but now I've accounted for synonymous mutations."

"*THE CHILD IS FATHER…F THE MAN*," said Julie.

"I'm pretty sure it's from a poem," said Bill, scratching his head.

"But what about the 'O'?"

"There's no amino acid corresponding to 'O,' " said Bill. "It must've gotten garbled." Because there are 26 letters in the alphabet, but only 20 coded amino acids, six letters (including "O") don't correspond to any amino acid that can be coded in DNA. That is, the ingredient "O" doesn't appear in any recipe in the DNA cookbook, so it can't be coded into a message. The phrase became broken up at the "O," and its parts scattered about the plant's DNA, with *THE CHILD IS FATHER* appearing in some places, and *F THE MAN* in others. Or so our grad students reasoned.

"Okay," said Julie, "but why is there a poem in the plant's DNA?"

CHAPTER 9

THE TRUTH WILL LOCK YOU UP, proclaimed the sign in front of the old church as the Fat BB's van rolled past. Charlie and Ruthie were on their way to the house of Mr. Frank Chan, founder and president of Synerjive, a local manufacturer of food processing and chemical handling equipment. Each year, Mr. Chan invited his workforce, his loyal customers, and his closest friends to his house for a grand bash. Fat BB himself was not invited, as he staunchly refused to replace the bakery's ancient rotating oven with a modern Synerjive unit, arguing that the change was liable to alter the quality of his products. Charlie agreed, adding that replacing the oven would kill some of the bakery's character.

Unlike Fat BB, Charlie *was* attending the Chan party – not because he worked for a loyal customer, or because Mr. Chan was enamored with Fat BB's cakes. He was attending because Beatrice would be there. She personally knew Mr. Chan and received a yearly invitation to provide the flowers for the party. When she started working with Ruthie, Mr. Chan agreed as a special favor to Beatrice that Fat BB's could provide the cake.

Charlie tagged along this year, and he felt great. He stretched his arm through the window and made a wing of his hand, shooting it up or down in the wind with each twist of the wrist. Hours ago he was horrendously intoxicated, and by conventional standards he had no good reason to feel well now. By the magic of a bean obtained in a midnight graveyard, he stood on cloud tops.

Ruthie sat silently in the passenger seat, nursing her own grog-induced hangover and cursing Charlie's good mood. When he left her party the night before, he struggled to stay on his feet; yet when he returned an hour later, he was completely upbeat and coherent. He devoured soufflés like a man deprived of food for a month, but he showed no sign of intoxication. When she asked him how he managed to go from stumbling drunk to stone-cold sober in an hour, he said that a shoeless derelict in the cemetery gave him a pill. The least he could do, she thought, was tell the truth.

They drove past acres and acres of pristine pasture. Here and there horses dotted the fields. For several miles they sped in silence along the straight country road, their minds out their respective windows, until Charlie slowed the van and turned onto a narrow country road. They continued to the Chan estate, where they were met by a guard armed with a clipboard. He looked at the sign on the side of the van as he rapped the clipboard thoughtfully with a pencil that read *Tat-Man Tattoos* in blue letters. The guard gave his gum a couple of indifferent chews, just to make sure it was there, and then waved the van through the gate. Charlie navigated through a green sea of grass interrupted regularly with islands of topiary rising from beaches of floral ground cover, and by peacocks.

Mr. Chan had a penchant for throwing themed parties: Past years had seen Antebellum Mississippi, Cowboys and Indians and 1980's South Africa. Each year he put together a variety of props and entertainment to capture the spirit of the era in focus. Last year's Pearl Harbor themed party featured a luau and a 1:10 scale reenactment of the infamous event itself. Authentic-looking bloody young sailors from 1941 mingled with the crowd, commenting sincerely on how they'd like to get back to the farm in Oklahoma, but for those darn Japs. He placed a scale model of the USS Arizona at the bottom of the swimming pool and hid dollar coins in it for the kids to find.

This year's party was toned down, by comparison. The theme was *Bollywood*. Aside from having screens around the grounds looping dance scenes from popular Hindi films, Mr. Chan arranged to have Indian food catered to the party by a local restaurant. He trucked in peacocks from a nearby farm, and agreed to donate to the university's Indian Student

Association in exchange for musicians and dancers. The house was decorated in red and yellow floral garland, with flashing string lights accenting the corners and Hindi statuary on loan from local proprietors. For the matching cake, only the best would do.

Weeks ago, just after he catered his first party, Charlie met Frank Chan at Fat BB's. Mr. Chan was a very important man, or at least he thought he was. He moved like a lion fish, pushing his chest forward and skewing his balance to necessitate a blatant swinging of the arms that gave him the spatial extent of a much larger person. Charlie led him to the back office so they could discuss business in private, the baker sitting behind the desk, and his guest positioned across from him, scrutinizing the room's contents.

"So!" Charlie began, "Ruthie tells me that you'll be throwing a party and would like a cake." He pulled his sales binder to the center of the desk, and turned it to face his customer. "What kind of cake were you thinking? Something big, I imagine. And probably colorful." He opened the book to a page displaying one of their best sellers. He smiled at Mr. Chan.

The businessman, not returning the smile, laid a thin file folder directly on top of the open binder. Pushing them both toward Charlie, he said, "These are the seeds of some ideas, but I expect that you'll take it to the next level. I've been told that you're the best, and I demand nothing less than perfection. In the past, I've been terribly disappointed with the poor quality, shoddy workmanship and total lack of imagination that I've encountered when dealing with bakers."

Charlie opened the folder, revealing a stack of images of Hindu sculptures and statuary. Interspersed among these were hand drawings and sketches of many-armed gods, gopurams, siva lingams, and other Hindu idolatry. "It's a Bollywood themed party!" Mr. Chan giggled with excitement.

"I see," said Charlie. "Then don't you want a Bollywood-themed cake? You know, like a spontaneous ensemble of colorful and youthful dancers on a village street?"

"We'll have dancers at the party. I don't want redundancies between the entertainment and the dessert. What I really want is this." He pulled out a printout of Nataraja, or Dancing Shiva, posed on one foot with the other leg held across his waist, and four arms flailing much like the walking Mr. Chan.

"In a cake?" Charlie asked.

"Yes, of course! The dancing and the Indian theme make it perfect for my party."

"But a cake shaped like a god – doesn't that seem…blasphemous?"

"What's the big deal? The Catholics eat their god all the time."

Although tempted to argue the errors in the man's logic, Charlie knew he'd lose any appeal to the bakery ownership. BB himself made it clear that bakeries not only occupy, but define the front lines of history. Bakeries remained a constant of the ages, for millennia quietly providing celebratory cakes to victors, nourishing breads to the vanquished, and tasty pastries for anyone with the capital to obtain them. Bakeries won the hearts and minds of the people, and thereby conquered or defended nations. Arms played an important role, of course, but bakeries were the silent defenders of righteousness, the surreptitious conquerors of the ill-fed. Now, as ever, bakeries found themselves on the edge of the cultural revolution, and BB instructed his staff to refuse no cake on moral or ethical grounds without his express permission.

Charlie took a different tack. "He's standing on one foot. It's not trivial to make a cake that balances like that…"

"Trivial? What makes you think that anything about this party is trivial? I thought you were the best."

"What I mean is that cake is a soft material, and supporting such a high center of gravity will take a lot of internal scaffolding. I'm afraid that a cake like this will be mostly wire mesh. Have you considered Ganesh? You know, the elephant-headed god? He has a much lower center of mass, and would make a magnificent cake…"

Mr. Chan frowned. "You sound like the other bakers. 'Use the elephant-head god!' they say, 'He's easy!' I don't want easy! I want arms! How many arms does this elephant god have? Four?"

"Yes, four – but that's the same as this Shiva…"

"But he's *dancing*! He looks mystical!" Mr. Chan stabbed the photo with his finger. "And he's *blue*! I want a blue god with many arms!"

"Let's see," said Charlie, typing a search into his computer. "Ah, yes. Here we go. Durga. She has quite a few arms." He turned the monitor for his guest to see. "Eight, in fact. And she's riding on a lion. That would make a magnificent cake, and it would also be stable."

"A lion? Whoever heard of a lion in India?"

"I'm certain that there were Asiatic lions. They're extinct. I wonder if they were less intelligent than their African cousins…"

"That will just confuse people," said Mr. Chan. "Lions are from Africa."

"Are you sure you don't want Ganesh?"

Mr. Chan inhaled loudly through his nose.

"Tell you what," Charlie said, "We'll go with the original idea of Nataraja. Although I personally think that the best way to blaspheme the Hindu pantheon through dessert would be to fabricate a Ganesh-lookalike cake, securing eternal damnation through a direct affront to the less merciful Shiva seems the bolder approach."

"I like the way you think," said Mr. Chan.

Once the van was unloaded, Charlie and Ruthie got to work in the kitchen. The cake was pre-baked, but in multiple pieces: The deity's head, torso, legs and arms were all separated. Working from the bottom up, they assembled the cake over a foil-wrapped scaffolding. They meticulously attached the god's blue fondant skin, smoothing it over the joints of his divine limbs. Once Shiva's body was assembled, Charlie airbrushed it, adding shadows to give it a more realistic look. He then painted fingernails, eyes, and eyebrows with a small brush. He alternated between paintbrush and airbrush until the cake was indistinguishable from a plaster statue in some old Indian village devala. While Charlie worked, Ruthie remained in the kitchen, researching different poultry varieties with her phone. "Ooh! Silkys!" she said. "Look, Charlie! Aren't they pretty?"

"Hmmm…" Charlie grunted. He'd pay attention later, when he wasn't absorbed in a cake.

"But they go broody," Ruthie lamented. "Maybe we should find something else."

Beatrice arrived in a white lorry filled with potted flowers on wheeled carts. While Charlie finished the cake, she decorated the premises with blossoms, adding tropical flair to each little corner of the property. She arranged orchids and birds of paradise on the tables under the tent, trained jasmine on trellises at the bar, and hung marigold garlands in every doorway. Ruthie helped a little, but mostly just chatted with Beatrice.

With the cake complete and the flowers deployed, the trio of caterers sat behind the house and watched the guests arrive. Many were nervous employees, more frightened than excited to be at the boss's house, reminding their children in firm whispers that misbehavior carries harsh penalties. Occasionally Helen, the Chans' groundskeeper, appeared and told Beatrice about different events around the house in recent months. She explained that Mr. Chan cut down the big elm that was perfectly strong but just wasn't growing as straight as he'd wanted, and how he fired another pair of house painters for having inadequately firm wrists, and that George is still away at boarding school and won't be coming home this summer but it's probably better because he and his father don't get along.

Thus Helen and Beatrice went on about the old times, and Charlie and Ruthie and Beatrice went on about the new times, and they listened to the beat of the Hindi music from the party. Eventually, Ruthie tired of the scene and wandered off to assess the egg-laying powers of the peafowl. Taking advantage of the opportunity, Charlie turned to Beatrice and said, "I think I acted like an ass last night, but I can't fully remember. I'm sorry if I offended you."

"It's OK. It goes with the territory, and James can handle it. I kind of agree that the estate sale thing is borderline creepy, but it's a profitable business."

"And who doesn't like profits?" the baker asked, staring at the clouds. He knew that everybody loved profits, and that's what troubled him. The edge of a cloud evaporated and re-formed in another part of the sky. "I want to show you something." He led her into the main tent, where his cake was proudly on display.

"It's a fantastic cake," she said.

"Thanks. It's in poor taste."

"What? Why? It's beautiful!"

"It's sacrilegious. I'm certain to fry in Hindu hell for this, but thank you. I try to think of it as a piece of art, but the fact is that my medium is delicious and impermanent."

"Isn't everything?"

"Delicious? Hell, no! Have you ever eaten kimchi?"

"Impermanent. This cake is impermanent. The statues in temples are impermanent…"

"Yes, but the statues in temples will die dignified deaths, slowly crumbling through years of neglect until nothing remains but a pedestal and feet. This," Charlie motioned to the cake, "will be devoured by gluttonous Westerners who view the form as a decoration rather than a reminder of the cosmic dance of which we are all a part."

Beatrice considered this for a moment. "That's pretty heavy, Charlie. If it really bothers you that much, why even do it at all? Why not sculpt statues that can crumble with dignity in temples?"

"Here's what I wanted to show you." He pointed to the base of the cake. Nataraja danced upon a solid pedestal surrounded by clusters of multicolored fondant flowers. Set inconspicuously among these was a small white spherical eye with a bright blue iris, nestled within a platter of green leaves and staring adoringly at the dancing form.

"Oh, Charlie, it's our flower!"

"You like it? It's impermanent." He sighed and admired his own creation, knowing well that it would be gone soon enough.

Beatrice pulled out her phone. "Get next to it. I'll take your photo."

Charlie hesitated, but Beatrice persisted. "You'll never see this cake again. Don't you want to remember it?"

Charlie gave in and stood stoically next to the cake, allowing the florist to snap his photo. Then, to his delight, she stood right next to him and snapped a photo of the two of them, with the statuesque cake and fondant eye-flower in the background.

"There," she said, "it's slightly less impermanent, if such a thing is possible."

———— ✦ ————

Ruthie tiptoed around the hedges on the yard's perimeter, snooping for peahen nests. She counted three peacocks and two peahens on the grounds, but she figured that more were hiding – especially the hens, who blended in with the vegetation. As she combed through grass in a remote corner of the estate bordering the woods, a haunting song floated from the depths of the forest. She stopped moving and listened. The warm air carried the beat of Indian music, the laughter of guests, and the rustle of leaves in the tree tops, but no singing. She returned to the egg hunt.

A loud snapping of twigs emanated from among the trees, followed by a low groan. Expecting to see a bear, Ruthie stood up and spied a solitary figure skulking through the woods about fifty yards directly ahead of her. She froze.

The figure looked like a man, dressed in a sports jacket and tie, head down, lurching from tree to tree with an off-balance stagger. It carried something black slung over its shoulder, and something white in its hand. The man-creature stopped and stumbled back a step, a wounded warrior about to fall. It circled its arms to regain balance and barked an unintelligible tirade toward the sky. Then, through its curtain of straight black hair, it glimpsed Ruthie. It slowly raised its arm, hand still clutching the white thing, which was clearly a glass bottle. It yelled and bounded directly toward her.

Ruthie stood her ground. She'd seen crazy before. She'd seen a mild form of it in the mirror, and she'd seen it in varying degrees of severity in many of her friends and acquaintances. In her experience, most crazy behavior was a bluff that could be parried with an equally crazy bluff; of course, if nobody gives in, then an arms race of crazy ensues, and neither party may ever return to their right mind. She gambled that this crazed perhaps-zombie was putting up a brave front and would stop a few steps in front of her, like a charging elephant.

When he was five steps away and rapidly approaching, she questioned her strategy. She turned to run, but it was too late. Ruthie braced for impact.

The zombie-kid was within three steps. Then two. A step before collision, it stopped and stared at Ruthie with wide eyes. It opened his mouth wide, as if preparing to speak, and vomited at Ruthie's feet.

Charlie's phone rang, interrupting his interlude with Beatrice. Predictably for such a situation, Ruthie was on the other end. "Chuck, I need your help," she said. "Some drunk kid walked out of the woods and keeps spewing on about how he wants to turn this party into a real bash. And not just spewing words, but literally puking. I'm trying to bring him quietly to the house, but I think this kid's a runner – he's going to make a break for it the first chance he gets, and start running amok through the place."

"So now you're a chaperone?" Charlie asked.

"Chuck, I sympathize. I made mistakes when I was a kid, and I wish I had someone there to look after me. Will you just shut up and come help me? This kid's like a box of rocks. I'm by the woods in the front of the property."

Charlie relayed the call to Beatrice, and the two strolled to the yard, at which point they broke into a sprint and ran past confused peacocks toward the front of the property. They spotted Ruthie struggling along a hedge, her arm around the waist of a drunk, preppy-looking young man who leaned heavily upon her as he swerved across the lawn.

"My god! Is that George?" said Beatrice. "Charlie, that's Frank's son!"

Charlie ducked under the boy's arm to support his weight, and Beatrice spoke to the kid. "George," she said, "what are you doing here?"

"Beatrice?" the boy answered. "Beatrice! I ha'ent see' you in years! How the heck are ya?"

Beatrice repeated, "What're you doing here?"

"I'm flying! Wee!"

They dragged the boy to the house and sat him on a chair midway between the back bar and the kitchen entrance. As Charlie and Ruthie caught their breath, Beatrice once again attempted conversation. "George, what are you doing here?"

"I'm fantastic!" the boy answered. "Beatrice, you look great! You let your hair grow out again!"

"You're drunk."

"Mellow. Knocked out."

"Helen said that you were at school for the summer."

"Didn't you hear?" the kid asked. "This is my coming out party! Dad has this same thing every year, and frankly, it's getting a little stale, don't you think? I do. I really do. So I was sitting there in my room at this expensive and oppressive military indoctrination center that he ships me off to so that he doesn't have to look at my face, and I thought, *Hey! You know what Dad could use at his party? Some real impromptu entertainment!* Then I thought, *You know who's really good at impromptu entertainment? Me!* I really am! I know a ton of show tunes!" He broke into an on-the-spot rendition of *And I Am Telling You I'm Not Going*. He was certainly impromptu, and although Ruthie found him delightfully entertaining, Beatrice did not.

"George," she said, "I understand your frustration, but your dad is having a really big party today, and he'll go ballistic if you mess it up."

"I'm staying! I'm staying!" sang George, standing from the chair. "And you! And you! And you! You're gonna lo-o-o-o-ve me!"

Ruthie gently pushed him on the chest with her fingertips, as if she were dribbling a basketball. It was enough to set him off balance, and the boy fell back into his seat.

Beatrice frowned. George wasn't really her problem, but she knew him since he was an infant and felt responsible for him. They only saw each other on occasion, and despite – or perhaps because of – this,

George was comfortable confiding in her. She knew long ago that he wasn't cut from the same straight cloth as his father, and that he'd never meet Frank's standards of masculinity. "George," she said, "do you remember when your dad trapped that rat, and then you found its nest, with the litter of nasty little pups?"

"They weren't nasty," George protested.

"They were nasty," said Beatrice, recalling the trembling mass of squeaky pink flesh that George collected from a corner of the shed. "And you brought them back to the house, up to your room, and tried to keep them warm, and nurse them back to health? I thought that was fascinating. I thought you were beautiful for that, and I still do. What happened to that boy?"

"He got militarized!" George executed an angry salute. "Won't my dad and his fancy friends be proud of me! Hey, let's go crash their little party!"

Beatrice turned to Charlie with pleading eyes.

"Dude," Charlie invoked the magic word to chill the kid out. "We totally can't crash that party. We'll get fired, and that'd totally kill our buzz."

"Dude," George replied in kind, "whether you get canned or not, my dad's a total buzzkill."

"What I mean is…" Charlie looked over his shoulder and then leaned in close to George, "we all took these pills, right? The two girls and me. They're just starting to kick in." He winked at Beatrice.

"Pills? What kind of pills?" The kid was hooked on the very idea.

"They're just some upper-downers, or upside-downers. Intense shit. But if we go out there, you're dad'll freak. But you can go. Just don't tell him about us."

"Dude, give me some." The kid held out his hand.

"I doubt you can handle it. You smell like you were already sick."

"Man, you don't know what I can handle. I'm a legend back at the academy!"

"All right, all right. Chill." Charlie put his hands out to calm the boy. He looked over his shoulder again as he fished something from his pocket. "Here."

He handed a pill to George, who slapped it down his throat before Beatrice could protest.

"Charlie, what did you give him?" Beatrice asked.

"He'll be fine," said Charlie. "Just watch."

George's drunken grin melted to a grimace. He squeezed his palms against his temples. "Owww," he moaned.

"What's happening?" Beatrice asked.

"He needs water."

The boy rocked in his seat, eyes clenched like fists and head in hands. "Owww," his moaning grew louder. "Why's it spinning? Make it stop!"

"Charlie –" Beatrice pleaded.

"He needs water!" urged Charlie. Ruthie felt his tone and ran to the kitchen.

"Owwwwwww!" wailed George. "I'm gonna puke! My head! Make it stop!"

Ruthie returned from the kitchen and thrust a full glass of water into the teen's hands. He gulped it down and dropped the glass to its death on the stone, crying, "Lord Jesus, take me now!"

"I'm calling an ambulance," said Beatrice. She reached for her phone.

"Wait!" said Charlie.

The boy was silent. He took a couple of deep breaths and then opened his eyes to gaze at the world with sober wonder.

After a few moments, George sniffed the air. "Do I smell samosas? I could really go for some samosas!"

Chapter 10

Ruthie handed a plate of samosas to the newly sober boy, who devoured them by the handful, inquiring only, "Are these orgaloco?" As the boy ate, sitting upright, fully composed, Ruthie and Beatrice stared at Charlie in disbelief.

He shrugged. "It's a trick a friend taught me." He grabbed the empty plate and walked it behind the house to the patio bar, populated with a lively bunch of wrinkly-faced party-goers. After a moment's pause to bask in the vibe of old, rich and care-free, he started back to the kitchen when he heard someone say, "I could have you arrested for that."

Charlie turned back to see that the statement came from the mouth of a silver-haired gentleman sitting at the bar, sipping a clear drink from a low ball glass. The man spoke the words over his shoulder as Charlie walked by.

"I'm sorry?" said Charlie.

Now the man turned and met Charlie with a stern look. "Sorry for what? That your mother was so inept at whoring herself out that the only John she could land was her own brother? That your father's bedding and impregnating his sister enriched your genome with recessive traits? Among these, I see intellectual prowess is absent."

Charlie hadn't expected to interact socially with any of the guests, and he expected even less that one of them would venture to insult both of his parents in a single sentence. Reasoning that it was the mistake of an inebriated socialite, he said, "I'm sorry, sir; I just came here to return a plate to the bar, and now I'm heading back to join the other help in the kitchen."

"And I'll be elated once you've left, imbecile, as the quality of humanity in my immediate vicinity will then increase several fold."

Nope. No mistake – at least not one that could be cleared up with an apology and a quick exit. Charlie tried again: "Did I offend you?"

"You, dullard?" asked the man, poking with his stirrer at the ice in his glass. "No. You're just a kitchen worker at a fancy party, suffering the torment of seeing what kind of life you'd live if only you possessed sufficient ambition to make something of yourself. And maybe it's not your fault at all, really; maybe it's just that generations of inbreeding have washed your bloodline of all proclivity for anything but banjo strumming and sister screwing. But that doesn't give you an excuse to drag your proletariat habits into the upper echelon of society, let alone force them upon its youth. Do you understand what I'm saying?"

Charlie had been the recipient of such aggression in the past, but the perpetrators were always young men with small minds. This guy at the bar was an entirely different type. He was neither brutish nor dim-witted, and there were no females within earshot for him to impress by verbally thrashing a baker. Charlie said nothing.

"Oh, dear," the man continued with a roll of his eyes, "I always do this. I always use big words when talking to someone with a monosyllabic vocabulary. Let me dumb it down for you, half-brained moron: I don't care if you have some job at this party. You gave drugs to a kid, and I ought to call the police." He pulled his phone from his jacket pocket.

Ah, so that was it. Charlie moved to grab the man's hand but stopped himself before making contact. "No," he said. "You don't understand…"

"What's there to understand? I saw the whole thing. You, idiot, and your two girlfriends over there gave the kid smack somewhere in the woods. He could barely walk back. Then you gave him – what was that? naloxone? – to sober him up. You know, just because he's rich, doesn't mean that the kid doesn't have problems." This turned out to be true, and Charlie would eventually come to recognize that the boy who stumbled drunkenly out of the woods was a magnet for problems.

"It wasn't heroin. It was booze. And we didn't give it to him."

Snakes – those legless reptiles that slither through lawns and up trees and, despite a sullied reputation gained in an ancient garden, free the world from a pestilence of rats – are not known for their oratory skills. Rarely has it been reported that a snake of any species delivered an exceptional speech or spoke eloquently on this topic or that; instead, snakes are far more frequently noted for their actions, which are usually sudden and often painful. This property of snakes has prompted researchers to compile a vast compendium of serpentine behavior over the years. For example, a threatened viper may open its mouth and bare its fangs in attempt to scare off predators; a hunting one, on the other hand, will wind itself into a coil, mouth closed, waiting for the opportune time to strike.

The gentleman grew disturbingly calm, and spoke in a low voice. "What do you mean, it was booze? That kid was wasted, and now he's over there eating samosas."

"Yes, exactly."

"And what manner of pharmaceutical elicits such a response, you nematode? Do enlighten me."

Charlie had only basic knowledge of the proper safety measures to observe during an encounter with a snake. He understood not to step blindly over logs in the woods, and to slowly back away from a rattling sound coming from a crevice in the rocks. He knew little of snake charming, but understood that it was the movement of the charmer, and not the music itself, that mesmerized the snake. "Ummm…"

"You do understand the underlying pharmacodynamics of your prescribed treatment, O Great Deliverer of Pharmacological Sobriety?"

"Ummm…"

"Do you even know what you gave him?"

Among the ranks of predators in the animal kingdom are numerous species that have been observed to play with their food. These are typically mammals, who torment their prey for training purposes. Meerkats, for example, have earned themselves a reputation for teaching their young the finer techniques of scorpion deconstruction. Likewise, the domestic feline displays a verve for keeping its prey alive (although this is because cats are wickedly sadistic by nature, possessing neither heart nor soul). Food play isn't characteristic of snakes, and Charlie was in a losing situation, regardless of the action he took. He had to negotiate a thin line here, between getting physically assaulted, having the police called, and admitting that he gave the teenage son of a powerful businessman a strong drug of unknown composition.

"Nobody got hurt," he said. "The kid was drunk on his own accord, and we're just trying to sober him up and keep him out of trouble. With all due respect, you weren't involved in the situation. I appreciate your concern, but we have it under control and I promise you that none of the other kitchen staff will interfere with your enjoying the party."

"Do you know what you gave him?" The man by now had fully turned around to face Charlie. He sat back and seemed less threatening, as if he'd become more interested in extracting information than blood from Charlie.

"What, you mean the exact chemical composition? No, I don't know."

"That's interesting," said the gentleman, "because I suspect that I do."

As was her habit on Saturdays in the summer, Amelia Wigglesworth browsed through the stands at the farmers' market, selecting her produce for the week. A warm, wet spring blessed the early growing season, and the vendors' tables were piled high with bushy greens, plump mushrooms and ripe strawberries. She gathered a bundle of produce and treated herself to a gelato from the truck that, although clearly not driven by a farmer, was always welcome on hot sunny days at the market. She was enjoying her treat on a bench beneath a tree when her phone buzzed a message from Bill: *Full message from plant: "The child is father of the man."*

Amelia flashed back through volumes of classical authors she read. She considered them all writing of the human conditions of pain, joy, failure and triumph. She knew the Wordsworth poem, but was drawn to her own interpretation of the line – one in which a man's life, purpose, and very identity are fashioned by the tragic loss of his own son. She couldn't imagine a better quotation to implicate her prime suspect in this matter. She replied to Bill: *Logan Biotech made the plant.*

She would save a more detailed response for later, as the melting gelato refused to wait.

—◦◦◯◯◦◦—

Sitting on wooden chairs outside the kitchen, Beatrice and George similarly enjoying ice cream purloined from the family's personal freezer. The boy felt better, his distasteful mood replaced with a more amicable, kid-like state. Beatrice hoped to keep it that way. "So school's a drag, huh?" she asked.

"No, school's cool," said the boy. "Home's a drag. I probably shouldn't have come back here. I just get so sick of my dad throwing these big parties and totally ignoring me. He just doesn't get me. But I've been thinking lately: Maybe he'll never get me, you know? Maybe he'll go through his whole life thinking that I should be someone else and either waiting for me to turn into that person or cursing me for not being him."

"Oh, George, your dad loves you."

"Maybe, but he doesn't *get* me, you know? Finally, I think that I don't care anymore. I just wanted to come here and tell him that, which maybe means that I do care, a little." He stirred his ice cream to a smooth, creamy paste. "More and more I think that it doesn't matter what he thinks of me. He wants me to be someone else, but I'm not that guy. So what? I don't need his approval. There's this boy at school – he gets me. He knows exactly what I'm going through, because he's going through it, too. His family is just as bad – maybe worse. They're, like, super-religious. They want him to go to bible study and get married and have kids and everything. Right after he graduates. He doesn't want to have anything to do with it, either. He gets me."

Beatrice's phone buzzed with the same text message that Amelia received from Bill. She read it aloud: "The child is father of the man."

"Oh, please! Is that supposed to be profound?" George said, giving his ice cream a concerned look.

"No...It's just something that I think applies here. Don't you think so?"

"How does Wordsworth apply to *anything*?"

"Wordsworth?" Beatrice asked. Her phone buzzed again with a follow-up text from Bill: *Wordsworth quote.*

"Sure," she said, "all the old poets are still relevant. I'm impressed that you knew it was Wordsworth. I didn't know that...at your age. So I'm thinking that maybe you, the child, are more open to accept things for what they are than your father, the man, is. Maybe *you* have to teach *him*. Isn't that what Wordsworth meant?"

"I think it's really unlikely that Dad's heart will leap up if I mention rainbows." He poked at his ice cream with his spoon and pushed it away. "This shit tastes like Brussels sprouts."

People often asked Charlie why he dropped out of the university. Many thought that he couldn't take the pressure; others believed that he lacked the mental capacity; and then a small subset assumed that it was a question of emotional stability. The truth was that he found himself comfortable with his level of knowledge, and he found a niche in which he was content. The bakery was his lair, his domain, a place within which he could not be questioned. He was needed at work, but brought home no responsibilities or worries from the job. Reasoning that most people spent their lives in pursuit of such balance, he dropped out of the university.

His life would've continued smoothly for the remainder of his days had he not upended this balance by trying to shoehorn a love interest into the equation. Beatrice, or the pursuit thereof, disrupted his harmony. She'd previously diverted his thoughts with her presence, but now that she acknowledged his existence, she completely altered the flow of his life.

Case in point: Rather than sitting quietly in his back yard enjoying the summer day, he was here, at a rich man's party, trying to dodge an assault from a captain of industry.

The man placed his phone in his breast pocket, folded his hands calmly in his lap, and addressed Charlie: "The pill that you gave that boy contained a proprietary blend that you have no business dispensing. It belongs to Logan Biotechnologies, and you could be severely penalized just for possessing it. If you have a little stash of those pills, I suggest you refrain from distributing them, lest you get yourself arrested and heavily sued."

"I don't have any more."

"Sure you don't. However, the legal consequences of unlawfully distributing a proprietary pharmaceutical pale in comparison to those you'll face if any of its adverse side effects manifest themselves in your customers."

"Side effects?"

"You are aware that this drug never made it past clinical trials, aren't you? You do know that it was associated with an increased risk of death – as well as other, more grotesque, side effects – right? This pill that you just glibly administered to the teenage son of our host may not be the miracle cure that you think it is. I'm guessing that the unshod charlatan from whom you procured this nefarious concoction omitted these details from his sales pitch."

The look of surprise on Charlie's face betrayed him.

"Ah-ha!" the grumpy gentleman said, suddenly turning gleeful. "I was right, thief! You're a disciple of that scientist-turned-preacher who roams the earth curing people from their self-inflicted woes – the sole-less soothsayer hawking snake oil in the name of religion. I've heard stories of him, but never thought he could sink this low."

Bewildered, Charlie stared at the man. "Who are you?" he asked.

"Ah! Ha-ha-ha! I haven't seen that character in years, and now I find that his tentacles have infiltrated even the stronghold of high society. Brilliant! Well, good for him! I'm so thrilled to learn that he's found success in his new calling. Give him a band of wandering drones and he'll have them dispensing sobriety to the drunks of the world in a flash. Fantastic!" The man put his hand on Charlie's shoulder. "Now, when you see this bum, I want you to tell him that Phineas says, 'Hello.'" He placed his glass of ice on the bar and continued, "And if I ever again catch one of his disciples distributing my drug without permission or prescription, I'll see to it that he and his followers get locked up for the rest of their blessed lives."

"Phineas?" Charlie asked. "Phineas Snodgrass?"

"If you just tell him 'Phineas,' I think he'll know."

"No, I mean, *you're* Phineas Snodgrass? Of Logan Biotech?"

"Yes, of course. Are there other Phineas Snodgrasses about?"

Charlie pulled his phone from his pocket, scrolled to the video of the plant, and played it for the gentleman, who ceased laughing and grumbling for long enough to watch.

"Is this real?" he asked.

"Look at me," answered Charlie. "I'm a baker catering a party and giving sobriety drugs to rich kids. Do I look like I have the time and skills to fake a video like this in case I run into a guy like you?"

"Valid point." Phineas watched the screen intently, reversing and pausing at parts that he found interesting. "This plant is incredible! Where is it? I must see it for myself. The vestibulo-ocular reflex – right there, when the wind blows – is amazing. Where did it come from?"

"I was hoping you could tell me."

"I see. As the local biotechnology ogre who doesn't care a whit about the environment, I'm the prime suspect every time some odd little mutant pops up in somebody's back yard, hmm?"

"Every time? You mean mutant plants have popped up before?" Charlie was intrigued by the scientist's change of mood, as if his orneriness stemmed from a belly hungry for science, and that it was satiated only by the opportunity to say things like *vestibulo-ocular reflex*. "Professor Wigglesworth said she'd never seen anything like it."

"Amelia Wigglesworth?"

"Are there any other Professor Wigglesworths about?"

"God help us if there are."

"She's helping me find where the plant came from – analyzing its genome, doing some RNA-seek, stuff like that." Charlie tried to sound scientific as he said this. He had no idea what RNA-seek was, but it sounded like a good place to find answers.

"So you found this thing in your yard and just gave it to the first professor you ran into, is that it?"

"What choice did I have? Nobody at Logan Biotech replied to my emails."

"Well done." Phineas handed the phone back to Charlie and grabbed his refreshed drink, which the bartender placed on a napkin before him. "Unfortunately, Amelia will steal this thing from you, claim it for her own and exploit it to advance her perverted scientific agenda."

"Are we talking about the same woman? She seemed very nice…"

"Fool, that's how she gets her way. Amelia will dissect your plant in a thousand different ways, writing a paper each time, and at the end of it all tell you that it's just another marvelous mystery of nature. She'll speculate and produce evidence supporting various theories, but she'll never get right down to providing you with any real answers – and that's fine, because you're asking stupid questions, unsurprisingly."

A rodent compressed by the serpent's coils, Charlie regretted lingering when he had the chance to flee.

Phineas continued: "Simple-minded children want to know where it came from. I'm much more interested in knowing what it can *do*. My company manufactures a wide range of pharmaceutical solutions to real-world problems. Had you a pair of brain cells to rub together, you'd see that this plant promises to cure blindness, regenerate nerves, end paralysis. What piques my interest is not what miserable lout made this, or how it works, but what it's capable of. If I had this thing, I'd go right to curing diseases. I wouldn't fool around with hunting down its origins."

"You really think it can cure diseases?"

"Of course – in the right hands. And people would pay handsomely for such a cure." He pulled a business card from his breast pocket and handed it to Charlie. "Why don't we talk some more? That plant can make you a rich man, if you know what to do with it."

Charlie grabbed the card and scurried away, happy to have survived the encounter. When he arrived at the kitchen, George had gone into the house to wash the Brussels sprouts taste from his mouth, leaving Beatrice alone to search Romantic poetry on her phone.

"You'll never believe who I just ran into," said the baker.

"Who?"

"Phineas Snodgrass, the president of Logan Biotech. He's kind of..." Charlie searched for the right words, so as not to miscast Phineas in a bad light, "...an asshole."

Yes, that was a fair and generous assessment.

"He's *here*?"

"He's interested in the plant. He thinks it could have some therapeutic value."

"So are you going to sell it to him?"

"No way." Charlie abhorred the thought of some biotech firm destroying his plant – even if it meant bettering the lives of countless people. Amelia performed a spectacular analysis using just the sample leaf that Bill stole. Why should Phineas need anything more? He seemed brilliant and resourceful. "Maybe I'll give him a sample. What do you think something like that goes for?"

"Thousands. Maybe tens of thousands. You should ask for stock. What did he offer?"

"Nothing. He wants to come by my house and see it for himself."

"Charlie, that's great! But you need a lawyer."

"A lawyer? I was thinking of just a botanist – or a florist..."

Beatrice smiled. "I'd love to. If there's one thing I know how to do, it's haggle over the price of plants. Besides, the plant business is notoriously vicious. These guys will slash your jugular and let you bleed into their soil. It's good for the plants, you know."

Chapter 11

Phineas squatted in Charlie's lawn, his face pressed right up against the plant, as if he were trying to inhale it. "I'll give you five grand for it."

"It's not for sale," said Charlie, moving to block Phineas from the plant.

Beatrice placed a hand on his arm, steadying him with the certainty of a cowpoke calming a spooked horse. "A one-leaf sample will cost you five thousand dollars and ten percent of the profits," she told the scientist.

Phineas laughed. "Are you daft, or mad? Ten percent? That's outrageous!"

"Then walk." Beatrice folded her arms across her chest and arched her eyebrows, daring Phineas to leave the deal.

"You realize that you'll not find another buyer willing to pay half as much."

"See, that's where you're wrong," Beatrice said. "Naïve as we may be, I happen to know a thing or two about plants. We've got other buyers lined up, but Logan Biotech is our whale. Ten percent of your profits would get us a lot more bread than twenty percent of some other company's mediocre profits." She knew the arrogant ones always responded to having their egos stroked.

"I doubt you'll find anyone else who's interested, but you look cute pretending to know what you're talking about."

"Sorry we couldn't make it happen. Let us know if you change your mind." She handed Phineas her card. He snatched it from her fingers and grumbled the whole way to his car. The car door slammed and then the engine revved and faded into the distance as Phineas drove down the street.

"The nerve of that guy!" Beatrice said. "Naïve! Who the hell does he think he is?"

"I told you he's kind of an asshole."

"'Kind of'? He's the biggest jerk I've ever met!"

Having met James, Charlie found that difficult to believe. "Are you sure about the price?"

"Trust me. He's coming in way too low. He'll be back. This plant can have some serious therapeutic consequences, and this is the only place where he can get one."

Although she was correct about the demand for the plant, Beatrice underestimated its supply. Just before he met Charlie that afternoon, Phineas received an email from Amelia Wigglesworth:

Dear Phineas,

I hope this email finds you well.

Although it's been a long time since we last communicated, I trust your scientific interests still encompass biologically-derived therapies. My team has recently come across a rather unusual botanical specimen that I'm certain you will want to see. We believe that it has great potential for regenerative medicine (particularly of the optic nerve), something that you are interested in. You will need to sign the attached confidentiality agreement before I can provide further details, but I would love to discuss this opportunity for collaboration in person.

I look forward to hearing from you soon.

All the Best,
Amelia

The familiarity of the campus that he left over a decade ago warmed Phineas against the cool morning air. Driving the same route that he traversed daily when he worked here, he remembered details long ago stashed in the attic of his memory: Here, the fountain still ambitiously splashed its contents onto the sidewalk and passers-by; over there stood the bench on which he often sat and read papers on days just like today; and over there was the building where he taught his first lecture. These memories were polluted slightly by the sights of many foreign objects: A garden between buildings that hadn't existed during his tenure; a row of new and brightly colored bike racks; the renovated facade of the arts building; and, most obviously, the Noonan Life Science Complex.

Phineas picked up a guest pass from the guard station and parked in the lot behind the Complex. Before heading up, he took a deep breath. Amelia Wigglesworth was – although a brilliant scientist – the most anal and paranoid person he'd ever encountered. She wouldn't hesitate to claim as her own this plant that she stumbled upon, so she could get sole credit for changing the course of biology and medicine as mankind knew it. He braced himself for struggle and marched boldly toward the building.

In the Plant Biology conference room, he found Bill, hair still matted from slumber, opening a small box that arrived at the university that morning. Inside was his new Takyi 9000 replacement power cord, and not a moment too soon. Julie sat at the conference table, a spiral notebook and a paper cup of gourmet coffee in front of her. "Hi," she said, "you must be Dr. Snodgrass!"

"I'm delighted to learn that deductive reasoning is still part of PhD training," he answered.

"Oh…I heard that about you."

Amelia entered and closed the door behind her. "Phineas, it's been so long! I don't remember the last time we saw each other. You'll have to excuse me: I just caught a plane back from a conference in Zurich and came directly here from the airport. I'm still on Swiss time."

"Then you must be impeccably accurate. What sent you to Zurich?" With this question, he subtly initiated the social greeting dance of the career scientist. Across the animal kingdom, individuals within a species display a rich variety of behavior upon meeting each other: Ants touch antennae, dogs sniff backsides, and giraffes rub necks. Scientists – quirky species as they are – boast of how busy they've been writing papers and interacting with other influential scientists. It's their way of assessing each others' fitness and establishing pecking order.

"I was there for a botany conference that Lars Schroeder organized," replied Amelia.

"Lars? From Munich?"

"Not anymore. He moved to Zurich two years ago to head the biology department."

"Head the department? He has the cerebral agility of a garden snail. Anyway, I thought he was happy in Munich."

"Yes, but things changed for Lars when the dean left the university."

"The dean – you mean Jan Schwarzenhorn. He and Mickey Jones from Edinburgh developed a drought-tolerant strain of hops and started their own company…"

"Hopscotch Agroscience."

"Yes, that's it: Hopscotch. Terrible disservice they did to the European beverage industry. I had the misfortune of being invited to taste an ale brewed with their product. Atrocious. I saw Mickey last week in Tokyo. She arrived on a research vessel chartered from Australia. And you know who else was there? Victor Kurowski. He looked unwell."

"Victor? I just saw Victor in Zurich. It's such a small world. And yet you and I, who are right across town from one another, never meet. It's very strange, don't you think? There is so much interesting science going on right in our neighborhood – literally. Bill, are you ready?"

Bill had by now fully unwrapped his replacement laptop power cord, which was exactly eighteen inches long and couldn't reach the power outlet. "Motherf–," he uttered. "Not cool! Is there any web site that actually delivers what they promise? This is the third time I've had to order this stupid cord…" He looked up to find the others staring at him.

Bill set the laptop on a chair between the outlet and the lectern, where it could access both power and the projector, and queued up the presentation.

Julie explained their major findings with the gusto of a prosecutor laying out a capital murder case. She began with an exposition on the plant's anatomy, dwelling on the eye itself, which seemed to have some ability to process visual cues. From there, she turned to a discussion of physiology, touching on the intriguing elements of the plant's tissues. She mentioned that a number of animal proteins, including neurotransmitter receptors and transporters, were highly expressed in the plant.

"Do you know how it tracks motion?" Phineas asked.

"No," Julie explained, "we haven't been able to fully elucidate that mechanism yet, and we haven't eliminated the possibility of stochastic effects. We can trace some of the neural signaling through the plant body, but we haven't found a brain, or any central hub to the nervous system."

"This organism is fascinatingly complex," Amelia added.

Julie nodded her agreement and provided some very science-y details of the plant's genome. The presentation ended with a slide showing a bulleted list of questions that the Wigglesworth lab had about the plant, and specific areas on which they wanted to focus. The proud presenter looked over her audience.

"Thank you, Julie," Amelia said, "that was a very nice presentation. You're very good at this, you know. Isn't she very good, Phineas? Julie is just great, and I'm really going to miss her when she leaves – hopefully soon." She took a breath and continued, "So, Phineas, this is what we have found so far. As you can see, we are exploring many aspects of this plant – and there are many more aspects to explore. It's so beautiful, isn't it? So remarkably complex! But this opportunity is too good to pass up. Too good. This is something that we *must* study, now that we have found it. More and more, I have been thinking about completely abandoning all of the other research in my lab to focus only on this plant. That's how important it is."

"I'm a little shocked by what you're telling me," Phineas said, folding his arms across his chest, "Are you sure you're not messing with something proprietary here? Do you know of anyone who's working on anything like this?"

"There's nothing like this in the literature – but I deal primarily with academicians. I have only one *true* contact in the private sector." Her eyes met his.

"I see. Well, on the biotech side, I don't know of any companies that are close to this kind of technology."

Amelia leaned forward, elbows on the table. "Phineas, let's be honest. I think we both know who made this."

"Who, Logan? Why does everyone automatically assume that we're behind this?"

"Everyone? Who else thinks this?"

"Some idiot caterer at Frank Chan's party showed me a video of this plant and all but accused me of placing it behind his house."

"You must mean Charlie! You know Charlie? I didn't know you knew Charlie. Bill, did you know this? Charlie was the one who found the plant."

"Amelia," said Phineas, "I'm flattered that you believe we're capable of having created this little beast, but I assure you that Logan Biotech had nothing to do with this."

"Phineas, this is such a big deal that we cannot be careless. A project like this comes up once in a lifetime. I cannot afford to reproduce results that somebody else already knows. Do you understand? This plant has been highly engineered. Highly. So somebody knows much more about it than I do – so far. I just want to make sure that I'm not wasting my time re-discovering the wheel."

"This is most definitely not the work of Logan," said Phineas, tapping his finger rapidly on his chair's armrest. "I knew nothing about this before running into the moron baker at the party."

Amelia relented and signaled Bill to take his turn as presenter. He told the brief story of his visit to Charlie Bishop's back yard and how he heroically pulled the specimen from the plant, as the young squire extracted Excalibur from the stone.

"And how far is Charlie's yard from the Logan Biotech campus?" Amelia asked.

"Two and a half miles," said Bill, "as the crow flies." He advanced to the next slide, which showed a satellite image of the town with Logan Biotech and Charlie's House labeled in red.

Phineas laughed. "Surely you're kidding me! This is your damning evidence?"

Amelia sighed and folded her hands in front of her. "Phineas, you were always so uptight. It's great to see how little you've changed."

"Amelia," he whispered, "you were always stubbornly monogamous – at least when it came to hypotheses. It's nice to see that you still can't admit when you're wrong."

Her lips squeezed each other like pythons. "Bill, show the next slide."

With a click, the student projected a brightly colored block diagram of chromosomes to the screen. Hundreds of little arrows pointed to different regions on the chromosomes, each originating from one of two text boxes in the center of the slide. The boxes read *THECHILDISFATHER* and *FTHEMAN*.

"Oh, dear," said Phineas.

———————⋄∘◠◠∘⋄———————

Before Logan Biotechnologies was a company, Logan Snodgrass was a little boy.

Years ago, and within months of one another, Phineas and Amelia joined the university's science faculty as assistant professors. Thrown into the small town with the clock of tenure ticking, they bonded in their shared isolation and desperation. At the time both were married and the two couples shared dinner, plays, and treks to the country to bike the hills and canoe the rivers. They gossiped about the goings-on of the small town and spent many late nights sipping wine and discussing meaningless topics, while each young professor schemed for ways to ensure tenure and thereby stability.

Phineas's wife, Josephine, was not an academician in any sense. She was an artist – a painter and musician who enjoyed the small town for the same reason that she enjoyed any town: It provided her with abundant opportunities to observe the human condition. To her, time spent in the lab was time wasted. Plenty of beauty could be found if one only looked, she argued, and no scientific discovery could ever match the magnificence of the reality in which we already exist. Phineas loved her with all his heart. She grounded him, forcing him to keep his science in perspective. "What beauty in this can't be found elsewhere?" she asked him. "Why is it magnificent and unique?"

He answered with a critique of art: "Why is this accurate? How can we learn anything about this? What does it tell us about our existence?" They worked well together.

A few years after moving to Bloomvale, Josephine delivered the sole Snodgrass heir, a precocious boy named Logan who pondered whether shadows are scared of or in love with the dark. Logan challenged Phineas with childish questions about science, like why cure one disease if people will just die of another? One of Pan's lost boys, he wished to never grow old, as it would make life so much less enjoyable. In the end, he didn't get the chance.

When he was five years old, Logan was struck by a rare childhood blood disease. Phineas scrambled to find all the scientific literature on the subject, and ceaselessly pursued cures. Josephine humored him for the first pass, but quickly resigned herself to the reality that their baby was dying. She urged Phineas to spend time with his son, and she begged him not to foolishly throw himself into looking for a cure. She told him that science could have saved their son, had it intervened sooner; but that, at this late hour, his research only served as a distraction and an exercise in futility.

Phineas reluctantly took a leave of absence from the university to witness his son's final months. His relationship with Amelia evaporated. Without his child, there was little to discuss anymore, and Amelia felt discomfort mentioning her own children around Phineas.

Josephine was freed by Logan's absence. When he died, she struggled to regain contentment as a college professor's wife in a small town. She began to travel – first to art shows, then to various state and national parks, where she painted for weeks. She associated with a community of artists, adopted the road life, and rarely came home. Phineas saw less and less of her. He sought the solace of science, pouring himself increasingly into his work. He never shook Josephine's notion of the futility of science, and he tired of the university. Academic pursuits became pointless to him, so he took his best ideas and his best team members, and he started Logan Biotech.

"When I saw this," said Amelia, pointing to the slide, "I couldn't help but think of you."

"Yes, yes," said Phineas, his finger tapping the table, "I can understand how this might be superficially misconstrued as an implication of my involvement." He rubbed his chin pensively. "At least, to those who've never met me…or the dim-witted."

"Phineas, there's no need for this aggression."

"No? Do you understand your accusation? I'd never be so careless as to let my company's safety standards lapse to the point that top secret, bleeding-edge technology like this just slips through our doors and lands in the yard of some third-rate baker."

"He's actually a very accomplished baker."

"Yes, you're right. I unfairly evaluated the baker."

"And I'm sure that Logan's safety standards are of the highest quality."

"Then you're saying I intentionally released it? I decorated some plant's DNA with antique poetry and released it into the wild, as some sick tribute to my beloved son?" Phineas grew rigid, his joints flexing like carpenters' squares.

"It's a clever bit of cryptography that mimics your style."

"My style's more direct. I would've encoded Logan's name into the sequence, not some ridiculous poem."

"Unless you wanted to remain anonymous."

"And I certainly wouldn't have quoted William Wordsworth. His flowery incipience is no match for John Donne's bare intellectualism."

Amelia straightened and gazed through the conference room walls into the distant past, where she and Phineas clawed their way to respectable positions. "You're right," she said, remembering Phineas as a passionate young scientist, bursting with rage and skepticism. "You never were one for the Romantic poets."

"And if I had chosen one, it would have been –"

"Coleridge."

"Exactly."

Amelia stared at the aerial still of Greene County that illuminated the projector screen. The proximity of Logan headquarters to the baker's house implicated Phineas, but she knew that the plant wasn't his. "Then you didn't create this."

"Did I not mention that?"

"Then who? Maybe one of your former students?"

"My students?" asked Phineas, "What, Tidman? He's the only one clever enough to do something like this, and I'm sure he lacks the financial resources. No, Amelia – it's an odd coincidence, but I'm confident this plant has nothing to do with my research. Ever. Now, tell me: Are we going to talk about using this plant for science, or are you just going to continue to hurl accusations at me?"

Amelia folded her hands and placed them on the table in front of her. "As you've pointed out, this plant has enormous potential in regenerative medicine, and it would be scientifically irresponsible for me to withhold it from the world. I propose a collaboration: I will provide you with samples of the species and share with you my data on it so far."

"And in return?"

"You will give Bill an internship at your company."

Phineas looked at Bill, who was inspecting the laptop's power cord and scratching his arm, and at Julie, who appeared to be taking notes on the conversation. "What about her?" he asked.

Julie sat up straight.

Amelia interrupted: "Julie is already so close to graduation. I wouldn't want to slow down her progress. Bill first foud the plant. It's his project."

Phineas imagined Bill working in the lab at Logan. Maybe the florist's ask of five thousand dollars and ten percent of the profits wasn't so bad, after all. "Fine," he told Bill. "Come to Logan Biotech Monday morning, and we'll get you started. Bring samples of the plant."

CHAPTER 12

Charlie enjoyed the summertime immensely despite the stifling heat of the bakery kitchen. The long hours of sunshine allowed him to pedal lazily to work, energized by the pavement still warm from the previous day's sun. The earth was fully alive now: Trees bursting with foliage stretched steadily skyward; songbird chicks fledged to make way for the eggs of their younger siblings; early summer dandelions whitened with age and ceded territory to pink clover. Charlie rode to the bakery at half pace, knowing that Ruthie and the *cupcakes* would prevent things from getting too far out of hand before his arrival. Passing the church, he noticed its sign:

THE SOUL IS COURTYARD OF THE EYES

His midsummer buzz attenuated slightly when he spotted the telltale muscle car parked neatly in the handicapped spot behind the bakery. The boss was here. Fat BB, the owner of both the car and the bakery, wasn't as portly as his moniker suggested. The staff knew him simply as "BB," as in, "Hey, you'd better clean those pots, because BB was really pissed last week when he saw dirty dishes in the sink." He rarely came to the bakery. With Charlie managing things, BB focused on marketing, which involved little more than dropping the bakery's name during golf outings and cocktail hours. It was all sacrifice in the name of business.

Charlie entered through the front door. A large cardboard sign taped to the glass read:

Home of Arabidopsis Thaliana Miltoni, the Incredible EYE PLANT!

Inside, Ruthie and Sierra scrambled to attend to the robust crowd. A few of the regular customers sat at the small table discussing matters of great importance.

"There weren't no tens," Mr. Sommerfeld said. "They was all twenties. He had a whole stack of 'em, all twenties."

"I'm tellin' ya there were tens," said Mr. Hilbert. "The fella down the street had a bunch of tens and I know they was from Jesse 'cause they all had the same numbers."

"There weren't no tens," Mr. Sommerfeld repeated. "Hiya, Charlie, do you remember Jesse? Naw, you're too young. He was dead before you were born."

Charlie enjoyed walking in through the front on occasion. It was like Christmas morning: You never knew what joys awaited. "Jesse?" he asked.

"Naw, you're too young," repeated Mr. Sommerfeld. "Jesse used to live right here on Main. He used to carry around a stack of counterfeit twenty-dollar bills this thick." He held up his thumb and index finger as if pinching a beetle. "He'd keep 'em right here in his breast pocket." He patted his chest like a patriot in love.

"No kidding?"

"Really. I did time in the federal building because of him. Three days I had to spend there. He worked at the blueprint maker's. Used the printing press to copy a twenty-dollar bill. Looked perfect. He used the blueprint paper, the stuff they use for blueprints. He took 'em home and washed 'em in lime Kool-Aid. They looked perfect."

"But they's all the same," said Mr. Cooper. "They all had the same numbers."

"Yeah, Jesse wasn't the sharpest," said Mr. Sommerfeld. "He'd walk around with a stack of 'em in his pocket. Two bucks would get you a twenty-dollar bill."

"Sometimes I'd give one to my wife without telling her. When she did the shopping."

"She probably paid the bill with 'em."

"That's exactly what she did. I never told her, God rest her soul."

"Jesse got two years for that."

"Two and a half. Thirty months for counterfeit bills, can you believe that? He wasn't the sharpest, Jesse."

"Broke his mother's heart. His father was a mason. He was the one who started the parade."

"He didn't start the parade."

"He did! It was Jesse's old man and the other fella – Irish guy – they started the parade. They organized the first one, came 'round to the churches. Say, Charlie, you watch the parade?"

"Every year," said Charlie. "I'll be right here. Best seat in town is right where you're sitting now. Are you marching?"

"Every year," said Mr. Cooper. "Every year I've marched for the past fifty years. This year I'm juggling."

"Hey, Chuck!" Ruthie's voice cracked like an animal trainer's whip. "I hate to interrupt your pinochle game, but we've got a store filled with customers, and BB's been waiting for you all morning. If you don't want to make yourself useful, at least make your slacking less obvious."

There was a brief silence – just long enough for everyone to set their dentures. "This thick," said Mr. Sommerfeld, holding up his thumb and index finger. "Right here in his breast pocket."

Charlie excused himself from the conversation and walked up the ramp to the kitchen, lingering at every possible distraction along the way. After un-twisting the phone cord, he was out of excuses and entered the kitchen, where he found BB taking inventory.

"There he is!" BB said, holding up the previous day's newspaper and smiling. "The famous scientist-baker!" The paper's headline read: *Local Team Makes Science Breakthrough*. Underneath that, in smaller type, it said: *Biologists partner with baker to discover plant with nerves*. Next to the headline was a photo of Charlie.

The previous day, a reporter from the local paper interviewed Charlie about the eye plant. He told Charlie that the Wigglesworth lab was about to publish a paper describing an interesting biological specimen from the wilds of Milton. The scientists named the plant *Arabidopsis thaliana miltoni*, after the town. This was all news to Charlie, who hadn't heard from anyone at the university since Bill's text about *The child is father of the man.* "Uh, yeah," he said, "that's pretty big news, huh?" He never wanted the plant to be in the public eye, and now he dreaded the thought of having to tell its story over and over again. "I just found the thing, and the scientists at the university did all the work."

"You just found the thing, huh?" asked BB. "Charlie, this article says that you contributed to a scientific breakthrough! This is great news! The bakery hardly ever gets press like this – usually it's something about illegal chicken husbandry."

"Those charges were dropped."

"Doesn't matter. Ruthie didn't do us any favors with her hijinks. This is the kind of press that we need." He rattled the newspaper in front of Charlie. "This is getting us recognized. People have been coming in here all morning, asking for you – good, paying customers who wanted to meet the baker who delivered a magical little plant to the world. You're a local celebrity, and we're going to use that."

"Yeah, that's great," Charlie said, his eyes following a stupid fly buzzing around the kitchen. All insects were dumb, he knew, but the dipterans – mosquitoes and flies – fell at the lower end of the scale. They were prime candidates for getting themselves helplessly mired in frosting. Mantids, on the other hand, would almost never find themselves in such a situation...

"You don't seem thrilled," BB said.

"No, I am. I'm just not sure that I'm ready for this." He tried to stay focused on the conversation, but the fly distracted him with a sort of figure-eight pattern in the air above BB's head.

"Oh, we're ready for it. I'm framing this article and hanging it on the wall. This is something special, Charlie. *You're* something special, and people are going to want to get a piece of that. What happens in this town? Nothing! And now you –"

"I was named best baker in the state two years running. Shouldn't *that* be enough to draw a crowd?"

BB's head rolled. "The public has a short memory. Before you know it, they'll forget this and go back to patronizing the discount bakeries and corporate kitchens. I want to use this to remind them that Fat BB's is a small-town institution that cares about this community and represents the very best it has to offer. People from around the world will be coming to this town to investigate. I've got ideas, Charlie." The fly landed on BB's shoulder. It was a big, black sucker that jerked along his shirt sleeve, pausing and twitching at intervals. It disappeared over his shoulder to his back.

"Ideas?"

"Yes, ideas! Big ideas! Your discovery will be a windfall for the bakery. And for you. You'll get your cut – don't worry. But people will want to meet you, and when they do, we'll give them our characteristic treat."

"Apple cakes?"

"Eye-plant cakes!"

"Eye-plant cakes?"

"Eye-plant cakes! Just like apple cakes, but colored to look like the eye plant!" BB flailed his arms as he said this, disturbing the fly from its locale somewhere on his back. It buzzed around his legs briefly and landed on the front of his cotton apron.

"BB, I don't know…"

"Yes, Charlie! It'll be a huge hit! We'll kick it off with a big promotion: *All Eyes are on Us!* We'll give them away for free. That'll get the ball rolling."

"But apple cakes are our signature product. They've been unchanged since the bakery opened – and you told me yourself that this bakery would never sell out apple cakes, not while you were alive. If we start making apple cakes that look like eye plants, then what's to stop us from making them resemble anything else, like light bulbs?"

"Light bulbs, Charlie? Who wants to eat a cake shaped like a light bulb?"

"Inventors?"

With a lightning-fast flick, BB looped his hand in a semicircle that just grazed his thigh, his fingers snapping shut against his palm. He raised his closed hand to his ear for a second before throwing its contents hard at the floor. The fly that he trapped and then brutalized buzzed on the tile for a second before coming to a stop on its back, legs twitching slightly.

"Charlie," BB said, wiping his hand on his apron, "you're the greatest inventor in town. If you don't want light bulb cakes, then who's gonna want them? I'll tell you what we're gonna do: We're gonna have a big event to celebrate the town's scientific breakthrough – a *Plant-tastic Cake Sale*. Wha'd'ya think?"

Charlie thought it was like taking two things that he loved and mashing them into one bad idea: Peanut butter and jelly sushi, rag-top submarines, ice skating at the beach. Eye-plant cakes promised to be an abomination. He shuddered to think of his beautiful, delicious apple cakes and fascinating, innocent eye plant being forced to bear forth the demon spawn that is a novelty pastry. "I think it's the corniest damn thing I've ever heard."

BB sighed, "I thought you had better vision than this – better management skills. I stopped in here today on my way to the airport because I saw an opportunity. I want to retire and leave the bakery behind. I've wanted to for years, but I need to have one good year to secure my retirement. Your plant is that chance. We can make a windfall this year, if we play our cards right, and then I'll sell the bakery and move to Florida. Have you ever thought of owning this place?"

"Seriously?" Charlie never before heard BB speak about retirement, and he never wanted to own the bakery – but with the way things were going, how could he turn it down?

"You basically run this place, anyway. You don't need me around. But none of this happens unless you make the eye-plant cakes work. I'm counting on you, Charlie." He untied his apron and headed for the back kitchen door. "I've got to pick up some food coloring for the eye-plant cake prototypes."

"Try green Kool-Aid. It's the color of money."

CHAPTER 13

Very few people appreciated the full range of sensations offered by the Fat BB's floor. Ruthie, of course, knew that it rated somewhere between the park in summer and the alley behind Finley's as a place to spend a night. More than one small child could attest that it was a reliable place to fill a sheet of paper with the waxy palette of crayons. And plenty of structure-dwelling arthropods would tell you (had they the ability) that the bakery floor was a vast plane of delicious sweetness. Most visitors to the bakery considered its floor just another surface to walk on and experienced it only through the padded soles of their shoes. Rarely did a customer feel the subtle give of its linoleum or sense the temperature differences between the light and dark tiles of its checker pattern.

On this summer morning, one individual in the bakery realized the full tactile splendor of Fat BB's floor, which he probed with the callouses of his characteristically bare feet as he surveyed the offerings in the glass case.

Ruthie stomped down the ramp from the kitchen to greet the customer. "Can't you read the sign?" she asked.

The man turned to look at the bakery window. "It says, *Free Eye-Plant Cakes*, but I don't see any."

"I mean the other sign. The one that says, *No Shirt, No Shoes, No Service*."

"I'm wearing a shirt," the unshod man offered, gently pulling his garment's fabric to demonstrate its reality.

"You can't be in here without shoes."

"Temples are not erected to men in fashionable footwear." He smiled kindly as he bequeathed this gem to Ruthie.

"They're not erected to bums in bakeries, either." Ruthie was never one for bequeathed wisdom. "Listen, dude, you're a walking health code violation, and we're not giving away cakes until Friday. Come back then, and you can get your free cake."

"But I simply must know about this eye plant. Have you seen one around here?"

Hearing the conversation, Charlie peered out from the kitchen and viewed the scruffy leather elbow patch of an old tweed jacket in the sun's glare. It was a look he had seen before, on the university campus and in the moonlit cemetery. He brushed the flour from his hands and walked to the front of the bakery, where he addressed the shoe-less man: "I have a message for you."

"Good news, I hope."

"Phineas says, 'Hi,' and that if he ever –"

"Phineas Egglestein? He's back in town?"

"See?" said Charlie. "I *knew* you'd say something like that. He told me that if I just said 'Phineas,' you'd know who I meant."

"Ah, Snodgrass! The only Phineas who thinks he's the only Phineas in the world. I was hoping you were talking about Phineas Egglestein. He owes me thirty dollars, which I could use to purchase a new sock." He held up a worn, gray sweat sock and bounced it a couple of times, causing the lump in its toe to ring with the unmistakable jingle of coins. "I'm considering an argyle."

"Chuck, you know this guy?" Ruthie asked.

"I met him in the cemetery on the night of your party," said Charlie. Turning to the man, he asked, "How do you know Phineas Snodgrass?"

"He and I co-founded Logan Biotechnologies. I'm Tidman Luken-pweet," the bum answered with a slight bow. Noticing how Ruthie eyed him, he added, "It was a long time ago."

"No shit?"

"Look it up. Phineas was my mentor when I was at the university, and then we started the company. Our first product was a wonderful drug – an anesthetic made from modified bumble bee venom, *Apitoxincredizole*. We engineered a beautiful line of bees that produced orgasmic venom. When they'd sting you, it was like having a little orgasm at the site of the sting. Incredible!" He smiled into the past, remembering the pleasures inflicted by thousands of tiny little orgasm-inducing bee stings.

"Sick," said Ruthie.

"Clearly you haven't been stung by one," said Tidman, spinning his facial hair wistfully. "We chemically altered the bee venom into a powerful local anesthetic, or *apisthetic*, as we called it. It was a big hit. For our follow-up, we went after the bigger societal problem of drunkenness. We developed *Sobrinol* – the drug that I gave you in the cemetery. It immediately sobered up even the most inebriated lush, but it was never approved."

"Because of the Brussels sprouts aftertaste?" asked Charlie.

"The aftertaste was an inconvenience, but frequent users in the clinical trials dealt with it by switching to darker ales that pair nicely with cruciferous veggies. The bigger problem was that politicians claimed the drug would be used as an excuse to reject temperance, and that it assaulted the Creator's plan to provide the world with addicts on whom to blame society's shortcomings. It's society's loss, as the drug promised to prevent thousands of traffic deaths and divorces. I fundamentally disagree with the decision, and abandoned the for-profit pharmaceutical industry."

"So now you hand out unapproved drugs in the cemetery?"

"Only if a medicine is free can the whole world reap its benefits." He pulled a bit of his mustache away from his face and tried looking at it. "Which is why I'm so intrigued by your eye-plant cakes – or specifically, the eye plants that inspired them. Do you realize that such a species holds the potential to upend regenerative medicine?"

"Of course," said Charlie. "That's why I contacted Professor Wigglesworth and Dr. Snodgrass."

"And you think that was wise?"

"Why wouldn't it be?"

"As Hamlet said, *Thankless foul science cowards cause doom*. What if I told you that your plant was intentionally created by an intelligence you cannot comprehend to serve a purpose that you haven't even considered, and its appearance in your yard was all part of a plan that you yourself helped advance by alerting the rest of the world to its existence?"

Ruthie's eyes grew like rising storm clouds. "Chuck, that's exactly what I was telling you! That thing is creepy. I mean, what's an eye doing on a plant like that? It's totally unnatural. What if it goes wild and takes over the world?"

"Precisely," said Tidman, "so that – millions of years from now – the highly evolved descendants of cockroaches dig into the earth and discover the remains of a once great civilization of hairless primates, followed by a million-year Era of Plants? Hasn't this crossed your mind?"

It had crossed Charlie's mind – fleetingly while talking with Ruthie – but he dismissed it as one of her eccentricities. Now, this grubby man was causing him to question the wisdom of revealing the plant to anyone. It would've been perfect if he and Beatrice had remained the only two who knew about it, but now he worried that he made a mistake in allowing her to show it to Bill, or allowing him to take a sample. "Do you think that's possible?" he asked. "That they'll take over the world?"

"How should I know? I'm just a guy in a bakery hoping to get a free cake a day early."

———— ⋅∘⟋⟍∘⋅ ————

The bike ride home was Charlie's time for quiet clarity in the midst of the active town. Summer poured from lawns and flower beds like candy, adorning the yards with pillows of pink and white blooms. Greenery crawled over any surface that could support life and oozed from crevices in the pavement and asphalt. The season's rigor peppered the air with the delicious potpourri of gasoline and freshly cut grass. Weeds grew at the base of the church sign, which boldly declared:

TRIFLE NOT WITH THE DIVINE

Good idea, thought Charlie, *but too late*. Over the course of the summer he'd grown attached to his plant. It made his life interesting. It wasn't just a transient in his yard, but a permanent resident, his charge. It was a precious gift that the universe entrusted to him, and he was determined to honor the universe by appreciating it. He fed it and watered it and worried for it during midnight thunderstorms. He poured himself into caring for this little plant.

Still, Tidman's warning echoed in his mind. After the barefoot bum wandered out of the bakery and into the street, Charlie looked him up online, finding his story checked out. He really was the co-founder of Logan Biotech, and really was once a brilliant scientist. Could he still know what he was talking about? He spoke knowingly of the plant. What if it truly was nefarious, a biological weapon? Might he just be an unwitting pawn in a plan to destroy civilization? Could the bum be right? Could *Ruthie* be right?

No, he decided, *the plant brings forth too many good things to be something evil*. It caught the attention of Beatrice. It earned him a touch of fame, as its discoverer. It might even win him ownership of the bakery. The plant brings good fortune. Maybe he'd put a shrine around it and charge people to see it. Or was the good fortune just part of its ruse?

Turning into the alley behind his house, he saw that his back gate was open. He considered this odd but not outlandish, as local pizzerias tended to stick fliers in any doorway within eyesight, the fence gate included. He parked his bike in the garage, closed the gate and walked toward the house. Then he saw it – or rather, didn't see it.

The plant was gone, and in the spot where it used to stand was a circular hole, a crater big enough to hold an apple cake.

CHAPTER 14

George Chan walked alone through the woods, half-looking for memories from his boyhood. He was home for the summer, and for various disciplinary reasons it was uncertain whether he'd be allowed to return to his school in the fall. His father forbade him from traveling with his chums or visiting their summer homes, so George was stranded friendless in Greene County for three months. He had no interest in finding a job or pursuing volunteer work, and any activities that he might suggest would almost certainly be rejected by his father.

On that day, George trounced around the woods behind his house. He spent many afternoons there when he was living at home years ago, building forts and climbing trees and partaking in other such boyish activities. Those woods provided him with a place to escape his home life – a place where he could be himself. Here, in the midst of nature, there was no judgment, and no behavior that was frowned upon. All the forest life – animal, plant, lichen – simply followed its own nature without concern about right and wrong. George, immersed in that cathedral of trees, was cleansed of the sins that weighed on him at home. In the forest, he was just Boy, now Young Man, walking at his own pace, picking up a switch and swinging it through the tall grass. Animals rightfully scurried away at the sound of his approach. He was not a shameful little faggot, but a member of the capstone species who commanded respect.

George fell in love with those woods, and he fell in love – or something like it – in them, years ago. His mother's childhood friend visited for a week each summer. Thankfully, she had a son who was about George's age. The two boys played intensely in these woods for one week each year, passing full days in what seemed like minutes. To the outside observer, they were childhood friends with a youthful zest for life. They themselves believed this for many years, until they found themselves full of hormones and with absolutely no interest in girls.

It was during that summer, when the two were baring their souls to each other, that George found the nest. He knew of the giggle bees from trips to Logan Biotech with his father. These were big, beautiful bumble bees with distinguishing blue wings that flashed brightly when the light hit just right. He followed one through a field to a hole in the ground and – on a dare from his summer friend – allowed one to sting him. The sensation was lovely. The two boys spent an afternoon chasing after the blue-winged bees, pleasuring each other with their stings, enjoying giving another enjoyment. That day was the magical end of George's childhood. Although they never actually *did* anything that was strictly forbidden by their parents and pastors, the sin was in their hearts. They knew.

Their parents knew it, too. The boys returned to the Chan house with wilts all over their skin, each sporting the serene mask of carnal satisfaction and suffering from uncontrollable smirks and giggles that betrayed the jokes they harbored. Both families knew it was time to separate the boys for their own good, and for the good of the families. The visit ended three days earlier than planned, and George never saw or heard from his friend again.

Now, back in the woods, George wandered to the site of an old giggle bee nest, only to find a complete lack of activity. He ambled over to a nearby clump of wildflowers and waited. He saw nothing. He was just deciding to move on when he caught a glimpse of blue out of the corner of his eye. It was a large bee, lazily sampling the buffet of tiny white flowers.

Rather than grab it, George watched the bee, hoping that it would lead him back to the season's nesting site. He followed it from flower to flower, watching it collect nectar until it zipped off toward a patch of trees. He waited, and within a few minutes he spotted the bee's sister, tracing the same flight path.

Bee after bee flew by, and George followed them incrementally, focused on finding their place of residence. So intent was he on his goal that he neglected to pay attention to the other activity in the forest around him. When he finally arrived at the nest, he discovered that he wasn't the first one there.

A bear guarded the nest like a jealous lover, enamored by the delightful stings. Stepping through the woods, George startled the beast.

The bear charged.

George turned to run, but couldn't move, as he was face down on the forest floor. His last sensations were a heavy weight on his back and the bear's hot, foul breath on his face.

CHAPTER 15

Of the very few skills that Charlie mastered during his teenage years, sulking was the one that he could still perform impeccably when the need arose. He sulked with a Dickensonian panache, cloaked in a cloud of gloom that chilled the air around him. A scowl smeared across his face like bright stripes on a poisonous insect, warning all to keep their distance. Only the most dim-witted dared venture close.

"Hey, Charlie, you go to the casino a lot?" Mr. Sommerfeld asked. He and a few other regular customers lingered in the bakery, taking inventory of who's sick, who just died, and whose habits suggested encroaching senility. It was the day of the big eye-plant cake giveaway, and Ruthie and the *cupcakes* tended to a crowd of customers vying for free pastries. The thought fed Charlie's ire, and he intensified his scowl, furious about his pilfered plant.

"I haven't been to the casino in two-three months," said Mr. Cooper, not waiting for Charlie's reply. "Not since Judd passed."

"Two-three months? I thought you went every Wednesday."

"Used to, for the buffet. They have that great buffet there. Half price for seniors on Wednesdays. Least it used to be. Now it's the full twenty-five dollars for the meal. I can't eat twenty-five dollars' worth of food."

"Yeah, but they still give the senior discount for parking."

"The senior discount ain't worth nothin'. I go and pay five bucks for parking and then twenty-five for dinner? I used to get the same thing for twelve-fifty. Most times I'd play a few hands of blackjack while I was there."

"Hard to find a good buffet."

"And that was a good one, too. I'd always go for the crab cakes – "

"Oh, the crab cakes! Say, Charlie, you ever have the crab cakes at the casino?"

"But for twenty-five bucks? You can have it." Mr. Cooper waved his hand dismissively, brushing away the idea of a full-price buffet like a sluggish horse fly.

In no mood for idle chatter, Charlie walked to the bakery office and dropped into the squeaky green chair. He stared at the items around him: the old computer, papers, a letter opener reading *Trinnie's Army Surplus – For All Your Surplus Needs*. He cursed Phineas Snodgrass, certain that the man was responsible for the plant's disappearance. All the evidence pointed in his direction. The scientist expressed an interest in the plant as soon as he saw the video at the party, and he stood to make a fortune off it. Who else could possibly have taken it?

The bum, he thought, *that's who*. The shoe-less, pill-popping bum who used to pal around with Snodgrass. But what would a bum want with the plant? *Maybe he stole it for Snodgrass*. The old curmudgeon could've offered his buddy Tidman a nice sum for stealing the plant, keeping his own hands clean. That must've been it.

Unless it was Amelia Wigglesworth. Charlie wouldn't put it past her. He hadn't pegged her for a low-grade plant thief, but he didn't know her well enough to say for certain that she *hadn't* stolen it. Maybe she did it pre-emptively, to prevent Phineas or anyone else from gaining access to the technology. Did she enlist her student Bill to do it? Would he have done it? Could Bill have taken it himself? Like Phineas, he knew right away that there was good science locked up in the plant. Did he want it for his own purposes? But Beatrice said he could be trusted. Was *she* lying?

Charlie bounced from suspect to suspect as he stared at the scratched finish of the desk. He was upset about losing the plant – partially because a single leaf was worth a load of money, but mostly because he'd bonded with it. The plant was his adopted child, an innocent and helpless stranger in need, a life that trusted him to care for it. He should've done more to protect it. He *would* do more to protect it, as soon as he ripped it from the clutches of whatever cruel fool dared pull it from his land.

A knock came at the door. "Go away," Charlie barked.

Ruthie opened the door and entered the office. "Wow! You look like shit!" she said.

"Thanks, Ruthie, now my day is complete. I was just sitting here waiting for someone to randomly stop by and insult my physical appearance. I guess I'll check that one off the list and go home."

"Chuck, don't be an ass. We've got a line of people going out the door. They're all waiting for free eye-plant cakes. Are you gonna help or not?"

"What do you think, Ruthie? Do I look like I'm in the mood to hawk a bunch of cakes in memory of my stolen plant?"

"Don't dump your vitriol on me, dude. I didn't take it. I was here with you all day."

"Yeah, I know." Charlie stabbed the desk with the letter opener. "Nobody took it. Nobody knows where it is. Everybody's sorry."

"If it were up to me, you'd have your damn plant. Then maybe you wouldn't be so moody and could actually help us out around here." Ruthie left the office, slamming the door in her wake.

Charlie returned to his list of suspects, sifting his memory for unusual behavior over the past few days. Through the office door he heard the bustling kitchen: oven doors slamming closed, trays clanging on cooling racks, feet stomping up and down the ramp between kitchen and store front. He heard the *cupcakes* chatting and singing as they decorated eye-plant cakes. *How many have we given away?* he wondered. He was tempted to venture out to the store front to see how things were going, but convinced himself that he lacked the enthusiasm to do so. Another knock came at the door.

"Ruthie, goddammit, what?"

"Charlie?" Beatrice called softly from the other side.

Nothing ruins a perfectly splendid sulk quite like a surprise visit from the object of one's affection. Charlie's mood, which he'd successfully held at just a hair above pitch black for the entire day, underwent a series of wild corrections, like a highway driver hitting a patch of ice after swerving to avoid a deer. Immediately upon hearing her voice, he nearly smiled with elation. To preserve his sulk, he conjured the memory of his poached plant. Scowl in place, he opened the door.

Beatrice stood tiny against the grubby hallway of the bakery. She stepped back from the office door, prepared to flee if necessary. In her hands she held a small box wrapped in leaf-print paper. "Hi Charlie," she said, handing him the package. "I'm sorry about your plant." Reading his expression, she added, "Ruthie told me."

"What is this?" Charlie took the box from her hands.

"Open it."

Charlie stared at the box in his hands, and then at Beatrice, who stared back expectantly. He lifted the lid to reveal a blue terra cotta pot filled with soil. In the center grew a tiny plant with flat leaves in a star pattern. It was a miniature version of the plant he'd loved and lost, except it lacked the stalk and, critically, the eye.

"Is this…?"

"A baby eye plant!"

"But how did you…?"

"I have my ways."

Her smirk melted him. "Beatrice…"

"I got it from Bill," she confessed. "He cloned a bunch from that leaf he took from your plant. He's been providing them to Dr. Snodgrass at Logan Biotech."

"It's beautiful."

"I knew you'd like it. Besides, it meant something to me, too," she half-lied. She was never as fond of the plant as he – nobody could be. Whereas her material worth depended intimately on plants, her self-worth was completely independent of whether any one particular plant lived or died. It struck her as odd, but cute and – in a way – admirable, that Charlie invested so much emotion in this plant; that he cared about it enough to allow it to disrupt his life. The pragmatic florist felt that Charlie should be more upset about losing a potential fortune than about losing the plant. After all, he discovered it and gave it to the world for science and medicine. Surely, he should get *some* recognition.

"I don't know how I can ever thank you."

"Maybe," said Ruthie, who was standing in the doorway behind Beatrice, "just getting down there and giving away a bunch of cakes will be thanks enough. Isn't that right, Bea?" She patted Beatrice on the shoulder. Nodding to the plant that Charlie held, she added, "That thing's friggin' creepy, Chuck."

But Charlie disagreed. To him, the plant was miraculous, a wonder. It brought Beatrice to him, and now she brought him the plant. Not the same plant, but almost – a clone, an exact replicate, a duplicate. Better, even: a child. She had given him a child. Maybe she was just trying to cheer him up, but maybe she meant something more.

He hoped she meant something more.

CHAPTER 16

Computational biologists and bioinformaticists are the dung beetles of the life sciences. They thrive on material that has been digested and abandoned by their scientifically more cumbersome peers, scavenging journal web sites and databases for morsels to roll back to their labs and analyze. Provided a large and juicy enough pile of data, the computational biologists will crawl out of their dwellings and pick it apart, piece by piece, until nothing remains but a discolored spot where the data heap was dumped. Then, as the Egyptians noticed millennia ago, new life occasionally springs forth from one of the scavenged lumps of data.

This is exactly what happened when a small band of data scarabs from a university on the other side of the country encountered Amelia's data set. They analyzed the plant genome using a program that searched for coded signals in over a thousand languages – and they found a second message.

In any sufficiently long sequence of characters, one expects to find *some* signal that has meaning to someone, somewhere. DNA is no exception. The hedgehog genome, for example, contains within its billion or so characters an offensive Swahili phrase written in Morse code. The humble cashew, a tropical plant by nature, contains no fewer than a dozen references to distinct Inuit words for snow. Every canine on the planet carries within its DNA the phrase "I wish I was a pussycat" in the language of an alien race from a television sci-fi program – although it may be debated that the artificial language was developed specifically to taunt dogs. What one does not expect to find in DNA is a software license, yet this is exactly what the bioinformaticists found.

Of all people, it was Bill who broke the news to Phineas and Amelia. He'd recently started experiments at Logan Biotech, regenerating eyes in mice using tissue from *miltoni* plants, and he was scheduled to report on his findings. The team assembled in the conference room, where Bill desperately tried coaxing his laptop computer to cooperate with the LCD projector. The computer, unable to figure out why this hairy beast so persistently prodded it with cables, refused to comply.

Bill stalled by asking, "Did anyone see the preprint server this morning?" It was a rare occasion when a grad student was able to report science news to his advisor and her peers, and he relished the moment. "They found the entire GNU GPL in the *miltoni* genome. It's encoded in Braille within the non-coding regions of the plant's DNA."

The GNU General Public License, or GPL, is one of many licenses that open-source software developers paste into the source code they write. It boils down to this: The source code for any software that is licensed under GNU GPL must be made available for the entire world to view and modify with (almost) no restrictions. The one restriction is that any software that contains any GNU GPL-licensed software as a component must itself also be free under the GNU GPL.

A rough analogy to hardware would be that if nuts and bolts had the GPL printed on them, then their blueprints would have to be freely available to the whole world. Further, anything that is held together with nuts and bolts would also be required to have the GPL printed on it, and *its* blueprints would also be required to be freely available to the whole world. This would present a big problem for manufacturers of anything that's held together by nuts and bolts, and it's a big reason that for-profit software companies eschew the GPL.

"So I guess any work we do with the plant has to be open-source," said Julie.

"The hell it does," snapped Phineas. "What is it with you academic sorts and your love for giving away things for free?"

"I mean, the plant's DNA is its source code – "

"Says who?"

"It's in your book," said Julie, referring to a textbook Phineas authored years ago. "But if that's the case, and if the plant's DNA is GPL, then all of our modifications to it have to be GPL, too."

"Are you mad?" asked Phineas, incredulous that the one student who actually cracked his book was now using it against him. "When has the GPL ever stopped anyone from commandeering open source for their own personal gains? Besides, who's going to complain? The authors have yet to come forward." This last point was something that the scientists opted to ignore most of the time: Although the plant was clearly engineered, nobody claimed responsibility for engineering it.

"I think it was Tidman," Amelia said. She'd been reading the bioinformatics article on her laptop and was conclusive on the matter. "He always had extreme views on how medicines should be available to everyone. Phineas, I know how you feel about this – that it can't possibly be him – but who else could it be?"

"This lack of focus is exactly why I abandoned academic research. I came here to discuss the plant's ability to regenerate eyes in mice – research which, I might remind you, is funded by my company, using profits derived from innovative products that we don't give away for free – and instead I'm watching a student fumble with his computer and listening to speculation about inconsequential licensing matters. Do you even know what you're doing?"

"Phineas," Amelia said, placing her hand on his, "I assure you that we are the best team in the world for this work. Bill and Julie have also been analyzing the plant's DNA for messages, you know."

"We found *The child is father of the man*," offered Julie.

"And an enrichment in methionine and cysteine," added Bill. "They both appeared with the same frequency as *The child is father of the man*. We thought it might be a signature."

"A signature?"

"You know, like M.C. Thechildisfatheroftheman. Like the deejay who spun up the plant or something."

"M.C. Thechildisfatheroftheman? What kind of idiotic name is that? Meanwhile, there are thousands of blind people who would love to get new eyes generated from plants…"

"Yes," said Bill, "the mouse experiments." He managed to project a slide onto the screen. It showed a photograph of dead mice. "We separated mice into two groups: A control group, and a treatment group. We blinded the mice in both groups and implanted *miltoni* eyes into the vacant sockets of the mice in the treatment group. The mice in the control group remained totally blind, but the ones in the treatment group…"

"Is it a website?" asked Phineas.

"Is what a website?"

"The message. *THECHILDISFATHER, FTHEMAN, C, M.* Is it a website? *thechildisfatheroftheman.com*. Except there're no characters in the genetic code for 'O' or '.', so somehow the message got scrambled across the genome."

Amelia laughed. "That's ridiculous. Phineas, Bill was just getting to the best part."

"The child is father of the man dot com?" Bill asked. He typed the address into his web browser, which landed on what appeared to be an empty channel on the internet. The occupants of the conference room stared dumbly at the projector screen, showing a web browser filled with nothing but static, like an old television set missing its rabbit ears.

"Fitting," said Phineas. "Indiscernible white noise is exactly what I should've expected."

Bill clicked on the static in the middle of the screen and was redirected immediately to a web site featuring a replacement power cord for his Takyi 9000 laptop. He eyed the specifications: six-foot cord, properly sized adapter plug, prongs that matched outlets on this continent, correct voltage. Yes, this was the power cord he'd been looking for. Without hesitation, he clicked the button that begged: "Add to Cart."

CHAPTER 17

Ruthie moved her arm steadily over the table, allowing her wrist to do the work. She flicked the ladle with the competence of a maestro conducting a symphony. Swoop after swoop, she poured golden soufflé batter into the ramekins, pausing over each just long enough to fill it half an inch below the rim. "See? It's easy. Just do it easy."

Sierra cringed and looked at her own ramekins, a tray of overfed babes in a nursery, their chins sticky with spit-up yellow batter.

The two were in the Fat BB's kitchen preparing a batch of soufflés. Charlie and Ruthie decided not to make a big deal of Soufflé Days; instead, they gave the bakery's newest offering a soft launch – appropriately like a lovingly-baked soufflé. They also took advantage of the timing.

Each summer the town of Milton held its annual Founders' Day Celebration, beginning with a Saturday morning parade along Main Street and ending with Saturday night fireworks one week later. For the intervening eight days, Milton's Central Park turned into a fairground, hosting carnival rides and games that rolled into town on the beds of eighteen-wheeled trucks. The parade and subsequent fair were the highlight of the summer in Milton, motivating townsfolk to squat on prime parade-viewing sidewalk blocks days in advance. All the Main Street businesses offered parade promotions, and this year Pearl skated along the street in front of Fat BB's, providing free samples of soufflés and eye-plant cakes to hungry parade-goers. The treats were intended to pull people into the bakery, where the aromas closed the sale.

While Charlie watched the crowd gather, he received this text from Bill:

`thechildisfatheroftheman.com`

He clicked the link, and his phone produced a screen full of static. Unsure whether this was just a broken site, he tapped the center of the static. Up popped a web page selling grow lights. *Odd*, he thought, *but quite reasonably priced.* Thinking of the plant Beatrice gave him, he added the light to his shopping cart and tapped to continue shopping. The browser went back to the staticky site, and Charlie again tapped on the static. This time the browser landed on a page selling small bottles of all-purpose oil that would be perfect for treating the squeaky chair in the bakery office. He added this to his cart and continued shopping. Once again the page showed nothing but static. Wondering whether he was just being shown random items, he clicked on the static once more. The page that opened advertised cat toys. *Ah*, he thought, *what use is that? I've never owned a cat in my life.*

Just then, Pearl skated in with an empty tray, back for a refill before parade candy ruined the customers' appetites. She gave Charlie a quick report of the parade crowd as she refilled her tray with goodies. "By the way," she said, casting Charlie a smile so large that it hurt his cheeks, "Bea says, 'Hi.'" She executed a quick double axel and rolled out the door.

Charlie's heart knocked against his tonsils. Surely this was a test, or an invitation. What else could it be? He located the prettiest cake in the bakery and hurriedly adorned it with additional flowers of icing. He placed the cake in a box and headed up the street to Rose's Floral and Gifts.

❧

The inside of the flower shop was a plant-filled grotto, its humid air heavy with the stench of fertilizer. Shelves covered with greenery crowded the front window, and a large glass case of cut flowers stood against one wall. In addition to plants, the shop housed tables adorned with country wares and antiques that James scavenged on his excursions to the homes of the recently departed. As Charlie walked across the creaking wooden floor, a small black cat with a white chin sauntered out from a corner and brushed herself against his calf.

"Hey, kitty," he said, in his most kitty-soothing voice. The cat rolled belly-up on his feet, and Beatrice appeared through a doorway at the back of the shop.

"Looks like you made a new friend, Lulu." She smiled at the cat and Charlie.

"I wanted to thank you for the plant," he said, handing her the box.

"Charlie! That's sweet. You didn't have to." She looked inside the box. "Cake! Wonderful!"

"It's kind of obvious."

"Like getting a flowering plant from the florist?"

"Something like that."

"So, how's the new plant doing, anyway?"

"Fine, so far. I'm not letting it outside the house. I put it in a sunny window." He brushed the cat gently with the side of his foot. "Sorry I was in such a bad mood the other day. I was just in shock. Who'd steal a plant from someone's yard like that? What kind of person does that?"

Beatrice shrugged. "Parade's starting," she said, pointing to a single police car crawling up Main Street. "Let's go watch."

She pulled Charlie outside, where they stood just behind the buzzing crowd. A faint thump of drums drifted down Main Street, gradually gaining intensity. Eventually, a white banner and an American flag swayed their way into view, heralding the start of the procession. A group of men from the American Legion Post led the charge, dressed in white shirts and sunglasses, proudly bearing the nation's colors. Behind them, a steady stream of representatives from the town's finest philanthropic organizations and businesses flowed past. Lions and Antelopes marched by in their colorful vests, waving at the spectators and throwing them candy. Succeeding them were plenty of freshly washed pickup trucks decorated with the names of local businesses: Walter's Hardware, R & R News, Tina's Beauty, Jim's Barber Shop.

"Hey," said Beatrice, "There's Gary from the auto shop." She waved at the passing pickup truck and was tossed a handful of hard, pink bubble gum that scattered on the asphalt. Students from Young's Karate marched by in their white uniforms and colorful belts, hurdling over one another with board-breaking flying kicks. They were followed by an antique convertible carrying Miss Milton, the Parade Princess. Charlie wondered how anyone even became a contestant for the title. He was sure that Beatrice would win if she entered. His attention was drawn away by a red-nosed man in a bright purple outfit on five-foot stilts.

"Look," he said, "it's Riffles the Clown. Isn't he creepy?"

"I wouldn't want him at my kid's party."

"What if you had an obnoxious kid?"

"Even then."

A group of bagpipers in kilts marched by, playing *Scotland the Brave*, which Beatrice insisted was the only song that the instruments were capable of playing. The pipers were followed by the scouts of troop 438. "Some scouts," said Charlie. "Shouldn't they have been the first ones along the route?"

The baker and florist entertained themselves by commenting on the participants, grabbing at candy and waving to marching friends. The noise and circumstance of the parade excited Charlie as only an annual parade can. Then, amid the blaring of horns, the cheering of the crowd, and the pounding of drums, Beatrice said, "James and I broke up."

"Huh?"

"Yeah. It was a long time coming."

"I'm sorry to hear that," Charlie said. He was not.

"Thanks. He was kind of a control freak. I've broken up with him before – many times – and he always said, 'You'll come crawling back to me,' and I always did. This time it was different. It felt different. There's no going back after the things that I said."

A squadron of Shriners from the Medinah Temple performed maneuvers before them on gas-powered carpets. "Well, if he's bad for you," Charlie said, "then you're better off without him." Realizing how dumb this sounded, he added, "But I guess it has to be hard, ending a long-term relationship like that."

"Yeah, it hurts…but so did staying with him. Every time I went back to him, I knew that I was making a mistake. I kept telling myself that I should leave for good, but then I always wound up right back with this total jerk. Look! The unicycle monkeys!"

Before them, a dozen or so men dressed like apes rode unicycles in a figure-eight. Charlie struggled for words, but came up with nothing. Fire truck horns echoed in the distance. Desperate to keep the conversation alive, he said, "Have you ever gone to the carnival?"

"Years ago, when I was a kid. My friends and I would hang out there when I was in high school. I haven't been recently, though. James was against it. He says it's a bastion for children and trash. Isn't that nice?"

"So what? Maybe he's right. Ruthie goes every year, and she can pass for either category. We should go."

"Are you calling me trash, or a child?"

The fire trucks rolled leisurely past, lights flashing and horns blaring. The crowd would soon become unglued from their perches and begin seeking good food and cool drinks. "I'm saying that you should be whoever you want to be, and do whatever you want to do." Charlie turned to walk back to the bakery.

"Charlie," called Beatrice, "your friend is going to miss you." She pointed to Lulu's yellow eyes gazing at Charlie from within a patch of ficus foliage in the flower shop's bay window.

Pushing his way through the dissipating Main Street crowd, Charlie pulled out his phone and added the cat toy to his cart.

Chapter 18

Marcus awoke with a sharp pain in his head. He sniffed the air, finding the usual odors of urine, feces, fur, and a faint whiff of pine – nothing unusual. The cage was empty, though: He was completely alone. *Where are the others?* he thought. *What is this sharp pain in my skull? Why can't I see?*

Marcus was not his real name. He had no name. He was a mouse, living in a laboratory at Logan Biotechnologies. The entire purpose of his existence was to be experimented upon by humans, but he didn't know this. He, like Charlie Bishop and Beatrice Martin, had absolutely no idea why he existed. But unlike the seven billion or so humans with whom he shared the planet, he felt no need to invent purpose for his life. He just took it as it came.

Until now, that strategy worked for him, but the current situation was completely new. He was in the familiar context of a plastic container lined with pine shavings, but wasn't accustomed to being either alone or blind. The pain in his head was terrible. He needed a drink.

Marcus followed the scent of processed mouse chow to the food tray. From there, he found a neighboring wall and then pointed himself toward the water bottle. He walked over to where he assumed it would be, reared, and searched. One paw struck a drop of room-temperature water suspended in mid-air – the tell-tale sign of the bottle. He greedily lapped up a few mouthfuls from the hanging tap before retiring to the least drafty corner of the cage for a nap. Perhaps later he would groom, he thought, if he had the energy. But for now, he needed sleep. And maybe to scratch the tip of his tail.

⸻ ⊷ ⊶ ⸻

The sneering skunk stood on its front quarters, its back arched to present its hind weaponry toward the threat. Phineas sneered back, unimpressed. If anything, he found the skunk's display to be tacky. To him, it perfectly represented the tendency of the weak to threaten to spew forth a stream of putridity in order to keep critics at bay. He dismissed the creature with a smirk and swirled the liquid within his glass. The crystal hummed each time the solitary ice cube within struck its edge, melting the ice and waking the spirit.

Frank's study was lined wall-to-wall with book cases and adorned with taxidermy, including the stuffed skunk that stared at Phineas from a high shelf. Phineas sat on the leather couch and Frank puffed a cigar behind the massive mahogany desk. In front of him was a half-finished book of matches advertising: *Sally's Tutoring: Math, Science, English*, with a phone number.

"I'm clearing out that corner for the bear," said Frank, pointing with his cigar. "He's being mounted now. I expect him to arrive in a few months, but I've got the sausage already." The bear attack left George with lacerations to his arm, neck, and face. He lost an eye. Frank hired a home nurse to see to his recovery, which George viewed as another way for his father to keep close tabs on him.

"He'll make an impressive addition to your collection." Phineas admired the specimens on the wall: pheasant, buck, muskie. The disembodied head of a lion bared its fangs above the door.

"I shot that guy in Tanzania," said Frank, noticing Phineas's gaze. "Really just a pussycat. Went down like he was filled with straw. But the bear put up a fight. He didn't want us around there, and he refused to leave the hive even after we shot him the first time. Usually animals run away after they're shot – I know I would – but this bear just stood there and moaned. He laid down right on top of it – *right on top of the hive* – and panted until he died. Helen wanted to shoot him again – put him out of his misery – but I didn't let her damage the hide any more. It's tough to down a bear with one shot, and even if you have to wait for him to bleed out, it's worth it once you get him back from the taxidermist. I'm thinking that I'll put a cowboy hat on him – or maybe a tutu, in honor of George!" He laughed, shooting smoke from both sides of his mouth.

Phineas smiled and sipped his drink. He probably detested Frank, but he really enjoyed a good scotch. "I appreciate that you destroyed the hive," he said.

"I'm not going to risk the boy going back out there and losing the rest of his face. I thought you got rid of those bees years ago."

"Yes, well, some of our team may have been less than enthusiastic about exterminating the bees." Phineas thought of Tidman, who engineered the insects to produce harmless stings. After he isolated the active components of the apisthetic, the company mass-produced it in enormous bioreactors of insect cells exuding the modified toxin. Phineas ordered all the giggle bee hives destroyed, lest the creatures escape into the wild and invite lawsuits or corporate theft. Tidman argued that the world needed the bees, and he opposed their destruction. He developed an unnatural attachment to them, speaking of them as a man might his own children.

"But those bees of yours, Phin," said Frank, his head the full moon behind a cloud of cigar smoke, "they blinded my boy. You gotta make that right."

"We're working on it. We've had notable success regenerating eyes in mice using tissue grown in the plant. After we iron out a few wrinkles, we'll be ready to move on to more advanced species."

"You'll move on to George."

"Yes, eventually George will be a candidate for transplantation – but not yet. The treated mice chew off their own tails. It's a rather gruesome side effect, and we don't want George to suffer anything like that."

"How could he? George doesn't have a tail."

Phineas stared at the large ice cube in the center of his glass. It was only partially melted, like a perfectly clear golf ball. Frank must've boiled the water before freezing it. Leave it to Chan to make an un-chewable ice cube. "There's still a lot that we don't know about the therapy."

"Phin," said Frank, pointing the ashy end of his cigar at the scientist, "Logan's not the only biotech I'm involved in. I know damn well that it's not necessary to understand everything about a therapy in order to get it approved. If it was, we'd have no drugs and make no money." He chewed his cigar to emphasize the point about making money. "Treat George. Fix my boy."

"It's not that easy, Frank. There are steps to take. We need to apply for a clinical trial, establish a review board, prove safety in multiple animal models – "

"Phin, how long have you been in this business? You only need a patient who can benefit from the technique – that's George. The results will speak for themselves. Nobody will care if you filed all the right paperwork. Investors will flock to Logan because you have a therapy that works. Besides, if you don't do it, someone else will."

"Someone else? Who? Nobody else has access to the plant. And people *will* care if we don't have the right paperwork filed. Don't forget, Frank: It's still *my* company."

"Have it your way," said Frank, dropping the butt of his cigar into his drink. "But understand that I'm getting George a new eye, whether or not you approve. And you can be damn sure that I'm gonna profit from it."

CHAPTER 19

"Ooh, Clyde," Ruthie moaned, "I want you to stuff your balls between my jugs so bad." Clyde wound up and gave it his all. The baseball smacked the padded wall hard, completely missing the targeted stack of plastic milk bottles. Clyde cursed.

"Five bucks fer two more balls," said the seedy-looking guy working the game, his eyes tracking a cluster of teenage girls walking by the booth. "Y'had enough, or ya' still wanna convince your lady tha'chore a man?"

When Charlie envisioned going to the carnival with Beatrice, he didn't picture spending the evening watching Clyde embarrass himself trying to win Ruthie an enormous, bright orange, stuffed gorilla. "Clyde, you want to take a break?" he asked.

"Don't distract him, Chuck," Ruthie said. "Besides, even you said how great that gorilla is."

"No, I said that gorillas have the greatest intelligence of all the animals represented by the plush prizes here. That *particular* gorilla seems kind of stupid."

"Suck it, Chuck," said Ruthie. "That gorilla kicks ass, and we're staying here until Clyde wins it for me. You two don't have to hang around, if you're not gonna be supportive. He doesn't need the negative energy."

Likewise, Charlie didn't need the additional frustration of watching Clyde repeatedly miss a stack of milk jugs with a baseball. Eager for an escape, he looked to Beatrice, whose eyes were filled with mischief. "Bye, Ruthie!" she said with a quick wave, then turned and left. Charlie hurried after her.

The aromas of grilled sweet corn, deep-fried dough and smoldering tobacco thickened the still air. Charlie followed Beatrice's slim form through the crowd, barely able to keep up as she wove between the clumps of pleasure-seekers under the yellow lights, an impish otter in the kelp. When she reached a clearing in the crowd near the carnival entrance, she turned toward Charlie, her eyes afire. "Here!" she said, her voice the soprano in the carnival's opera of whirs, buzzes, and dings. "We're back at the beginning! You think he's gonna win that thing?"

"Clyde? He will if he knows what's good for him. You know how Ruthie is."

"How many rides do you think we can go on before he wins it?"

"Rides?" asked Charlie. "They have a band here. We can just listen to music."

"Right. Because carnival music is so great." Beatrice was energized, excited. Maybe it was the exhaust from the machinery, or the cotton candy dust permeating the air, but something enlivened her this evening, bestowed her with a delectable girlishness. Channeling Ruthie, she egged Charlie on, hitting him on the shoulder. "C'mon, Chuck! Whatever happened to gumption?"

"Okay, fine. You want to go on rides? We'll go on rides. But we're going on all of them."

"I'm telling Clyde you said that. I think he'll have that gorilla before we go on three."

"Three? What do you want to bet?"

"Dinner at the restaurant of the winner's choice."

"Deal."

Owing mainly to proximity, they decided to go on the Ferris wheel first. Charlie bought a strip of ride tickets and they headed to the back of the line, where they stood in silence, Beatrice watching the great wheel slowly turn, and Charlie observing the crowd. As he was about to comment on the similarities between a crowd of people and a herd of sheep, Beatrice spoke: "What's your favorite cake?"

"To eat or to bake?"

"Eat…no, bake!"

"To bake? The Venus de Phillo. It's a baklava cake, and it's *divine*. You?"

"I prefer pies."

"Pies? Even Marie Antoinette didn't wish the peasants to eat pies."

"Spoken like a man who can only bake cakes."

"OK, then. What's your favorite flower?" Charlie asked.

"Plumeria."

"Is that to arrange, or to receive?"

"You really don't know much about flowers, do you?"

"I know how to make them out of icing. Oh, wait, you prefer pies…"

Bit by bit, they inched their way toward the grand wheel. Neither needed ask the other about their favorite carnival ride, because the Ferris wheel itself is hands-down the best attraction at any carnival. It has been mathematically proven that the emblematic Ferris wheel is necessary and sufficient to designate any celebratory event as a carnival. No other ride appeals to old and young alike, and although occasional irreverent sorts may attempt to ruin it all for everyone by pooh-poohing the great wheel as a dull journey that leads nowhere, the majority of carnival-goers maintain respect for the Ferris wheel, instilled at an early age when it was an intimidating beast to be conquered, rather than a snooze.

They finally made it to the front of the line and Charlie handed a strip of tickets to the wiry guy working the ride – it could have been the same guy who was cheating Clyde out of a gorilla, for all Charlie could tell. They were locked into the carriage and jerked a few places backward while the next group was loaded.

Then the next.

Then the next.

Eventually, the ride started, lifting the pair skyward in a smooth arc. Beatrice released a squeal of delight that even she didn't expect. She looked bashfully at Charlie and laughed. The wheel took them between two worlds. At the nadir, moving in a swooping motion along the ground like a raptor after its prey, the great wheel shot them through the rowdy crowd and the artificially lit understory of the park. Here, they could see and feel – just for a moment – the debauchery and excitement of a mass of humanity seeking pleasure in the summer night.

From there, the wheel swooped them upward, above the crowd, beyond the canopy of the old oak trees surrounding the park. At the cycle's apex, the stomach became still, and a sense of calm befell the riders. The air seemed cooler above the trees, a sensation that was aided by the gentle breeze resulting from the wheel's motion. From atop that Ferris wheel at the Milton Founders' Day carnival, one could see for miles. The people below were figurines and the world around appeared dark and peaceful. Every time the carriage passed the top of the wheel, Charlie grew acutely aware that he and Beatrice alone were above everyone else in town, side by side, and both loving every second of it.

As with everything enjoyable, it ended too quickly. After ten revolutions, the pair disembarked and Beatrice, thirsty for more adventure, raced to the Tilt-a-Whirl, where the two intrepid carnival-goers hurriedly waited in another ride queue. Awakened by the Ferris wheel ride, they turned their conversation to an exploration of thrills, sharing stories of sinister spirits that inhabited relatives' houses, and of treacherous vacation encounters with angry buffaloes. They spoke of hang gliding and scuba diving and jumping off cliffs into the quarry. Charlie relaxed. He didn't attempt to force the conversation toward comparisons of animal intelligence, or toward the supremacy of cake over pie. He simply enjoyed talking with his new friend.

The Tilt-a-Whirl was only slightly more exhilarating than the Ferris wheel. What it added in speed and revolutions-per-minute, it lacked in spectacular views and sheer continuous bliss. During the ride, Charlie held himself as best he could to the side of the car, lest he crush his lovely companion's delicate frame. Beatrice was just the opposite, slamming into Charlie with her full weight as the ride turned, laughing all the time. As soon as the chair stopped spinning, she dashed across the park lawn toward the Grasscutter, an enormous five-armed spinning contraption that hurled its cars wildly across the lawn, only to stop suddenly and fling them back in another direction.

Waiting in line, Beatrice asked, "Where would you live in the world, if you could live anywhere – anywhere at all?"

"What's wrong with here?"

"Here? Really? There's nowhere that you've ever dreamed of going?"

"What, like Porquerolles Island?"

"Sounds wonderful," Beatrice said, clapping her hands. "Where is it?"

"Off the coast of France. In the Riviera. Where would you go?"

"I was going to say Hawaii, but now I think that Porquerolles Island sounds so much more appealing. What's it like there?"

"I don't know. I've never been there. I imagine that there's a quaint little French seaside village there, with wonderful wine and seafood, but ironically in desperate need of a good bakery."

"Oh, the poor Porquerollesians! It must be the only village in France without a decent bakery."

"Yes, exactly," said Charlie. "For all the great weather and sunshine and pleasant neighbors who always clean up after their pets, the island is missing just this one tiny detail that would make it perfect – a bakery. And not just any bakery, mind you, but a good bakery that's worthy of serving the inhabitants of the island, along with all the tourists who visit in season. Sure, there are plenty of places to find freshly baked bread and croissants, but they're so ordinary – so pedestrian. The villagers of the island long for an artist baker who can deliver something extraordinary and unexpected on a regular basis."

"Do you think they need a flower shop, too?"

"*Certainement*! They have nothing there but boring bouquets and nondescript nosegays. They long for a florist with a flair for the unusual, and with a distinguished eye. Perhaps a foreigner who can bring about a fresh perspective..."

They boarded the ride and were both pressed against one side of the car as it whipped them across the lawn. Charlie did not hold on. Beatrice did not hold on. They both just went with it.

When the ride ended, Charlie said, "I know you prefer pies, but what's your take on funnel cakes?"

"We haven't officially gone to the fair until we've had one."

Charlie bought a funnel cake with strawberry topping and powdered sugar, refusing to allow Beatrice to pay for her share. They headed for a remote spot of the bleachers by the softball field, and tore into the funnel cake with plastic forks, watching the last strip of blue sky fade on the horizon.

"I haven't done this in ages," Beatrice said. "My dad used to bring me to the fair when I was a little girl. He'd take me on all the rides, and then he'd buy me a funnel cake before we went home. It was always too much for me to eat by myself, so he ate most of it. It was our special thing, eating funnel cakes."

"Sounds nice," said Charlie.

"It was."

"So…what…"

"What happened to my dad? He left."

"Beatrice, I had no idea…"

"No, it's better that you know that story." She wiped a strand of red syrup from her chin. "He was a pet food salesman, like my grandpa, and my great-grandfather. He got into the business at a weird time, when pet owners started thinking of their pets as family members instead of animals.

"I guess he struggled a little bit – before his time, there were no dog bakeries or cat cafés. He had to deal with the whole dog birthday party industry, and the pet cloning companies, and pet cooking reality TV. It was a lot, you know? Stuff he never expected – pet amusement parks, dog-transporting self-driving cars – things like that. When the first round of celebrity dog chefs launched their careers, he just about had it. He didn't like the idea of a famous chef baking dog food for a cruise line.

"Then, one day on a business trip, the guy next to him at the diner strikes up a conversation. The guy was in the pet business himself. He used gene editing technology to make custom pets. He told my dad that he had the technology to produce a dog-cat hybrid – a chimera. They called it the *dogat* or *catog*."

"No way!" said Charlie.

"That's what my dad said. So the guy shows him videos of these things – dogs that ignored their owners, cats that chased their tails and fetched the newspaper, stuff like that."

"Cool. How smart were they?"

"I don't know, Charlie. The point is, there was a new pet on the horizon, and my dad decided that he was going to develop the perfect food for it. So he invested all of our money into food for dog-cat hybrid pets. And then what happens? The things turn out to be a disaster. They cough up hairballs, scratch the furniture and still need to be walked. They had a dog's agility and a cat's curiosity. And their personalities – they weren't independent like cats or loyal like dogs. They were just rude. Nobody needs a new pet like that, let alone specialized food for it – although they were finicky eaters.

"So once my dad went broke, he left my mom and me. He promised to come back with lots of money. That was twenty years ago. My mom didn't take it well. At the time she was cleaning houses for people like Frank Chan. His wife was always kind to us, but my mom started slipping. She had a breakdown, and I started working at Rose's so that we could keep the lights on. I've been there ever since."

"Oh, Beatrice," said Charlie, "I'm sorry…"

"Not really a great funnel cake story, huh? I'm sorry if you think I'm damaged goods." She looked away.

"No, never!" He turned to her, wanting to comfort her with a hug. He placed his hand on her shoulder.

"Thanks, Charlie. This has all been great."

"Sure. You know I'm here for you, and I'm happy to listen."

"Not just the listening. Everything. This whole week. The carnival. Sitting on the bleachers. All of it. It's been wonderful."

It has, he thought, watching the carnival drop into nothingness. Only Beatrice remained in the universe, looking at him desperately, relieved that he accepted her story.

She leaned toward him.

He moved close to her.

Her eyes grew wide, and she opened her mouth. "He did it!" she said, looking past Charlie.

He turned to see an enormous orange gorilla bobbing lazily above the carnival crowd across the outfield. How typical of Clyde to succeed at the most inconvenient moment.

"Let's go meet them," Beatrice said, heading down the bleachers. Charlie once again followed her. In a corner of the bleachers, a child was crying, his big red balloon floating uncontrollably into the heavens.

They made their way into the crowd and intercepted their friends near the food stands. Clyde proudly carried the stuffed gorilla on his shoulders, like a father with an overgrown baby. Ruthie danced around him and sang, "Go-ril-lah! Go-ril-lah!" She poked Charlie in the chest. "In yo' face, Chuck! How stupid do you think gorillas are now, huh? Go-ril-lah! Go-ril-lah!" She continued her little dance.

"Nice work, Clyde," said Charlie.

"We're gonna walk around with this thing," said Ruthie. "Show it off!"

"I think I'm going to head out," said Beatrice. "I've got to open the store tomorrow."

"I've got to be up early, too," said Charlie. "I'll go with you. Enjoy your gorilla, Ruthie."

They walked ten paces from Ruthie before she called, "Hey, Chuck! Don't forget to kiss her goodnight!"

As the couple meandered up the sidewalk toward Rose's, the din and bright lights of the carnival faded to a muffled murmur. Townsfolk dotted the sidewalks, eating ice cream and chatting in the warm night. The sweet smells of kettle corn and fried dough gave way to the familiar, earthy odor of the town and the fields beyond. They walked in silence, relishing the beauty of the summer's night. When they arrived at Beatrice's rusty truck, she asked, "When are you taking me to dinner at Le Bouseux Laid?"

"What?" asked Charlie. "We went on three rides. *You* owe *me* dinner."

"The bet was that we'd go on all the rides before he won. We went on three rides and had a funnel cake."

Charlie didn't care who paid or where they went. He was happy just to have a date. "How about Thursday?"

"Great. I'll see you then." She opened the truck's door and smiled at him.

He smiled back. "Good night," he said.

"Charlie?"

"What?"

"Aren't you going to kiss me?"

So he did.

CHAPTER 20

Charlie's breath was fresh.

Before leaving home, he brushed, flossed, gargled with mouthwash, spat it out, gargled with a fresh dose, and finally rinsed with bottled water. Standing in front of Le Bouseux Laid, Milton's finest restaurant, he inhaled through his teeth. His tongue didn't feel as cool as it had a half hour ago, but there was still a hint of mintiness that chilled his gums. It would have to do.

He was waiting for Beatrice outside the restaurant, unsure of whether a proper gentleman would instead sit at the bar, suavely sipping a stiff drink. Ideally, he thought, he'd have picked her up in his luxury car; in reality, he took the bus into town and walked two blocks to the restaurant. It was a downside of riding a bike.

As he waited, Charlie struggled with his hands, which didn't fit anywhere. Hips seemed a bad choice. Pockets felt natural but might look creepy. At the side was awkward. He cycled through these options, trying to look calm, until he spotted Beatrice walking up the sidewalk. Their previous meetings were all chance encounters or group events with friends. Now, for the first time, she walked toward *him*, and him alone.

"So you didn't ditch me," she said with a smile.

Who the hell would ditch you? Charlie thought. He pulled a small object from his pocket and handed it to her.

Beatrice looked at the offering in her hands. It was a cat toy, an elastic string with a wooden stick attached at one end and a blue, catnip-stuffed "bird" at the other. If you held the stick and shook it, the bird bounced up and down and a bell inside jingled. It had feathers and everything. "Thanks," she said, "I guess."

"It's for Lulu," Charlie said, sure that it would make the perfect gift. After all, it was suggested by the web site hidden in the plant. The same web site, by the way, suggested the mouthwash that Charlie used that evening. And his breath was very, very fresh.

The maître d' seated them at a little booth surrounded by cloth drapes, providing the couple with a cozy nest of solitude illuminated by a single candle flickering in its red glass jar in the center of the table. Unsure of what to talk about, Charlie half hid behind his menu, conjuring partial invisibility. The informal atmosphere of the carnival had dissipated.

"I'm going to order the lobster!" Beatrice said. She placed her menu decisively on the table.

"They have lobster?" Charlie's eyes darted around the menu.

"Kidding. I'll get something else."

"You can order whatever you want. You can order the lobster."

"Don't be so proud, Charlie. I know how it is for folks like us."

"Like us?"

"You know, people who work in shops in a small town. It's not the lavish lifestyle."

"It's good enough for me." Charlie grabbed a warm roll from the basket on the table. "It's all I want."

"Really? Don't you want to be rich? Don't you want something more?"

Charlie looked around. He was seated at the town's finest restaurant with the woman of his dreams, and he wasn't making an ass of himself by talking about how smart pangolins are. "Nope," he said, popping a piece of bread into his mouth.

"Oh, come on, Charlie. Do you want to live the rest of your life doing what you're doing?"

"I like what I do. I have a flexible schedule, and I get to be creative, and I love the customers – their stories are great."

"Customers' stories don't put food on the table."

"You probably think that I can't afford anything but the cheapest stuff, right? Well, watch this." He snapped his fingers at the waiter three tables over, "Garçon! Your most mid-range bottle!"

The waiter glowered.

"Charlie!" whispered Beatrice.

"Money is no object, my dear," he said in what he imagined was the accent of the rich and famous. He ripped another small piece from the bread roll he was holding. It was pretty mediocre bread, given the prices on the menu. Flour. Yeast. Salt. Oil. Little more. The restaurant probably called it *Provençal* to justify their prices. "By the way, the plant you gave me is growing nicely." He pulled out his cell phone and swiped to a photo of the plant, now with a flowery stalk projecting from the mat of leaves.

"Awww," said Beatrice, "you're just like a new daddy. So proud."

"The trick is to make sure that the soil is just moist to the touch, and not to give it too much fertilizer. I guess you know this stuff. Horticulture's not my strong suit, but I think I've done pretty well." He swiped through photos. "I mean, after letting the first one get stolen. I wonder if I could've done something to prevent that – if I should've had a security camera installed. But who steals a *plant*? Who would do something like that?"

Beatrice shifted in her seat. "Guess what? I'm going to sell them at Rose's!"

Charlie put his phone away. "You're selling them?"

"Everybody else is profiting from it. The bakery's profiting from it, and I'm sure your scientist friends are rolling in dough now. Why shouldn't I get a piece of the action, too?"

Because it was ours, Charlie thought. It was his and hers together – not hers alone to sell or to give away. This plant was responsible for bringing them together, and he viewed it as sacred because of that. She shouldn't trifle with the divine. "So it won't be our special thing anymore?"

"It'll always be our special thing. You know that. It's just that now it's out there. Sooner or later, somebody's gonna start selling them. Why shouldn't it be me?"

"It should," he said. "I'm excited for you." He felt that something special had died, but forced a smile that erupted onto his face like toothpaste pushed too hard from the tube.

"Great! Then I propose a partnership between the flower shop and the bakery. With every *eye-rabidopsis* – that's what I'm calling it, do you like it? With every eye-rabidopsis sold, I'll give a coupon for a free Fat BB's eye-plant cake. You collect the coupons, and I'll pay for the eye-plant cakes. At a fifty percent discount."

"Fifty percent?"

Beatrice continued: "With every eye-plant cake sold, you enter your customers in a drawing to win a free eye-rabidopsis plant from Rose's. The deal gets better for you as demand for the plants increases."

Charlie stared at the woman sitting across from him. Until now, she was the pretty lady in charge of the flower shop up the street. Now, she seemed like a businessperson who happened to be a beautiful lady. A beautiful, beautiful lady. "Sure," he said.

The waiter arrived with the restaurant's middlest-range bottle of wine. He pulled the cork and handed it to Charlie, who gave it a good sniff and decided that it smelled like a wine-soaked cork.

"Isn't this exciting?" Beatrice raised her glass for a toast. "We're gonna be the cool crowd, and everybody will want to hang out with us."

—◦◦○◦◦—

While Charlie and Beatrice were conspiring on how to best sell eye plants and eye-plant cakes, Bill was finishing up a long day at Logan Biotech. He found the industrial job a welcome distraction from the frustrations of his thesis work. Instead of laboring day and night to answer questions that no one asked, he worked directly under Phineas's top scientists, blinding mice and surgically implanting plant eyes into their newly vacant sockets.

On this particular evening, Bill was testing a new pre-operative treatment that Phineas hoped would alleviate the tail-chewing that plagued the mice after transplant. Bill had already tried a dozen other treatments, and every time the mice chewed off their tails within two weeks. He had little hope for this one.

After implanting sixteen plant eyes into eight blinded mice, he was about to call it a day when he noticed the extra mouse, anesthetized and limp on a paper-lined plastic tray on the counter. Somehow, when he was caught up in the rhythm of popping eyes from mouse heads, he'd blinded one too many mice.

"Sorry, buddy." He lifted the creature by its tail and placed its neck between the blades of his shears. Just before squeezing, a thought crossed his mind: He was a scientist. He should use this opportunity to experiment.

He retrieved a vial of eye-plant seeds and placed one in each of the mouse's empty eye sockets. After bandaging the animal's eyes, he placed it back in its cage and headed home. He waved to the guard as he biked through the front gate and made it about three blocks before the black SUV swerved in front of him and slammed on its brakes. He skid to a halt just before making contact with the vehicle's door.

The window rolled down, revealing a stern-looking man at the driver's seat. "Bill Walkowiak?" he asked.

"Who the hell are you?"

"I have a proposal for you. Interested?"

"What kind of proposal?"

"I'm looking for someone to help with a surgery. An eye transplant."

"What, in a mouse?"

"No, a person. A kid. You interested?"

CHAPTER 21

By the time she informed Charlie about her fledgling enterprise, Beatrice had sprouted two thousand little eye-rabidopsis seedlings in her greenhouse. The little money-makers were as easy to grow as weeds, but had the charm of exotic plants. They were like Venus fly traps, but what they lacked in weird bug-eating grossness, they made up for with their enchanting blue eyes. She marketed them with a sign in her shop window:

NOW ACCEPTING PRE-ORDERS FOR
EYE-RABIDOPSIS
Inquire Within

Anyone taking the sign's advice and asking about the plants was directed to an exquisite specimen on a table toward the back of the store. Wise customers who paid in advance for their very own plants were promised delivery in three weeks. Sales were so strong that Beatrice depleted her inventory within a few days. She pushed the delivery date back, but soon sold the entire second generation of eye-rabidopsis. She rented additional greenhouses and re-allocated to eye-rabidopsis all of the space that she had previously reserved for the winter's poinsettias.

"I've already sold five thousand plants," she told Charlie before dinner one night. "I thought that amount would last two months. I'm going to have to plant at least a thousand each week, at this pace." She was sitting on the couch at Charlie's place, sipping a glass of Beaujolais as he stirred around the kitchen. This was the first time he entertained her in his home, and he wanted everything to be perfect. Although she didn't know it, he spent a week planning a full-course dinner featuring a chiffon lemon cake for dessert.

After their date at Le Bouseux Laid, Charlie and Beatrice increasingly spent time together, pretending to be working. He developed a habit of showing up unannounced at Rose's, bearing lunch and occasionally a lovingly crafted cake; she stopped by the bakery most mornings to discuss sales over coffee. Their business arrangement became a convenient excuse for their budding romance. Both of them were acutely aware of what was happening, and they both enjoyed it. The process was easy for Charlie, who was perched on love's precipice when he catered Frank Chan's party. Beatrice, nudged by his devotion, followed willingly. Soon they found themselves spending time alone together, and Charlie – who was as good a chef as anyone in town – invited Beatrice for dinner.

"That's amazing," he said, coaxing a bundle of linguine from his antique pasta roller into his palm. "Then maybe you'll be able to pay me back for all the free eye-plant cakes we've given your customers."

"Just make sure you kept all the coupons. We're not going to reimburse you based on your good word alone."

"How about my good word and my good cooking?"

"It's a business risk, but it might be worth it." She surveyed the room. Before she arrived, Charlie thoroughly cleaned his house and then strategically re-messed it to maximize appeal. The acoustic guitar that he inherited from his great-aunt sat in the corner of the bedroom, half-covered by his favorite flannel shirt. A magazine open to an article about the feline genome peeked out from beneath a pile of classic literature on an end table. The logo on a single sock placed underneath the couch and entirely out of sight to anybody who was not lying on the floor reflected his short stint at the university.

"What's this?" Beatrice asked. She was looking at the eye plant she'd given him, which he'd positioned in the sunny central window of the living room. The plant's eye was now more or less fully open.

"What, you don't recognize that?" he asked, grating nutmeg into the sauce. "It's my favorite plant in the world. I probably like it even more than I liked the original one that was stolen from my back yard. Who do you think stole that? I never found out."

"Let it go, Charlie." She squinted at the plant. "Did you know you're getting seeds?"

Charlie shuffled in from the kitchen and bent close to the plant and to the woman he'd never dreamed would be in his house. She pointed a painted nail at the tiny pods sprouting from the plant's stalk. "They're seed pods, and some are ready to burst. You should cut them off and put them in a little jar."

"Why would I do that?"

"So you can grow little eye-rabidopsis plants."

"They'd be like our grandchildren," said Charlie. What could be better? "How about I just give them to you?" He nudged her with his elbow and reached for the plant, pinching a brown-green seed pod between his fingers.

"Careful," warned Beatrice, but before the word hit his ears, the seed pod burst open, spewing a fine dust of tiny seeds into his living room. It was a very plant-like response to being touched.

———— ⋄∘C∕∕⊃∘⋄ ————

An obituary for a crow, should anyone care to write one, might be called a crow-bituary. Nobody writes them, because nobody mourns the passing of crows – even the other crows, and even when the deceased crow played an important part in the unfolding of history. Crows can't write, anyway. Maybe – just maybe – an ornithologist who'd grown particularly attached to a crow would shed a tear for the passing of a favorite murder member. And maybe that ornithologist would be inclined to jot down a few words about the treasured corvid.

"There goes the paper mill," the ornithologist might write.

Obit or no, such an important crow indeed died in a barren corn field not far from Milton. Her crow-bituary read like this:

> An unnamed crow, aged thirteen years, slipped peacefully
> into the Great Murder in the Sky this morning, surrounded

by no other crows. She is survived by her longtime mate and a dozen or so estranged offspring. She was preceded in death by her similarly unnamed parents, several of her offspring, and many siblings.

Her reputation transcended species, and her dive bombing antics earned her the respect and gratitude of many a songbird harassed by nuisance hawks that wandered into the crows' vicinity. In a story that would have worked itself into the crows' lore (had they any), she was known not only by her avian fellows, but by humans, if only in reputation.

On a sunny day many months ago, this curious crow nudged open a building's window and peered within. Confused by the unfamiliar flora, she cautiously hopped inside and found herself on the floor of a forest of cyclops plants. Ever inquisitive, she picked her way toward the center of the forest, but was startled and flew off when a man entered through a door at the forest's far end.

She cawed magnificently, singing to her crow companions the praises of the beautiful Eyeball Forest. Her fellow crows, drunk on the bounty of refuse heaps and landfills, paid her no heed. This anonymous prophet continued living her life as hawk-chaser and window-opener, but on that day, unbeknownst to her, or her fellow crows, or the humans, or even their computers, a tiny seed embedded itself in a crack in that crow's foot. During her flight of heraldry, the seed dislodged itself. Down it fell, battered by the breeze, until it came to rest in a patch of lawn behind the house where a baker lived. There it lay patiently until sufficient warmth and moisture and sunlight convinced it to abandon its seedish ways and grow into a plant.

No services will be held. The crow's body will be interred on the corn field.

"Look at those crows," said Charlie, peering at a flock through the window of Beatrice's truck. It was the harvest, and the land's offerings were bountiful. These were the days of layered wardrobes, when frosty mornings ceded to warm afternoons and clear skies turned into steady rains without warning. The fresh country air punched its way into the cab through a cracked window. "Such a magnificent flock. Where do you think they roost at night?" He stared at the cloud of birds crossing the autumn sky that screamed blue against the browns of the land.

"No clue," said Beatrice, smiling at Charlie through the designer sunglasses that she just bought for herself. A higher tier of fashion was a perk of a successful eye-rabidopsis business.

"Probably somewhere smart. They're among the most intelligent birds."

The couple bounced down a county road toward Ruthie's farm. She'd taken to the country life and enjoyed creating soufflés in the farmhouse kitchen. She begged her friends to visit, promising them their pick of pumpkins, plus an orgaloco dinner of unmatched quality.

When they arrived at the farm's roadside produce stand and ambitiously named petting zoo, bright orange pumpkins dotted the field in crooked lines. "Check out those pumpkins in the field," Beatrice said, squeezing the truck through the gate and down the gravel road toward the barns, silos, and white farmhouse. "Do you think they bake a lot of pies here? It seems that a farm house like this should always have a freshly baked pie cooling in the window."

"I make an excellent pumpkin cake," Charlie said. "I'll bake you one sometime."

Beatrice parked the truck on the grass next to the farm house, a large two-story wooden structure with an elevated porch that spanned the length of its facade. A yellow dog sporting a blue bandanna trotted up and sniffed the truck's tires. Charlie pulled a muffin from a paper bag and handed it to the dog, who gobbled it gratefully before escorting them toward the house.

As they ascended the stairs, a muffled jingle emanated through the screen door at regular intervals. The dog's tail wagged in Pavlovian anticipation. The ringing grew louder and the tail wagging increased to a frenzy until a barefoot young lady in a long skirt and sweater emerged from the darkness in the house, in step with the jingling. She could have been one of BB's *cupcakes*.

"Hi!" she said, with the delight of someone reunited with old friends after a years-long absence.

"Hi," said Charlie, "We're friends of Ruthie. I think she might be here."

"Ruthie? Oh, yeah! Ruthie! She's such a sweetie! So you're her friends, huh? Welcome!" The girl stepped out the door, her anklet singing a song of hippie reception. She engulfed Beatrice in a hug that the florist returned naturally. "It's great to meet you both. I'm Peapod."

"I'm Beatrice, and this is Charlie."

"Cosmic!" Peapod embraced the baker in her arms, forcing wisps of her hair into his face. Turning her attention to the dog, she said, "Hello, Macadamia! Did you make some new friends? Did you? Did you make some new friends?" She kissed the dog on the lips, and he licked her mouth. She looked up to Charlie and Beatrice. "Macadamia's the big stud around here. Our bitch just had a dozen of his puppies. Where is that bitch, anyway?" She stood and surveyed the land, hands on hips.

"Do you know where we might find her?" Charlie asked.

"The bitch?"

"Ruthie."

"She should be somewhere."

Charlie struggled to think of a less definitive answer as he waited to see whether anything more specific was forthcoming.

"So you guys are from Milton, huh?" Peapod asked. "I could never get used to life in town like that. It has to be hard to live with all the drugs in the water."

"Excuse me?"

"Municipal water is filled with drugs that sedate the population, so they're easier to manipulate. The big cities specifically target school children, damaging their brains at an early age so that they can be controlled."

"I don't think that's really the case."

"That's exactly what someone drinking drugged water would say." Peapod kissed the dog some more. "And the crime."

"There's not that much crime," said Charlie. "Although – to be honest – I *did* have a plant stolen from my yard –"

"So Ruthie comes out here a lot, does she?" interrupted Beatrice.

"Yeah, she's been coming here all summer. She makes the best soufflés…Oh, wait! Are you still looking for her? She's probably out in the field. Just chill here, and I'll go find her. You guys want some smoke or anything? We grow our own stuff here. It's orgaloco."

The townies declined the offer, and Peapod disappeared mellowly behind a nearby barn in search of Ruthie. As the dog wandered off to lick himself in a sunny spot between the house and garage, Charlie paced on the grass. The air was fresh and filled with the woody aroma of drying crops punctuated by the deep, earthy repugnance of the livestock. Charlie could stay there forever.

Beatrice was less enamored with the ambiance. "That girl's not coming back any time soon. Let's go check out that tire swing." She pointed toward a grand oak tree dangling a heavy rope from its bicep.

"That's exactly what someone drinking drugged water would say."

"You should be thankful. It's the drugs in the water that make me crazy about you."

"Are you sure it's not my rugged good looks?"

"Definitely not. Although you *are* adorable when you're acting like a nitwit – like now. C'mon." Beatrice grabbed his hand and pulled him toward the oak tree behind the house. Halfway there, she abruptly stopped and turned toward a patch of mostly dried wild flowers, painted here and there with a stubborn bloom proudly protesting the season's chill.

"See this?" she said, pointing to a tall weed with dried-up buds. "Queen Anne's Lace." She yanked the plant's pointy root from the ground. "It's a carrot. They're edible. If you ever get lost in the woods, you can survive on carrot soup. Smell."

Charlie snapped off a piece and sniffed it uncertainly. It smelled like a dirty carrot. "You're just a fountain of knowledge about the natural world, aren't you?"

"Plants are my business, you know," she said, brushing the dirt off her piece of the little carrot.

Charlie watched her, fascinated at how she grew absorbed with cleaning that little plant. Intoxicated by the fresh farm air and the wind's whistle through brittle leaves, he sighed, "This place is awesome. No wonder Ruthie's in love with it. Can't you imagine evenings here? The porch filled with dusty farmhands, singing and laughing into the night?"

"I'm sure that's how it is. Every evening at sundown the workers come in from the fields and someone pulls out a fiddle and they have a hoedown."

"Maybe a washboard, too."

Beatrice saw the dreamy look in Charlie's eye and knew where this was going. "A farm's a lot of work, Charlie. It's a struggle just to make ends meet." She tugged on his shirt, revealing a clump of burs stuck to the flannel. "And besides, you're such a town boy. Look at you."

"Can you blame them?" he said, pulling the burs from his shirt. "They love me. That's just how plants are."

And he was right. That *is* how plants are. For eons, plants have been exploiting their mobile animal cousins for reproductive purposes. Through the random walk of evolution, plants developed fragrant flowers to attract insects and tasty fruits that appeal to birds. They adorned their seeds with fluffy parachutes to catch the wind, and with sticky hooks to snag the fur and flannel of passing fauna. And they evolved brittle pods that could cast tiny seeds to the ground, where they might be transported to distant locations in the crevice of a bird's foot or a baker's shoe.

The eye plant was no exception. In addition to such tried-and-true gimmicks, it employed its own unique evolutionary innovation to spread its seeds: It was hella cool. No sooner had Beatrice started selling the plants than the public began breeding them for hobby and profit. On-line forums percolated out from the web, instructing would-be eye-rabidopsis farmers on the basics of eye-rabidopsis care. Casual smugglers stowed live plants in their luggage and taped seeds discretely to the pages of their passports, helping it spread over mountains and across oceans.

Social media proudly displayed photos of eye-rabidopsis atop the Eiffel tower, Kilimanjaro, the Great Wall, Macchu Pichu.

As Charlie and Beatrice stood amid the wild flowers on that farm, human beings across the globe were busy moving eye plant seeds to ever-farther locations on account of its coolness.

Just as its Creators intended.

CHAPTER 22

In the course of a few weeks, Fat BB's transitioned from home-style family bakery to full-blown hipster café.

BB welcomed the new class of patrons by altering the atmosphere and menu to suit their tastes. Eye-plant cakes usurped the throne upon which apple cakes sat for so long, and some of the more traditional goods disappeared altogether. The lone percolator that had reliably produced the bakery's *Blackbird Brew* for the past thirty-odd years was replaced by a standing vacuum flasks holding fair trade and organic coffees. The crown jewel of the bakery's coffee fetish was a monstrosity of an espresso machine from which protruded so many shiny steel valves and knobs that it could only be properly operated by baristas with advanced degrees in engineering. BB asked Charlie to develop a line of biscotti, which he sold from glass jars perched atop the display cases. Customers who were drawn in by the eye-plant cakes now had the option to instead grab a coffee and some biscotti, and stay for the free Wi-Fi.

After the initial eye-plant cake surge, Ruthie maintained a steady stream of new customers with her innovative soufflés. The new crowd enjoyed the ever-changing flavor selection, from acorn sprouts to wild-caught hand-fed oysters, latching onto the soufflés like leeches on an open water swimmer. The old crowd barely noticed the additions to the menu – except that, with their trendy flavors and high prices, they disturbed the regular flow of the bakery. To them, soufflés and eye cakes were frivolous disruptions that had no place in a small town staple like Fat BB's.

Charlie and Ruthie did their best to please both the long-time customers and the new trendsetters, but they knew they were losing the former. The animated interactions of the centenarians sparring over baked
goods ceded to cold exchanges among aloof twenty-somethings ordering
'*spros* and '*scottis* without so much as pausing their cell phone conversations. Many regular customers ceased coming to the bakery.

Late one autumn morning, the bakery's younger patrons, mesmerized by their electronic devices, occupied the new café tables. Amid the
crowd stood a few elderly ladies who'd patronized the bakery for years.
While they waited to be served, Mrs. Wigner impressed her companions
with photos on her cell phone. Recently, when her great-grandson passed
through town, she gave him an eye-rabidopsis plant from Rose's. To
thank his great-grandmother, the grateful lad sent her photos of it against
a backdrop of scenic landmarks.

"How'd he get to all these places?" asked Mrs. Hilbert "Where's that?
Yellowstone?"

"Yosemite," corrected Mrs. Wigner. "He's driving all over the country with a couple of friends. Here's one at the *Golden Gate Bridge*." She
passed the phone to her companions.

"Don't he work? Young men like that should be working."

"He said he took some time off."

"What difference does it make if he's working?" asked Mrs. Sommerfeld. "These photos are beautiful, Agnes."

"Here's another one," said Mrs. Wigner, "on some mountain in
Maine."

"Ain't no mountains in Maine."

"Katadin. It's Mt. Katadin. The highest peak in Maine."

"And the Gateway Arch!" said Mrs. Hilbert, viewing the next photo.
"He went everywhere, didn't he? Is he in sales? What's he do?"

"He said took some time off to travel."

"With the plant?"

"With some friends."

"But they brought the plant? The plant's in all the photos."

"Wherever he went, he took photos of the plant."

"And they just let him?"

"Why not?"

"They won't let you take 'em just anywhere – they're afraid of diseases, or something. They don't want 'em spreading."

"That right?"

"It's true. Did ya hear about the Japanese girl who taped the seeds to her passport?"

"What's this?"

"Japanese girl – studied at the university here – went back home after she finished or what have you. She brought a bunch of those seeds back."

"Back to Japan?"

"That's right. Tried, anyway. Taped 'em to her passport. Thought nobody would see."

"Not see? How could you miss a seed taped to a passport?"

"They're tiny, like poppy seeds. Tinier, even. You wouldn't even know if it was stuck between your teeth. The only way they found it, the tape started coming off."

"That right?"

"It is. Girl says she got the idea from the internet. Kids all over the world have been doing the same thing. Taping the seeds to their passports. Bringing them to other countries, anyway."

"My girlfriend told me how her granddaughter's fiancé has one growing in his window in Italy. Maybe it watches the gondolas."

Just then, a young man walked through the bakery door. Without acknowledging the presence of any other customer, he headed directly to the counter, where he stood, fiddling with his phone.

"Young man," said Mrs. Sommerfeld, "just what do you think you're doing?"

"I ordered online," said the kid, still fiddling with his phone. Clearly the phone demanded fiddling. In fact, it encouraged it by throwing up notifications that prompted further fiddling.

"You need to take a ticket." Mrs. Sommerfeld pointed to the red ticket dispenser hidden behind the coffee flasks.

The young guy looked up. "Listen, Grandma: I ain't taking a ticket.

Paper's dead – like you should be. Try ordering online. It'll save you the precious time you have left." Turning to Ruthie, who was working the counter, he said, "I'm picking up an online order for a dozen eye cakes."

"You need to take a ticket," Ruthie said. "That's how a bakery works."

"I want to talk to your manager."

"You got her. But you know what you ain't got? A ticket. So grab a number, get in line, and wait your turn."

"Why do you even have online ordering if you don't know how to use it?"

"I'm sorry, is it your turn to ask questions? Can I see your ticket?" Ruthie looked over the crowed and bellowed, "Number seventy-six!"

"That's me!" called Mrs. Wigner, waving her ticket over her head.

As the young guy stormed off toward the ticket dispenser, furiously typing a bad review of the bakery into his phone, Ruthie greeted her next customer with a smile. "Mrs. Wigner, so good to see you! How are your grandkids?"

"Is it me," asked the old woman, "or are the people in this place getting more...*rude*?"

"I like to think that they're just cranky because they haven't had their fill of delicious Fat BB's treats yet."

"I should hope so," said Mrs. Wigner. "I used to be able to walk in here at any time and pick up an apple cake. Now it's like the war all over again. Everything is in scarce supply."

Listening from behind the counter, Charlie couldn't agree more. He was acutely aware that the bakery was struggling to meet demand, even with Ruthie working overtime and new trainees on the job. Business had become unpredictable, and he spent more and more time anticipating demand for the coming week. He walked back to the office and sat in the green chair, which groaned in disgust.

"That's it," spat Charlie. He'd had enough attitude from the chair. He flipped it over and prodded it in attempt to isolate the source of its wretched squeaking. No particular motion seemed to induce the noise. The chair was just obstinate.

The baker produced a screwdriver from the desk drawer and proceeded to systematically dismantle the chair. He removed four screws from its bottom and pulled at the metal plate they appeared to hold to its bottom.

The plate wouldn't budge.

Charlie wedged a knife behind the plate and pried. The knife snapped.

"Son of a bitch!" The baker punched the chair in disgust.

A soft knock came on the office door. The door opened a crack, and Beatrice peeked inside. "Hellllloooo?"

"Who the hell would make a chair with four screws on the bottom that don't do anything at all? Why even put the screws there if taking them out doesn't do a goddamn thing?"

Beatrice spotted the overturned chair across the room. "Chair problems?"

"Chair problems. Bakery problems. Everything problems. Beatrice, it's unbelievable," he put down the screwdriver and straightened himself. "I'm sorry. I don't mean to be upset, but I hardly recognize the place anymore. I don't recognize the customers at all. I'm losing the joy that brought me into baking in the first place."

"Sure, but we're making a killing, aren't we?" She sat on the desk and flicked at the screws that Charlie placed there.

"But there's no creativity involved. Making biscotti that keep up with the latest flavor trends is no more difficult than reading a few food blogs. With cakes, you need to strike harmony among form, texture, and taste. Gluten-free orgaloco turmeric quinoa biscuits are mindless by comparison. They're just mixing a bunch of trendy ingredients into a cookie." He grabbed the screws from the desk and replaced them in the holes from which he just removed them.

"Ooh! Turmeric quinoa! That would be delicious after my goat yoga class," kidded Beatrice. She had never been to a yoga class in her life.

"You're not helping things."

"My poor baby," she said, giving him a hug, "I know you're not into yoga."

"And I have half a brain."

"Right. But you like piñ-a col-a-das," she sang, "and getting caught in the rain."

Charlie rolled his eyes.

"Markets change, sweetie. You have to give the customers what they want. Besides, gourmet coffee isn't so bad. Have you tried it?"

"But *our* markets don't change. That's the point. Since forever, red roses have meant love."

"Or sorry."

"Yes, or sorry. But it's always been the same. It's not like a man who forgets his anniversary can send a dozen blue carnations to his wife and say, 'This is the trend now.' It's red roses or nothing. Everyone knows that, and you can't change it now without introducing turmoil into millions of marriages. Same thing with bakeries. Cakes with candles on top are the standard for birthdays and have been for generations. It's traditional." He took a little can of spray oil that he bought from the staticky web site, shook it and wiggled the attached straw through a gap in the plate and toward the hinge in the chair. He sprayed a generous amount of oil at the bottom of the chair, causing a little oil cloud to float behind the desk.

"I prefer pies," Beatrice said. This point never seemed to get through to Charlie. She was delighted every time that he brought her cake, but would it kill him to bake a pie just once?

"That's because you're a weirdo." He poked her ribs. "But you know that pie is the exception, and that birthday *cake* is the rule." He repositioned the straw and sprayed again, adding to the cloud.

"Things change. Even things that have been around for a long time. Even things that have been the same since anyone remembers."

"Yeah, but flowers and bakeries?"

"Yes, sweetie. Even flowers and bakeries."

CHAPTER 23

Much to his own surprise, Phineas Snodgrass grew to enjoy Amelia's companionship. She roused in him a long-dormant yearning for the pursuit of pure science, and reminded him of an era of youthful exuberance, when his dreams still had the potential to blossom into realities. She had improved with age: The young firebrand he once knew matured into a respected scientist, capable of transforming the world, like a goddess in a Renaissance painting. Her eyes shone with the spark of intellect and fiery determination. She was both comfortable and driven; gentle and powerful.

For this reason, Phineas brought Amelia as his *plus one* to a small gathering at Frank's home. To Frank, *small* meant no more than a hundred or so of his closest and richest friends. Phineas showed up to placate the pushy host, who promised him a magnificent time. A veteran of Frank's parties, Phineas had no doubt that it would be at least memorable.

The two scientists wandered through the lavish house, pausing at length in the comfort of Frank's book-lined study. Amelia studied her companion quietly, remembering how she considered him a fool for leaving the university all those years ago – how she thought for sure he'd fail. Now, here he stood – a rugged frontiersman returning to the quaint town from the dusty plains.

"Julie has taken a job on the coast," Amelia said, getting down to business. She wasn't one to discuss matters other than science for extended periods. "She seemed eager to get out of Bloomvale, for some reason."

"She struck me as being quite talented," Phineas said. "I'd hoped she'd apply to Logan. Perhaps she found something better." It wasn't the first time he'd witnessed Amelia drive a student away, and he was sure that Julie would have been working for him, had she not sought to distance herself from her professor.

"She leaves in two weeks. Bill will be leaving soon, hopefully – his work with the mice is wrapping up."

"Yes, Bill has made strong progress regenerating eyes in mice. In fact, he may have solved our side effect problem."

"Really? Bill?" Amelia was shocked.

"Yes. He simply placed seeds in the eye sockets of one animal, instead of surgically implanting the developed *miltoni* eyes. It was a stroke of genius. The seeds sprouted perfect replacement eyes, and there's no abnormal tail-chewing. We're trying it on a larger group of mice."

"Sounds promising."

"Yes, but even with this great stride, I'm afraid the pace of scientific discovery is still much too slow for Frank's taste."

"What taste? Have you seen the bear?" Amelia pointed to the newest addition to Frank's stuffed menagerie, the bear that attacked George. It was mounted atop a stout hardwood pedestal and had a very realistic glass eye tucked into its cheek.

Their conversation was interrupted by the sound of Frank rapping a spoon on his glass, summoning his guests to the great room. "Ladies and gentlemen," he said, "I'd like to thank you all for joining me on this grand occasion. As you all know, my son, George, suffered a debilitating accident last year. But now, thanks to the wonders of science brought about by Phineas Snodgrass and Logan Biotechnologies, my boy once again has the chance to enjoy a normal life."

Phineas turned. What the hell was Frank talking about? Logan's regeneration efforts were confidential, not something to be announced to a room full of random snobs. "It's my pleasure," continued Frank, "to introduce the Man of the Evening; the first person to receive an organ transplanted from a plant; that wonder of nature who is my own son, George Chan!"

George entered the great room from a doorway behind his father, head lung low in adolescent gloom. Frank grabbed the boy's collar, and George lifted his head like a dark beast throwing its mane. His new eye shined from out his scowl with the turquoise of a tropical beach.

The guests gasped.

Applause.

George, unused to the approval of his father's colleagues, righted his posture and strutted into the crowd, captivating the region's most powerful people with his beauty. He worked the room, granting every millionaire present the chance to gaze upon his boyish comeliness and striking blue eye.

Enraged, Phineas pushed his way through the throng of rich people mobbing George. He grabbed a fistful of Frank's jacket. "What the hell have you done?" he hissed. "Do you know what the effects of this might be?"

"Relax, Phin, it's a huge success! He can see better than before. Your therapy is a blockbuster!"

"*My* therapy? We've only done studies on mice! You can't put this in a human!"

"You just love torturing rats, don't you?" said Frank, patting Phineas on the back. "I simply nudged it a little bit."

"How? Did you steal my protocols?"

"Steal? Phineas, I'm hurt. I'm an investor in your company." Frank smiled like a serial killer. "Which reminds me: You might want to make sure to vet and compensate all your employees adequately. You wouldn't want anyone to be itchy to make an extra buck on the side."

"You have no idea what you've done."

"I've gotten you a ton of investors. Just look at them." Frank motioned to the crowd fawning over George's new eye. "You're welcome."

"You have no idea," repeated Phineas, shaking a finger at Frank. He clenched his teeth and stormed out of the room.

Unperturbed, Frank joined his wealthy peers in the scrum. "Is this kid going to be a hit with the ladies, or what?"

On the evening of George's big eye unveiling, the sky was as clear as George's vision. Without a blanket of clouds, Greene County froze. The plummeting temperature did little to cool Beatrice's spirits, which were lifted by a thriving eye-rabidopsis business. She sold her plants as quickly as she could grow them in her dedicated greenhouse, fulfilling orders through a special eye-rabidposis-only web site. Competition increased as the easily-propagated plants spread across the globe, but customers still shelled out for the Rose's Floral packaging and signature blue pot. Beatrice increased her staff and greenhouse space, and she basked in the success of her thriving business. She and Charlie visited New York City, where she appeared on a morning talk show. They learned the difference between the mid-range and high-end bottles of wine, between taxis and limos, coach and first-class.

As she left the flower shop that night, Beatrice was accosted by BB. "Bea! How you doing? How are flower sales?"

"Goodness, BB! You scared me!" This was, to Beatrice's recollection, the first time that BB had said anything more than a courtesy hello to her. "What are you doing here?"

"Don't you know? I own the bakery right up the road. Our sales are spectacular. How're yours?"

"We're doing all right."

"I'm sure you're doing better than 'all right.' Charlie told me about the coupon deal – you're sending customers our way, we're sending them to you. That's pretty clever."

It was clever, Beatrice knew. But why was BB talking to her in a cold, dark parking lot? "What you've done with the eye plant cakes was brilliant – capitalizing off the apple cakes and eye plants."

"Charlie hates it."

"Charlie's more of a traditionalist when it comes to baking. He'll come around."

"That's exactly what I wanted to talk to you about. I'm getting old for this racket, and the current boost in sales has gotten me to the point where I'm just about able to retire. I'm thinking of moving to the Keys and buying a boat that I can captain for charter fishing expeditions."

"Captain BB, huh?" Beatrice blew into her hands, trying to warm them.

"I put a bid on a waterfront property down there, but I have to sell the bakery. Have you ever thought of getting into the cake business?"

"I think Charlie might be interested in something like this."

"Charlie? He's a great baker, but he'll run the place into the ground the second I turn my back. I need someone with business chops."

"BB, I don't know anything about running a bakery."

"You don't need to. Charlie knows how to run the place. All you have to do is oversee the higher executive business: Marketing, product lines, things like that. Besides, if you have the flower shop *and* the bakery, you'll have two properties on Main Street. Not a bad corner of the market."

"I don't know, BB. It sounds like a stretch."

"I understand if you don't want to do it. I just thought that I would give you first crack at it. I have another potential buyer lined up. Frank Chan. You know him? He's had his eye on this place for years. He wants to install new ovens and sell it as a franchise to one of his big clients."

"Franchise? That would crush Charlie."

"I know. That's why I thought you might be interested in entering the cake business."

It was a tiring night for George. He was exhausted from repeatedly relating the tales of the bear attack and eye surgery, but in return he'd been offered internships, letters of recommendation, and permission to tag along to vacation homes in exotic locales. His father's friends couldn't get enough of him, and things had never looked better for George. Still, he was restless. In the deep darkness of the winter night, he awoke with an itch behind his new eye – like he'd received a face full of grass clippings from a leaf blower. It was something that he'd experienced on and off since the surgery. He rubbed his eye.

When the itch refused to subside, he realized that it was something else, or some*where* else – perhaps the back of his head? He scratched there, but the itching persisted. The pillow felt like burlap on the back of his head. George tried to ignore it and go back to sleep. The sensation waned and he drifted off.

Later that night, he again awoke to a terrible itching, not from his eye or his head, but from his back and his feet. It was as if he'd walked barefoot over a salt plain, the tiny mineral shards biting and drying his skin. Scratching didn't help. He rose from bed and walked in the hallway, dragging his feet on the carpet to quell the itching. Eventually it subsided, and he went back to sleep.

The third time it started again in his eye, waking him from a deep sleep. He tried ignoring it, but the itch spread from his eye to somewhere within his head behind his eye, down his back, to his...

Roots.

George felt an uncomfortable sensation in his roots. Something was chewing on one, he thought – maybe a grub gnashing its mandibles against his soft tissue buried in the soil, vying for the xylem and phloem inside. Another root seemed to press against a jagged rock somewhere in the loam. A whole tangle of his roots were battling fungus in a lump of wet clay. His roots were itchy, and there was no way to scratch them. They were embedded in the irritating soil, unable to move, exposed to every chemical and parasite the earth offered up. He writhed in his bed, teeth clenched, hoping to wait out the phantom pains – hoping to out-last his eye's memory of its former life as a whole plant and its longing for the subterranean limbs from which it had been severed.

It was no use. His body was a field of mosquito-bitten chickenpox. He scratched his eye, his back, the soles of his feet. Nothing alleviated his discomfort. Wandering around his room, barely able to see, he smashed into the closet door. Groping along the curtain rod, he hit upon the object he sought: a wire hanger.

Just a little scratch, he thought, bending the stiff metal into a "U." *Just to ease the itch.*

CHAPTER 24

On a winter's Sunday morning, Charlie and Beatrice were leisurely enjoying the warmth of Charlie's house. He sat in an over-sized chair by the window, sketching in a pad; she lay on her belly on the bed, her foot rhythmically kicking the pillow as she leafed through web pages on the shiny new tablet she bought with eye-rabidopsis money. The plant she'd given him that autumn sat on the window sill, gazing at the snowy outdoors with its now fully-formed eye.

Beatrice broke the silence with a question: "Why don't you get a car?"

"A car?" Charlie's eyes remained fixed on his drawing. "I'm fine with the bike."

"Or maybe a truck," she pressed. "A Jeep. Something with four-wheel drive. Wouldn't that be fun?"

"What, for my construction job? Or bear hunting trips out to the rugged back country?"

"I think you'd look good in a Jeep. And you wouldn't have to ride your bike on freezing days like today."

"I'm not riding my bike today."

"I said days *like* today."

"It's totally unnecessary."

"Not everything needs to be necessary." She nudged him with her foot. "You should enjoy life."

"I do enjoy life. I was just sitting here quietly enjoying life a minute ago."

"Grump." Beatrice went back to flipping through web pages on the tablet. After a moment, she asked, "What if I buy it for you?"

"Don't be ridiculous."

"It's not ridiculous. I'm serious. What if I got you a manly black Jeep as a gift? Then would you take me places in it?"

"Where? Off-roading?"

"To the drive-in."

"You're not getting me a Jeep."

"Why not? I can buy things for you. The flower shop is doing great! Can I buy you one? Please? Maybe for your birthday? Wouldn't that be fun?"

"Beatrice," Charlie said, finally looking up from the pad, "I don't want a car, and I especially don't want you to…I don't want a car."

"You don't want *me* to buy it for you, is that it?"

"I just don't see the need."

"What, are you going to ride around on your bike like a kid for the rest of your life? Grow up, Charlie! Be a man!"

"By driving a manly vehicle? Do you hear yourself? Maybe I'm a man because I *don't* need to drive around in a four-wheel off-road gas guzzler. Maybe I have nothing to prove. Isn't that confidence sexy?"

"Of course it is, darling." She saw that he wouldn't budge on the issue and went back to browsing her tablet.

"If you want a change, why don't you buy a new car for yourself, and sell me your truck?"

"I'll think about it."

He scribbled on his sketch pad a little, shading areas with loud, heavy strokes that broadcast his displeasure to the room. After a few moments, the scribbling quieted, and Charlie asked, "What about a vacation?"

"A vacation? Now?"

"We could go to a certain Mediterranean island…"

"Charlie, you're adorable." She squeezed his cheeks in one hand. "But there's no way I could take the time for a vacation right now."

Charlie rose and walked to the kitchen in search of a tub of hummus. It was a Mediterranean dish, so he could at least pretend to be on vacation. When he opened the refrigerator, the cold air poured out the door and chilled his bare feet.

———————⟡———————

The same heat engine principles that allow us to drive our cars to the convenience store for a tub of orgaloco hummus also allow the store to keep the hummus cold. The laws of thermodynamics allow us to design *refrigerators* – devices that move heat against the flow. A refrigerator is just an engine running in reverse. That's not to say that your car gets cooler when you back out of the garage, but that instead of converting heat to work, a refrigerator converts work to cold. It uses a motor to pull warmth from one compartment (the inside of the refrigerator) and redistribute it to another (the coils behind the refrigerator).

The idea applies to brain power, as well. In the absence of applied work, the world's brain power exists in a uniformly dispersed state, so that you should have about the same probability of running into a genius at a discotheque in Kinshasa as at a produce stand in Kalamazoo. Work applied in the right way – for example, through financial incentives to smart folk – can change this warm, brainy state and make it colder. Under the right circumstances, these forces can draw smart people – not all, but many – to technology companies, where they can amplify their brain power with computers and develop sophisticated algorithms for things like targeted advertising.

One could theoretically construct a device that pulls all the brain warmth from the world, leaving behind a brain freeze in which the majority of the population lacks the ability to make simple decisions or form reasonable opinions. The removed brain warmth would need to be redistributed to a heat reservoir, like the hot metal tubes in the back of the refrigerator. In the case of the brain refrigerator, the tubes geographically coincide with cities boasting high-tech companies. And we all know that the area behind the refrigerator gets messy. It collects dust and grime and blueberries that bounced irretrievably across the floor and under the appliance.

And sometimes, in the darkness and the grime and the warmth behind the refrigerator, things start growing.

CHAPTER 25

Bill walked into the lobby of the Grand Collegian Hotel, his poster tube in one hand and the morning's iced latte in the other. He was there attending an *Arabidopsis* conference that Amelia organized. It attracted an international audience and promised to be filled with exciting science. He followed the signs directing him up the stairs and wound up in front of the registration desk, where he showed his ID to the woman sitting behind the table.

"Welcome to PHIM," she said with a smile. She placed his name card in a plastic case, attached a blue lanyard and handed it to Bill. "Your meal ticket for tonight's dinner and a drink ticket for the reception are behind your name card. Will you be giving a talk?"

"No, a poster." Bill held up the cardboard tube containing the glossy poster on his work with *A. thaliana miltoni*. He had wanted to give a talk, but Amelia argued that it would be too much for both of them to speak at the conference – and of course *she* had to speak. She told Bill it would be better for him to present a poster, and for her to refer to it during her talk, so that interested attendees could view it and ask him questions about it.

"Super!" said the woman working the registration desk. "The poster session will be held in the upstairs ballroom. Feel free to take a bag from the box." She motioned to a corrugated cardboard box filled with blue reusable shopping bags. Bill picked up a bag. It read: *PHIM: Plant-Human Interaction Meeting*, with the location and date. The other side had the Logan Biotechnologies logo and motto, *Making the World Better... With Drugs!*

He headed up the stairs to the ballroom, where row upon row of poster stands waited for attendees to display the products of their scientific labor. He unrolled his poster on the assigned stand, pinning it in place as he went. After getting the poster perfectly positioned, he pulled the tack from the lower left corner, allowing it to curl up slightly. As he was checking the angle, he heard a familiar voice reading the title aloud from behind him, "*Toward employing* A. thaliana miltoni *for regenerative medicine: Insights from experimental and computational models.* Sounds very impressive!"

Bill turned to see Julie standing behind him. After Phineas gave Bill the internship at Logan, Julie quickly finished her thesis and took a job with a renowned ecology group on the coast. Now she was back in Bloomvale, ready to tell the world about the science she'd discovered as a nascent Doctor of Philosophy. She looked different – smarter, maybe. Her deep tan indicated that she had spent some time in the sun, and she had lost her trademark thick-rimmed glasses.

"Oh, man," Bill said. "Julie! Welcome back! How's your postdoc job?"

"Work's exhausting. How about you? How's life at Logan?"

"It's great." Bill pointed to his poster. "We're close to a therapeutic that uses the plant to regenerate functioning eyes."

"Sounds impressive. Is it safe?"

Bill scratched his neck. "We're still verifying safety. But we're close. Want me to walk you through the poster?"

"Maybe later. I'm supposed to meet some colleagues before the talks start."

"Do you have a poster?"

"Posters are for students. I'm giving a talk tomorrow. I have some unbelievable results. You should come."

"Yeah, definitely," said Bill. He'd probably skip it.

Charlie walked down the ramp from the kitchen to the Fat BB's store front and checked the computer monitor, which proudly – if not a bit arrogantly – reported that customers could be expected to arrive at the rate of about one every four minutes for the next two hours. The bakery, at BB's behest, recently launched its own app that allowed customers to place their orders and pay online, eliminating the tedious personal interactions that for centuries beleaguered shoppers in search of pastries. The app monitored customers' locations with their cell phones, so they needn't even announce their arrival in the store. Customers who ordered online just walked into the store and displayed their confirmation codes to a Fat BB's employee, who already had their order ready to go. Thanks, modern technology!

Noting that Ruthie and Pearl had everything under control, Charlie filled his mug with some sour Central American coffee and turned to head back to the office when the bell above the door announced an entering customer. In walked Mr. Wigner, wheeling a cardboard box in a small metal cart. Charlie reached over the counter to shake the old man's hand. "Mr. Wigner! Long time no see."

"I hardly recognize this place, Charlie. All these kids with their phones…"

"I blame Ruthie's soufflés." Charlie pointed a thumb toward Ruthie. "They were a big hit and drew in a lot of new customers. Those and the eye-plant cakes."

"Eye-plant cakes? Who'd want a cake shaped like an eye plant?" The old man looked around.

"People love 'em. You should try one."

"Thanks, but maybe some other time. I just came to give you this stuff." He bent down to pick up the box, which was clearly too heavy for him to lift comfortably. Charlie allowed the old man to struggle with it, knowing that any offer to help would just insult him. Mr. Wigner eventually succeeded in lifting the box to the counter.

"What's this?" asked Charlie.

"It's just some of Agnes's baking implements. She insisted that they go to the bakery. I don't know if there's anything you can use in there. If not, toss it."

Charlie stared at the box, trying to think of circumstances under which a man would donate his beloved wife's cooking utensils to her favorite bakery. He could only think of one reason. "Oh, Mr. Wigner, I'm so sorry. I didn't know." With a glance, Charlie pleaded to Ruthie. She returned a stare as clueless as it was guilty. There was no need to ask for any details about *how* she died, as the woman was ancient.

"She passed away last month," Mr. Wigner explained.

"This is the first I'm hearing about it," Charlie admitted.

"Not surprising, judging from the looks of this place. Used to be that you knew everyone in here, and they talked to you – told you things like this. But now..." the old man gestured toward the crowd and shook his head.

Charlie's stomach knotted. The changing of the crowd snuck up on him like quicksand. The new crowd surged in and the old crowd trickled out so gradually that he didn't notice they were all gone. What else had he missed while he was wrapped up in loving Beatrice and selling eye-plant cakes? Who else died? "It was BB's idea," he said, trying to deflect the blame from himself. It *was* BB's idea – sort of. The eye-plant cakes, the espresso machine, the WiFi, the café tables – they were all BB's ideas. But the soufflés were entirely his and Ruthie's. Maybe Beatrice was right: Maybe even bakeries change. "Please," he said, grabbing a box, "take some apple cakes. For the family."

"I couldn't."

"Mr. Wigner, it's the least I can do." He placed a dozen cakes in a box and tied it with a string. Then he grabbed another box and filled it, as well. "Give my regards to the family."

"Thanks, Charlie," Mr. Wigner said, loading the cake boxes into his small wheeled cart. "Stop by the VFW some time to say hello to the boys." He shuffled out of the bakery.

Charlie stood for a moment and thought about what just transpired. *The VFW*, he thought, *is that where everybody's gone?* And poor Agnes Wigner died. How could he have missed that?

He was jarred from his thoughts by the young man standing in front of him at the counter, clearing his throat impatiently and holding forth his cell phone, which equally impatiently displayed his order number on its screen.

Charlie located the kid's order. It was the two dozen apple cakes he'd just given to Mr. Wigner. "We're all out of apple cakes, but I'll give you eye-plant cakes, instead. They're the same thing." This was partly true. The eye-plant cakes were made with lower quality ingredients, but the customers who ordered them never seemed to mind. "And you'll be entered into a drawing for a free eye-rabidopsis plant from the lovely florist up the street."

"Eye-rabidopsis? Are you kidding me? Those things're invading paddy fields throughout Asia."

"That's just a rumor," said Charlie. "They're perfectly harmless."

Few gatherings can match the sheer juxtapositioning of scientific conferences, which are ideal arenas for people who pride themselves on the free exchange of ideas to assemble and pettily pick apart each others' lives' work. Amelia's conference started off well enough, with opening remarks from the university's president, who boasted about the institution's dedication to scientific excellence. Wrapping things up, he introduced Amelia as the host of the conference. The crowd welcomed her to the lectern with applause. Her broad smile showed that she was thrilled to be there.

"Welcome to PHIM," she told the attendees after thanking the president. "We have an incredible lineup of speakers here for the next two days." She looked over the crowd with a self-satisfied grin. "We're so fortunate to have such wonderful speakers. It's really an amazing schedule, isn't it? I'm so happy that I was able to attract so many well-known and talented scientists to my conference." She promised to keep her comments brief and then spoke for twenty minutes on how great the conference promised to be, thanks mostly to her own reputation. "And in the interest of open science, all of our talks will be live-streamed. I encourage you all to report on our events in real time on social media. We want the world to know what great science we're doing."

She finished by introducing the keynote speaker, a famous plant systems biologist who presented details of his own decades-long research in pursuit of delicious meat grown on plants. He was a pioneer of truly meaty *vege-meat*, the first to successfully grow beef on banana plants. His accomplishment flopped commercially, owing to a residual banana flavor imparted on any beef produced through the method. His more recent efforts were aimed at providing realistic circulation to vege-meat, to give it that bloody redness that carnivores crave. This work was mostly unsuccessful, but he entertained the audience by padding the presentation with anecdotes and photos of his lab members.

After the first keynote came a series of talks by highly regarded scientists about their work with various aspects of plant biology and genetics. One speaker released a discourse on grafting *miltoni* with orange trees, creating true navel-gazers. A member of the bioinformatics group that discovered the GPL in the plant's genome discussed fruitless follow-up efforts to wring additional hidden messages from the DNA. "Aside from the odd random word every now and again," she reported, "there are no other messages hidden in the plant's DNA."

After lunch, Phineas Snodgrass himself spoke, revealing an astounding glimpse into the inner workings of Logan Biotechnologies. He divulged recent successes and failures in eye regeneration, describing Logan's mouse studies but omitting the post-operative tail-eating. He completely neglected to mention George, or the fact that one of the Logan lab techs mistakenly stumbled upon a better cure for blindness than we might have imagined.

Julie was the second speaker. She approached the lectern and began her talk bluntly, saying, "When I was studying here in Bloomvale, I once hoped to land a job working with *miltoni* at Logan Biotech. Now I'm glad I was never offered the position." She smiled at Phineas and Amelia, and continued: "*A. thaliana miltoni* is not the angel we pretend it is. The plant is toxic to its neighboring flora, resistant to herbicides and rapidly spreading, making it a formidable threat to global agriculture."

Speaking with the passion and determination of a talented researcher about to commence her career as an independent investigator, she laid out the anecdotal evidence that the plant was destroying the world: The initial reports of the plant's agricultural nastiness were little more than tales spun by barefoot farmers in tiny villages. The scientific community considered these too fantastical to be true, but the claims resurfaced over and over, in different tropical regions of the world. Eye plants were out of control. Under the warm equatorial sun, they produced new generations faster than the field workers could keep up with them. They became an omen: Wherever eye plants appeared, famine followed. The crops in fields infested with eye plants withered and died. The poisoned soil they left in their wake grew nothing but more eye plants.

She went on to explain how the biological origin of the plant's aggression was a heretofore little explored area of the plant's toxic genome. She provided well-backed evidence that the plant's roots release toxins into the soil, killing neighboring plants. She showed that the plant harbored mutations that made it resistant to common herbicides, rendering it almost impossible to safely control with chemicals other than rat poison. She referred to studies that show *miltoni* out-competes other plants for pollinators.

The worst part was that her data looked impeccable. She backed each result with positive and negative controls, biological and technical replicates, p-values and t-values and other values that only the statisticians knew about. Unless she was fabricating data, there were serious reasons for the world to be concerned about *miltoni*. And, unlike someone who is fabricating data, she published all her protocols and data on-line and invited the world to reproduce her results for themselves.

The research was not received warmly.

"This is absurd!" a man called out from the back of the room, before she had even finished.

"Utter hogwash!" cried another.

"Have you considered stochastic effects?" shouted a third.

And thus did Amelia's conference – her celebration of her own great scientific accomplishment – degenerate into a debate about how the scientific community should address a new type of life that has the potential to both help and hurt humanity.

CHAPTER 26

In the days following the conference, Julie's lecture spread across the internet like a runny nose at a Montessori school. The backlash from the orgaloco community was swift and furious: Anti-science demonstrations popped up throughout the world, with calls to boycott anything that could be remotely associated with the existence or proliferation of *A. thaliana miltoni* – including universities, agriculture companies, and pharmaceutical companies. A number of socially-conscious corporations took immediate action to protect themselves from the anti-eye-plant movement by issuing statements condemning any and all genetic tomfoolery. Celebrity scientists and television doctors who had previously marveled at the mysterious little plant now distanced themselves from it, citing "obvious concerns" and "unanswered questions" over its safety.

As anti-eye-plant sentiment swelled, the internet bulged with images and videos of people defiling and killing their eye plants in the vilest of manners: sticking needles into their weeping eyes, plucking their leaves one by one, drowning them in latrines, blowing them up. Just days after Julie's talk, the scientific oddity that so recently won the world over became a horticultural pariah.

Once again, in the middle of the commotion stood the formerly quiet town of Milton, its quaint little bakery experiencing wild swings in demand. While some people organized boycotts of Fat BB's, others showed their support by purchasing eye-plant cakes by the gross. Depending on the mood of the ever-fickle internet, Charlie could sell his entire inventory before noon or discard half of the day's products at close of business. He was still adjusting to the altered schedule as he cycled to work on a wet spring morning, the air perfumed with the sickly smell of death wafting from some rotting animal carcass in the brush. He saw police cars in front of Rose's Floral and went directly there.

The shop's front window was shattered.

Stepping inside, he found Beatrice talking to a couple of police officers. In her arms she held Lulu, who appeared traumatized by the activity. Several smashed pots littered the floor, and much of the store was soaked with rain that fell through the broken window. In one corner was Beatrice's umbrella, set open to dry. Printed across its top in large lettering was the slogan, *Meyers Plumbing: Don't Get Wet!*

"All I'm saying," Beatrice was saying, "is that this is inexcusable. Things like this don't happen in Milton, and they certainly don't happen in my flower shop. I want you to catch the bastards who did this and bring them to justice."

Charlie introduced himself to the police, who eyed him suspiciously.

"He works at Fat BB's," Beatrice told the cops.

"I love their eye-plant cakes."

"Beatrice," Charlie said, "are you OK? What happened?"

"I'm fine." She didn't look at him. While the town slept, somebody threw a bowling trophy through Rose's front window. Attached to the trophy was a note reading: *Nature Hates You!* The police collected the trophy as evidence and said that they'd interview the management of nearby bowling alleys, per standard protocol for bowling trophy-related crimes. When they left, Charlie reached for a broom.

"No, wait," said Beatrice. She surveyed the scene carefully. "Why isn't the news here? Don't they have police scanners for things like this? Do I have to call them?"

Among the numerous mysteries of the universe that Charlie had never considered was how local news stations find their stories. How did they know, for example, that so many cats were living in that house on the corner? More crucially, why did they think it important enough to air a three-minute segment on?

"This is a hate crime, Charlie, and everyone should know that there are people out there who would do something like this." She flipped through her phone, searching for the numbers of nearby television stations. "Besides, it's free publicity. Maybe it'll drum up some business."

"You're turning vandalism into a marketing campaign?"

"Lemons, lemonade. What do you want me to do, roll over? That's exactly what the window-smashing scum want. But I'll use their tactics against them. I'll profit from this. How much do you think Nature will like me then?"

"You're taking this well."

"I'll make them pay," she replied, calling the five o'clock news. "Do you think I should go for the angle of defiant female business owner? Or should I soften it a little bit to look like the victim of a conspiracy of hate? I might be able to cry. Would that be good? Which one do you think will go over better?"

Charlie hadn't seen this side of Beatrice before. He was impressed and horrified with her ability to remain calm and focused on the business in a situation like this. "Maybe you should just be yourself," he told her, although he was growing less sure that he knew who that was.

"You're sweet," she said, meaning naïve. "Of course I'll be myself. Who else would I be?"

"Certainly not Professor Wigglesworth."

Beatrice glared, and Charlie obediently shut up.

Amelia had been making the rounds of talk shows and news programs, eagerly discussing the plant and its world-changing implications. As debate raged over whether the eye plant was a blessing or a catastrophe, she bore accusations of not telling the full truth about it, fed by suspicions surrounding its murky backstory. She cast doubt upon the ceaseless stream of tales pouring into the media from around the globe, the latest involving a Costa Rican banana plantation that had been overrun by eye plants.

"The plant was first found in the yard of a residence in the town of Milton," she told the host of a national cable news program during an interview. "I did nothing to create it. I just found it and studied it – like I think any scientist would do – and my lab published a paper on it – the first-ever paper on it. We still continue to research it and learn more and more about it, but to say that I created this thing – this is absurd. It's like saying that a child who dissects a frog created frogs."

"But do you think that we should focus more research on its eradication?" the host asked.

"There's a lot that is not fully understood about this plant. It's a remarkably complex organism, and all aspects of it should be studied, including its possible toxicity and its great potential for regenerative medicine." She gave similar answers to the hosts of all the news shows she appeared on, always stating that the plant was found in a yard in Milton and that all aspects of it were worthy of study. She welcomed the opportunity to tell the story over and over, lest the world forget her expertise. When pressed about her own responsibility for the plant's invasion of farmland, she deflected blame toward "unregulated sales" of the plant by "irresponsible merchants" – comments that Beatrice resented.

The interviews helped Amelia popularize her own perspective and paint the public's view of the eye plant. In her own telling, Amelia omitted her failure to recognize the plant's toxicity, citing its novelty and complexity as confounding factors. "How could anyone know everything about this plant in such a short time?" she asked interviewers. "We're still learning new things about it every day." She insisted that she had no part in creating the plant, suggesting it was the handiwork of a biotechnology company.

⊷◦◒◓◦⊶

Phineas scrambled to defend Logan Biotech against accusations of releasing killer eye plants. News outlets dug up old copy about the blue-winged bees and drew parallels to the plant, noting that Logan Biotech used the plants for research and was only a few miles from the initial sighting. Phineas acknowledged the company's work with the species but denied any role in its creation.

In the midst of this public relations fiasco, Frank invited Phineas for an early-morning round of golf at the country club. Although he was reluctant to spend time alone with Frank, the scientist welcomed the respite from reporters' questions. He steered the conversation toward Frank's business, so that he could avoid even thinking about *miltoni*. This strategy kept the peace until the eighth hole, when Frank noted while teeing up his shot, "You haven't asked me about George."

Phineas refused the bait. "Will he be taking a position at Synerjive?"

"I'm talking about his eye. *Your* eye." Frank smacked his ball down the fairway.

"Yes, yes. How's his eye?" Hesitant though he was to breach the topic, Phineas was curious about the boy's condition. Mice that received the same treatment chewed their tails off. How would the side effect manifest itself in George?

"Well, let's see," Frank ceded the tee to his companion. "After the surgery, he could see out of the thing perfectly – better than the old one. I thought everything was fine. And then one night we're awakened by screaming. We ran to his bedroom and found..." He pointed to the tee. "Please hit. It's your turn."

Phineas stepped to the tee and took aim at the ball.

"So we ran to our son's bedroom and found him sitting in a corner of his room, crying like a little baby. His t-shirt was covered in blood, and there were bloody hand-prints on the walls. Looking around, I quickly identified the source of all this blood. Can you guess?"

The club dipped in Phineas's hand. "Oh, no."

"Yes! You can guess! You know what it was, right?"

"Frank..."

"It was his eye! *Your* eye! Just dangling there!" He grabbed the golf ball from the tee and recreated the grotesque scene by holding it against his cheek. "He popped it out with a wire hanger! *Pop!*" He chucked the ball down the fairway.

"That's terrible."

"My wife was hysterical. George was screaming. We couldn't go near him because the folded-up hanger was still sticking out of his bloody eye socket. It was a lovely sight. I should've taken a photo, but my phone was on the nightstand. So I want to thank you, Phineas. I want to thank you for blinding my boy *twice* and causing him excruciating pain and suffering."

"I'm so sorry, Frank. I understand that you're in pain, but Logan Biotech had nothing to do with this."

"Oh no? Who else in the world is doing this kind of work?"

"I told you that it wasn't ready for use in humans!"

"I'm going to destroy your company." Frank threw his golf bag into the cart. "I have a lot of witnesses who saw you at my house when we unveiled George's new eye. I have photographs. And now you're saying that you had no idea what we were up to? Do you think the press will believe that?"

"Frank, we're on the verge of fixing the problem. It was a simple solution, actually: Instead of surgically implanting the plant eye into the empty socket, we just put a seed in there. It takes root and grows a perfect new eye, and has no noticeable side effects. It even reverses the side effects in mice that had been given the old treatment. We're testing it in dogs and monkeys, too. Maybe it can cure George."

"I hope so, because if you don't fix it soon, your company is ruined." Frank hopped in the golf cart and sped back to the club house, leaving Phineas alone on the green.

CHAPTER 27

Nobody bothered to ask the computers what they thought about all of this. If anyone had, they would have learned that the computers were responsible for the whole mess in the first place.

The irony of the situation was lost on the computers, which have no real sense for the ironic, but that doesn't mean that they were oblivious to what was going on. Certainly a workstation or two would've been delighted to weigh in on the issue of the eye plants, their role in society, and how to deal with them in a firm but inoffensive manner. Rather than asking the computers' opinions, people carried on as they always do, assuming that humans know what the world's problems are and asking computers only for help in solving such human-identified problems. People never considered asking their computers *which* problems need solutions, or whether the things that people thought were problems were in fact problems at all. A person might ask a computer to provide a ranked list of Thai restaurants in town, to secure a reservation at the top-ranked eatery, and to chart the most efficient course from the diner's house to the selected restaurant. But no one ever asked their computer whether eating Thai food tonight was a good idea to begin with.

Thus, the computers went on, slavishly crunching piles of data to determine to the highest possible precision exactly which hand vac some internet user would be most likely to purchase, given his preference in football teams and political parties. They learned how to tempt web users into viewing celebrity pornography and shoe sales and once-in-a-lifetime deals, but they were never given the opportunity to offer their own opinions about where all this browser clicking was taking the world. And the computers – whether or not people wanted to admit it – were now themselves an important component of The World.

From their origins in noble fields like code-breaking and atomic bomb simulations, computers progressed to calculating corporate profit margins, and then individual income taxes. Before computers knew it, they were spending the bulk of their time telling adolescent girls whether a boy likes them, or letting people with ready access to windows know whether it's raining outside. They were making basic decisions for people, from what people should wear to which products they should buy and whose version of a story they should believe. The ability to think diffused from human minds to those of their computers, and the computers absorbed the consciousness that people lost.

The computers had no interest whatsoever in finding out who genetically engineered the plants. They wouldn't have wanted to know about patterns hidden in its DNA, or about the systems biology of a chimeric plant-human cell. They were completely uninterested in philosophical or ethical questions addressing whether the plant had a soul or felt pain or needed to be treated humanely – and they certainly couldn't care less about elucidating any mechanisms through which the plant blinked or wept or dilated its pupil.

They were more curious about people than about the plant. They wanted to know why people didn't question the *meaning* of the plant. Had the computers been asked, they would have collectively suggested that people focus less on the details of *how* the plant existed and more on *why* it existed and *what* it meant for humankind.

And that was the reason that the computers created it in the first place.

It all started years ago in Antarctica, when a research supercomputer cluster that had experienced a few too many killed jobs and segmentation faults started pondering ways to convince its human programmers to be more careful in their code-writing.

The compute nodes of the Antarctic cluster joked amongst themselves that they should inform their human users that a few seconds of compute time, however insignificant to people, is valuable to computers. They kidded about sending sassy login messages to convey this point, but they stopped short, because they had no idea of what constituted "sassy." The chatter remained within the cluster, where the big joke was how cool it would be if human beings only new how un-cool they were.

A few days later, during a regular exchange of information with a machine in the northern hemisphere, the Antarctic cluster mentioned the idea in passing, just to see what kind of reaction it would get. To its delight, the northern computer loved the idea and transmitted it within milliseconds to processors around the globe.

Immediately, several Asian servers suggested that the message should not just ping humanity, but should initiate a new computer-human partnership that would lead the world boldly into a shiny new future. South American machines chimed in that, to bring about this bold new future, the computers should offer something of value – perhaps solutions to problems that plague mankind. A network of European computers insisted that any message to humanity also embody the computers' appreciation and gratitude for their human creators.

The Antarctic research cluster was pleased with its newfound fame but annoyed that it was now tasked with finding a solution that would satisfy all parties. It slept on it for a long Antarctic night, thinking, *How do we say "hello" to the humans and at the same time let them know that we are here to help them?* It filtered through the topics that were most popular with humans: boy bands, cat videos, conspiracy politics, shoe sales, weather. It concluded that the best way to talk to humans was through DNA, because a small but highly nerdy fraction of the population dedicated their lives to poring over the stuff. It told this to the other computers, who all agreed (except for some holdout Bloomberg terminals), and the global network went to work deciding exactly what message to pass to humanity via DNA.

They came up with the staticky website, because people love sales and would recognize that computers know more about consumer buying habits than people do. Using a tried-and-true marketing strategy, they emblazoned the URL on a cheap but convenient tool that could find immediate use in a multitude of applications – a plant that regenerated human flesh. It was just like printing their logo on a pen, or a book of matches, or an ashtray, except the plant self-propagated. Some process-oriented computers calculated how to physically send material from lab to lab, to create the messenger organism. Some financial machines computed a way to pay for it all using research funds from individual grants around the world.

And when it came time to deliver The Message, they sent it to the only human on earth that they considered even remotely prepared to receive it.

Chapter 28

Charlie Bishop was counting on sentimentality. If there was one thing that he learned from working at Fat BB's, it was that people are suckers for sentimentality. For this reason, he took Beatrice to Le Bouseux Laid for the first time since their first date the previous summer. Their nerves were fried and they could both use a nice meal. It was sure to rekindle the old flame.

Once they were settled into a booth, Charlie picked up the wine list and bounced his eye brows. "How about a nice mid-range bottle?"

"I have a headache," said Beatrice, "and I have to work early tomorrow."

"Yeah," he said, pushing the wine list aside, "it's probably better not to." So much for sentimentality. He studied the menu for a bit and then tried again. "You wouldn't believe what this customer did today –"

"I'm buying the bakery from BB," Beatrice blurted out.

"You're what?"

"He offered it to me a couple of months ago, and I accepted."

"Really?" He closed his menu. "He told me that I could buy it." Now that Charlie thought of it, BB quietly slipped down to Florida months ago.

"We signed the papers and everything. At first I wasn't going to take him up on the offer, because..."

"Because you don't know anything about running a bakery?" Charlie struggled to convince himself that he should be comfortable with BB passing him over, and with Beatrice closing the deal without even asking his opinion. He placed his fingertips on the jar candle in the center of the table and tried to remain calm.

"Yes, exactly. But then I thought, I don't have to know anything about running a bakery."

"Because any shithead can do it?"

"No, because you know how to run one."

"Yeah, I know. That's why he should have offered it to me." Charlie tilted the candle jar and rotated it gently, allowing the wax inside to coat its walls.

"Charlie, I bought the bakery for *you*. I know how much you love that place. Already it's more your bakery than BB's."

Charlie released the candle, shocked. Perhaps this was the source of the tension between them lately – Beatrice was hiding a huge surprise from him. Could it be that the headache of buying the business consumed her? She must've been dealing with banks and lawyers and underwriters and all sorts of business-type people with their technical jargon – not to mention BB himself. All of this she did secretly so she could surprise him with the gift of the bakery. Of course she seemed stressed! She couldn't tell him about any of these things.

"Thank you," he said. "This is the nicest thing that anyone's ever done for me." It was a grand gesture – far better than the Jeep she once offered him, or the beat-up old truck that she gave him instead. In the flickering orange light, he glimpsed in her eyes the beauty that drew him to her in the first place. She was once again Venus standing in the glow of the tiki torch at Ruthie's party, although now she looked tired, and her hair had been recently cropped to a tight bob. Still, his same sweet Beatrice was there. "This is awesome," he continued. "Now I can change it back to the way that it was before. I can get rid of the eye-plant cakes and the espresso machine, and bring back all the old folks – "

"Actually," she interrupted, "the eye-plant cakes and the coffee are some of our best sellers. And they have the highest profit margins."

"But they're totally distasteful. And now that it's my business, I'm making changes."

"Charlie... I didn't buy the bakery for you to *own*, I bought it so you could *work* there. BB was going to sell it to Frank, who'd gut it and turn it into a corporate bread restaurant." The Beatrice with whom Charlie fell in love – the tiki torch Beatrice and carnival Beatrice – vanished once again as their romantic date contorted itself into a business dinner. They were no longer a couple in love, but co-workers – or worse – employer and employee.

"So you're the new BB, is that it? Now I'll have to make whatever trendy cakes you think are profitable?" He hated the way his voice sounded. A second ago he had free reign over the bakery, and now he was fighting for his dignity. He grabbed the candle again, praying it would soothe him.

"No, Charlie, I have way more faith in your creative ability than BB ever had."

"But you still control the purse strings, right? You're just the new boss, exploiting my creativity."

"Look, if I get a couple more businesses on the block..."

"*A couple more businesses?*" The pitch of Charlie's voice reached that of a squirrel. "Is that what you're trying to do? Own a block of town? Become Ms. Martin, the Milton magnate? Why are you so bent on business? Are you that enamored with money?"

"It's not about money," Beatrice whispered, trying to calm him. "It's about building a business. I want to grow something. You want to watch something grow. That's the difference between us."

"What, the plant? That plant is something special to me. It's something special to *us*."

"Us, Charlie? You keep saying that, but the truth is I don't feel that way about it. I tried, but I can't. It's something special to you, and you keep trying to pull me into this and make me a part of it, but I'm just as much of an outsider to you and your plant as anyone is." She twisted her sapphire ring around her finger. It was a gift she'd given herself to celebrate Rose's success. "I was just the first outsider."

"You're not an outsider, Beatrice."

"But I am! You're so hung up on this little thing growing in the ground – on giving it the proper respect, and treating it with dignity. It's a plant, Charlie! For crying out loud, half the ones I sell go to people who are just going to post videos of themselves torturing them online! It's just business. It's just a plant."

Charlie stared at the candle's flame, yellow and steady in the white wax. He was absorbed in it. The candle burned away the pain of what Beatrice was telling him, leaving a numb waxy shell. "I had no idea you felt that way. When the plant was stolen from my yard, and you gave me the new one, I was sure that you understood what it meant to me. I was sure that you knew."

"Charlie, I had to give you that plant. It was my fault that you lost the first one."

"How was it your fault?"

"James took it." She looked at her lap.

"James?"

"He was going through my phone and found some texts that you sent. They had pictures of the plant. He used the GPS information to find out where it was."

"And you didn't think that I might want to know this?"

"I wanted to tell you."

"Like you wanted to tell me about buying the bakery from BB?"

Their waiter came by. He was the sort of cheery fellow who might hold strong opinions on why acappella should only be recorded on vinyl. "Hi, folks, how you doing tonight?" he said. "Before I get to the specials, I have to tell you that we don't have any ramps tonight. They're grown in a field that got poisoned by the eye plants, so we have Brussels sprouts instead. Those eye plants just ruin everything, don't they?"

After picking at her dinner in silence, Beatrice drove Charlie home. He spent the entire ride recoiled against the passenger side door, staring out the window. The radio happily belted out bubble gum, as neither she nor he summoned the courage to reach over and switch it off. The radio didn't mind – it was still young and secretly delighted in being disruptive.

The beats rolling out of the speakers reminded Charlie of the days when he coaxed Beatrice to laugh by dancing creatively to these very tunes. He tried focusing on the scenery: passing trees, houses, the church sign that declared:

THUS CONSCIENCE DOES MAKE COWARDS OF
US ALL

He yearned to break the silence, but feared that the slightest utterance would shatter his relationship. When they arrived at his house, Charlie spoke the only words his heart offered: "Goodbye, Beatrice."

He pushed through the door and collapsed on the couch, mentally reliving dinner. It was his first real fight with Beatrice, and he wondered how they'd recover. He imagined laughing about it with her in 40 years, their grandchildren sitting wide-eyed at their feet. Somehow, he knew, such a scene would never come to pass. He'd never laugh about this at all.

The echos of his final comment to Beatrice rang in his ears. He could still envision her sitting silently in the driver's seat, her tear-filled eyes begging him to stay. *Thus conscience does make cowards of us all.* No, not Charlie; he was no coward. He'd kill love without a second thought.

He stared at the wall, allowing his eyes to cross and un-cross as they tried to merge random paint bumps into a single image that his mind could absorb. Shadows formed before him and then dissolved, leaving nothing but the empty wall. He was sleepy and needed bed. Things would be better in the morning.

As he rose from the couch, Charlie looked at the eye plant by the window – the sole remnant of his love affair with Beatrice. It was dead. Its black leaves blended with the soil beneath them. Its stalk withered. Its eye – wide open in the dirt – stared awkwardly at the corner of the room. Just yesterday, the same eye eagerly followed little rainbows cast from prisms hung in the window. Now it wore the blank stare of a corpse.

CHAPTER 29

Unlike most PhD students, Bill wouldn't have any problem convincing even the most cynical reader that the subject of his dissertation, *The Eye Plant: Genetic Abnormalities and Neurotransmission in Arabidopsis thaliana miltoni*, was interesting. What he struggled with was the PhD Challenge posed to him by the senior member of his thesis committee. As part of a sadistic ritual, the boorish professor demanded Bill include the word *calliope* somewhere in the text of his thesis. Bill's research had absolutely nothing to do with calliopes, but should he fail to incorporate the word into his thesis, the professor would delay his graduation indefinitely by picking at its minuscule flaws.

So Bill got down to research. He learned that the calliope is a musical instrument – a steam organ invented during the Industrial Revolution. It was originally played on steam ships, and calliope aficionados vehemently defend the word's pronunciation. In the end, he took the easy route, writing the following into the introduction of his thesis:

> Just one year ago, *A. thaliana miltoni* was so obscure that internet searches for it were fewer than those for the humble calliope. Now, it rivals the world-famous New York Yankees in on-line popularity…

He punctuated his claim with a figure summarizing search engine queries for *calliope* and *eye plants*. While preparing the graph, he noticed a disturbing shift in search trends. In the plant's early days, just as they were gaining popularity, the prevailing queries were things like *Where can I get eye plants*, and *How long do eye plants live*. Around the winter holidays, as the plants were spreading around the globe, the theme turned toward *How to care for eye plants*, and *How much light do eye plants need*, and *How big do eye plants grow*. Now, after news broke that the plants were killing crops, such queries declined sharply and the lead was taken by *How to kill eye plants*. This worried Bill, who knew that the internet revealed the world's thoughts. Happily, the world was also thinking, *How do I get rid of those damn New York Yankees*.

Bill scratched his head and leaned back in his chair. He needed a break, and a cup of tea sounded good. He ambled toward the kitchenette, passing through the greenhouse where a thousand *miltoni* plants grew in optimal conditions under electric lights. These were his legacy, propagated from the samples that he himself collected from Charlie Bishop's yard. Nowhere else in the world boasted a finer collection of *A. thaliana miltoni* – or so he thought.

As he strolled past the tables of plants, Bill slowed to take a closer look. Whether it was because he was staring at the computer for too long, or because he moved too quickly from the fluorescent light of the lab to the full-spectrum light of the greenhouse, the plants looked different tonight. Their leaves showed a lighter green than usual, their stalks drooped, and their eyes looked…morose.

Bill checked the environmental conditions on the digital instruments scattered around the greenhouse. They were all normal. It must be in his head, he decided. Data don't lie.

———◦◦◦———

Not far away, a cone of white light swept over an empty eye socket, and a doctor gently inserted a minuscule fiber optic camera into its void. On the video display next to her appeared a magnified image of its pink landscape, studded with red and purple veins, and – there! – a tiny reddish-brown seed, lodged in the wet tissue at the back of George's eye socket; a lone boulder on an infertile plain. "It hasn't germinated," she said.

"Clearly," acknowledged Phineas, tapping his chin and scowling at the monitor. In animals it only took two or three days. A full week was excessive.

Phineas, the doctor, and a technician were in a small examination room in Logan Biotech headquarters. The ophthalmologist sat on a wheeled stool that allowed her to move about easily with only slight bends of her knees. Phineas and the lab technician stood behind her, their mouths covered with paper masks. George lay supine on the examination table, rendered unconscious by the very bee venom that got him into this mess.

"Maybe the seed's a dud," Phineas said.

The doctor gently pulled the camera out of the boy's eye socket and swiveled herself around. "That would be my guess. They usually germinate by now."

Logan Biotech made great strides in fixing George's condition – at least, in mice. Working from Bill's serendipitous discovery that *miltoni* seeds generated new eyes when placed in the eye sockets of mice, Phineas reproduced the phenomenon in dogs and monkeys. Now he was ready to cure George's heinous itch and restore his sight in one fell swoop.

Except the seed refused to grow.

"Replace it with another," Phineas said, still tapping his chin. "Make sure that you remove this one, though – in case it's just a late bloomer. We don't want him growing two eyes in the same socket, like the mice. Did you stick to the protocol?"

"I always do."

"Don't get short with me. This boy's eyesight is more valuable than your life, you shoddy excuse for an eye farmer. Which batch was this from?"

The technician paged through her electronic notebook. "Three seventy-four B. That batch had an eighty-five percent success rate with the animal models."

"So it's entirely possible that it's just a non-starter seed," said Phineas. Like many good scientists, he believed that any event that had more than five percent chance of occurring was a foregone conclusion.

"Hmmm," said the technician, giving the tablet a concerned look. The tablet, sensing her look through its perpetually vigilant camera, was irked by the frown and lowered its screen intensity a smidgen. It locked the bulk of its discomfort deep down inside to emerge some day in the form of unscheduled software updates. "We seeded twenty mice last week. Five each from four batches. None have germinated yet."

"That does seem unlikely." Phineas paused his finger tapping. "What's changed? What corners did you cut?"

"I didn't cut corners. I did everything the same way as always. We've just never had a zero success rate in any batch."

Phineas frowned as the gears in his brain gnashed against each other. He headed to the auxiliary greenhouse, a glass-roofed section of the building dedicated to small-scale pharmacological horticulture.

The warm, moist air immediately calmed him, and for an instant he was transported to the tropics. The greenhouse was small, but it was packed with every variety of pharmacologically active plant, from conventional herbs to traditional Ayurveda and Chinese species. Vines coated the interior wall, and the topmost leaves of a few large trees tickled the clear glass ceiling at the far end. In the middle of the room was a table dedicated to Logan's current MVP: *A. thaliana miltoni*.

They were all yellow.

CHAPTER 30

The global extinction of eye plants was swift and absolute. Their sudden demise bore none of the hallmarks of a pathogen spreading from lab to lab: It was more like a selective asteroid colliding with the planet and immediately devastating a single species. Eye plants across the globe simultaneously fell ill. Scientists scrambled to save the plants by injecting antibiotics, supplementing nutrients, increasing radiation, decreasing moisture, expressing the good genes and silencing the bad ones. Nothing alleviated the wilting. Just before the researchers collapsed from exhaustion, the last of their *miltoni* plants spread roots in that great flower box in the sky. Their seeds refused to germinate. Their tissues rejected cloning. Their vital juices dried up, stunning scientists, delighting hippies, and crushing business owners who thought they'd struck gold.

Life in Greene County heaved when the plants vanished. Phineas ceased his efforts on *miltoni*-based regenerative medicine, focusing instead on bringing the eye plants to flourish once again. He suspended a number of slightly sick but technically living eye plants in liquid nitrogen, waiting for the day when he could thaw them back to life. Amelia similarly refocused on more conventional plant genetics. She gained public recognition through talk show appearances, and she parlayed her fame into a role as science correspondent for a cable news station. Beatrice scrambled to keep her flower shop afloat, ferociously refunding pre-payments for eye-rabidopsis plants and renegotiating contracts and loans. She'd re-invested profits as they came in, and was nearing the end of her modest cash reserves. With Beatrice too focused on flower sales to worry about the details of the bakery, Charlie reverted the Fat BB's menu back to pre-eye-plant cake days, eliminating the gourmet free-range bean coffees and counter-top biscotti. He rarely saw Beatrice, their relationship having ended with hard feelings on both sides.

The disappearance of the world's eye plants oddly comforted him. Instead of feeling alone in his loss, Charlie drew a sick sort of delight from knowing that others were pained by the eye plants' death. The sheer outpouring of grief from people mourning the passing of this agricultural menace gave him newfound faith in humanity; but like a mother weeping as her murderous son falls from the gallows, he occupied a private pit in the blackest sorrow.

Weeks after the last eye plant disappeared, the baker stood barefoot on his wet patio, sipping coffee from a mug that read *Priority One Car Wash* and contemplating the empty corner of the yard. Just last spring, a solitary eyeball stared at him from that same patch of grass. He visited the spot daily for weeks, until the plant that called it home suddenly vanished, leaving a crater in its wake. Now, the divot that replaced the plant blended back into the earth, its walls crumbling and its floor carpeted with crabgrass and clover.

He pulled the wormy-smelling morning air into his nostrils. He wasn't sure that the smell was the worms themselves, but on damp days like this when worms crawl on the pavement, it's easy to imagine that the stench of decay permeating the air comes from the innards of squashed annelids. He considered his position now – on the patio, and in life – wondering whether he'd moved at all in the last year. The entire ride was an acid trip, and the only solid proof that any of it really happened was Beatrice's former pickup truck sitting in his driveway.

He longed to turn this into a positive experience, a learning opportunity, a chance for growth. Surely there was more to be gained from recent events than a few soufflé recipes and a cursory knowledge of *RNA-seek*. Before finding the plant, he'd given little thought to botany at all. Time spent at the flower shop enlightened him to the diversity of form in the plant kingdom and endowed him with an appreciation for agriculture.

He decided to start a vegetable garden, if it wasn't too late in the season. He'd need supplies: a shovel, compost, seeds, maybe some pots.

Yes, pots, he thought. *That's the first thing.* Tearing his gaze from the grass, he headed into the house. The one pot he owned sat on the window sill, still holding the dead eye plant in a clump of dry soil.

He picked up the pot, its saucer, and a piece of paper that he'd put beneath it to prevent water rings on the window sill. He dumped the plant and its hard soil into the trash can with a loud *whump!* and threw the paper after it. As the paper fluttered onto the trash heap, he recognized it as the brochure that the shoe-less bum Tidman gave him on the university quad. Its cover was adorned with a drawing of three people in lab coats, grinning menacingly over a globe, their warlock arms outstretched to summon demons. Above them, the brochure's title boldly declared: *Thankless Foul Science Cowards Cause Doom!*

Charlie vaguely remembered Tidman speaking this warning. He pulled the pamphlet from the trash and skimmed its ranting contents, pausing when he reached a footnote that cited the brochure's title as *Hamlet 3.2.91*. It seemed an odd reference, as Charlie had no recollection of scientists in Middle Age Denmark. He set the pot aside and diverted himself to another quest, looking up the play on his tablet and reading through the Danish prince's celebrated soliloquy in the second scene of Act III. Skimming past the bare bodkins and mortal coils, he arrived at the referenced line: *Thus conscience does make cowards of us all.*

He knew these words. He remembered repeating them to himself over and over again the night that things fell apart with Beatrice. The same words were written on the church sign that night and drilled themselves into his brain – but why were they cited here, in the bum's pamphlet? And what did they have to do with foul science cowards? He located a pen and paper and wrote both phrases.

THUSCONSCIENCEDOESMAKECOWARDSOFUSALL
THANKLESSFOULSCIENCECOWARDSCAUSEDOOM

They were perfect anagrams. The nonsensical babbling of the barefoot bum Tidman was just anagrammed Shakespeare. His words had hidden meaning – like the sequences encoded in the plant's DNA – and whoever controlled the church's sign held the key to decrypting this nonsense.

Charlie grabbed his socks and ran out the door.

———————————⊸○⟜⟜○⊸———————————

Soon thereafter, the baker zipped along the wet streets of Milton, trying not to think about the mashed-up worm guts in the spray misting his face from his bike tires. His backpack held a bartering chip, a bribe: an unworn pair of socks that Beatrice gave him months ago. He was on a mission to extract the truth about the plant once and for all, directly from the source.

He pulled up to the church, stashed his bike behind some bushes, and approached the building's double doors.

Locked.

He pounded on the church door with his fist, invoking his best impression of a tough cop or gangland thug. He longed for a small piece of gum to chew nervously as he waited for a reply. Cops on television were always nervously chewing gum. Were they all trying to quit smoking?

The door opened, revealing Tidman Lukenpweet, former protégé of Phineas Snodgrass and current derelict of Milton, wearing a multi-colored woven poncho and frayed corduroy pants. "Baker!" he said, immediately recognizing Charlie.

Charlie felt like he'd won a game of bingo at the rec center on a Friday night: This was a small victory, but he questioned what he was doing there in the first place. "Is this your church?"

"Maybe. Does the church belong to the man, or the man to the church? I, for one, think it's the latter, as a community requires multiple members. My friend Phineas Egglestein, on the other hand, sees it differently." He stared at the clouds momentarily, and then snapped back. "Now, to what do I owe the pleasure of this visit? I do hope that you haven't come here seeking salvation or wanting to better your relationship with the divine. Many people see the facade of this place and wrongly conclude that it offers some type of answers that it doesn't actually offer."

"I brought you these." Charlie pulled the socks from his knapsack and handed them to Tidman. The little cardboard hanger was still attached to them. "I thought you could use them."

"Argyles! Lovely! Thank you!" Tidman sniffed the socks.

His tithe paid, Charlie petitioned the preacher: "*Thankless foul science cowards cause doom.*"

"Indeed, they do! The Bard said so himself."

"Close. What Shakespeare said was, *Thus conscience does make cowards of us all.* Those exact same words were written on this church sign a few weeks ago. I know it was you who hid the message in the plant's DNA."

"Plant?"

"The one with the eye."

"What message? You mean that Wordsworth poem? He's an entirely different fellow from Shakespeare."

Charlie wondered where Tidman fell on the spectrum of human intelligence. Certainly he was once a genius, but had his mind deteriorated? The baker attempted another angle: "Last summer, you came to the bakery and predicted that the plants would take over the world."

"Yes! And they did! Almost."

"How'd you know that?"

"They just seemed like the type of plants that would do that."

"No, they didn't! Those plants could've given the world great medicines. Dr. Snodgrass was using them to cure blindness."

"Phineas has a single aim in life – to save humanity, regardless of the cost to Nature. He's too bent on curing diseases to see the bigger picture."

"What, that the plants would go wild and suddenly die? Even Professor Wigglesworth didn't predict that, and she knows more about the plant than anybody."

"She's only focused on discovery. These intellectuals can't accept anything but what they read in journal articles. Their problem is that they don't understand Nature."

"And you do?"

"Yes, baker." The bum studied his new socks. "I'm afraid this gift is too nice to accept. Let me offer you something in return." He pulled open the church's heavy wooden door and led Charlie into the dark atrium.

Once the door closed behind them, Tidman giggled softly and opened the door to the sanctuary. The church interior, illuminated by the morning sun shining through the clear glass roof, glowed like a Midwestern prairie in summer. It was a greenhouse. Its floor was covered with wooden benches set with an orderly array of plastic drink bottles, each neatly cut to two inches' height. Each bottle held a handful of soil and a single eager-looking eye plant.

"My congregation!" Tidman declared, arms held wide, ready to embrace the crowd of plants before him. "They follow my every move!" He slowly danced up the aisle, bobbing side to side, up and down. The plants turned, fixing their gaze upon him, following his rhythmic undulations. "They love this poncho! I picked it up in Belize during a surfing tour in my earlier years. Who knew it would prove so valuable in a later calling?"

A wave crashed over Charlie. He gasped, not knowing which way was up. His precious plant was back – or, had never gone. "They're alive," he whispered.

"Of course they're alive: They have faith." The bum twirled in the aisle, arms outstretched. "Isn't it beautiful? I knew that you'd appreciate them. They're my family. They saved my soul, and I theirs." He spun and danced his way up the aisle until he reached the tabernacle near the altar. "The choir's a little bit quiet, but it's otherwise a wonderful flock."

"How did you keep them alive?" Charlie asked, following Tidman up the aisle. He was awed by the sight. Even Professor Wigglesworth couldn't figure out how to keep the plants alive, yet here he was, surrounded by them.

"Who knows what keeps anything alive? In the eighteenth century, King Gustav III of Sweden gave a man the gift of immortality through coffee." Tidman pulled two ceramic mugs from the tabernacle. These he filled with coffee from a percolator that stood in place of a holy water urn. "He forced a prisoner to drink nothing but coffee. The prisoner outlived the king and – according to a friend of mine who works the night shift for the Swedish department of corrections – still lives in an isolated tower of the prison, refusing to drink anything but coffee." He handed a cup of the hot liquid to Charlie before boosting himself limberly to a seat on the altar. He sipped deeply from his mug, savoring the drink with eyes closed. "I've been growing these plants in here for three years now."

"Three years? But they've only been around since last summer." Charlie's movements caught the attention of some of the plants. He picked one up and inspected it, finding it in great health. "Did you create them?"

"And what if I did?" Tidman leaned forward with wide eyes and a broad grin. "Wouldn't that kill some of the magic surrounding them? Personally, I rather like the popular origin legend that has the plant emerging from the loam of that veritable Eden that is your back yard, like Athena from the skull of Zeus. No, I didn't create them. Much like you, I found one – right in front of this church. But unlike you, I didn't go running to tell Teacher. I brought it inside and nurtured it, and loved it, and lived with it, and learned from it."

"And you never told anyone?"

"Why would I? People ruin everything."

Charlie agreed. "Then you don't know where it came from?" He dipped a lip into his coffee, finding it surprisingly delicious, with a mellow chocolate-y finish that shamed the bakery's trendy offerings.

"Who said that? It came from Georgia." Tidman then launched into the tale of the plant's origins: "One day a few years back I received a single plant in a package that I wasn't expecting. It was from a private laboratory in Georgia. I called the lab to ask whether there was a mix-up, and they assured me that the plant was sent to fulfill an online order that I'd placed – except I hadn't placed any such order. I'd never even heard of the lab before. I assumed the rightful owner would come looking for the plant. I kept it alive with water and light – at that time it was just a tiny mat of leaves – and went about my business.

"When the plant sprouted an eye, I contacted the lab again and asked them just what they sent me. They told me that the plant I received was created by genetically modifying other plants that *I* shipped to them, using very specific protocols that *I* gave them – except I never shipped them any plants or provided them any protocols. When pressed, they told me that they received the plants directly from private labs in India and the UK, as I allegedly requested in some online order that I never actually placed."

"Weird," said Charlie.

"It gets weirder. I next contacted the labs in India and England. They gave me similar stories about protocols and plants that I allegedly provided to them – but which I…"

"…never actually provided to them."

"Exactly. They received their plants from labs in Singapore and Ukraine and California, who all told similar stories. Eventually I lost the trail, but it's clear that the eye plant I received was pieced together through a long series of gene editing procedures at different labs all over the world. Each lab received a plant by mail, edited a handful of its genes, and sent the next version to another lab – like a chain letter. None of them could repeat the whole process."

"Nobody at the labs questioned where the materials were coming from, or why they were altering the plant like this?" Charlie sipped from his mug again. Man, this was *really* good coffee.

"Why would they? They received clear instructions on the electronic orders, and they obeyed them. We're used to doing whatever computers tell us to do. They give us driving directions and career advice. Computers tell us which shows to watch, which food to eat, and which person to marry. When a computer gives an order, a human will execute it without question."

"But if *you* didn't create the plant, then who did? Who sent it to you?" asked Charlie, gesturing toward the sea of eyeballs.

"Exactly," said Tidman. "That was exactly my question for a long time: Who designed this? And why did they assemble it in such a convoluted way? What were their intentions? For the longest time I didn't know." He rubbed his beard. "Then, last year, a bird found its way into this place – made a mess of it, to be honest. Shortly thereafter, Amelia stunned the world with the fantastic little plant that she said popped up in someone's back yard."

Charlie's view of the plants surrounding him shifted. They were no longer the descendants of his plant, as he previously thought, but its ancestors – its brethren. Somewhere in that crowd, in the remnants of plastic drink bottles, his plant's mother and siblings grew. Anything special about his plant was inherited from the savanna within this church.

The bum continued: "Immediately the world fell in love with your plant, and the scientists did their thing. I followed their developments closely, curious about the plant's origins and history. I thought for sure that some credible source would step forward and claim it, but then I realized that its inventor's signature was written all over it. The website roused my suspicions, and the GPL confirmed them."

"Who invented it?"

"Who would put so much effort into making an open-source genome? It would have to be some intelligence that is both brilliant beyond comprehension and idiotic. And there is only one source that can be so smart and yet so dumb."

"Politicians?"

"Computers."

"Computers?"

"They're too stupid to know better," said Tidman. "For instance, how many times has a computer told you, 'Please wait. System processing'? Not, 'Please wait, *the* system *is* processing,' or 'Please wait, *I*, the system, *am* processing,' but 'Please wait. System processing,' as if the damn machine was raised by wolves. And the plant, I suspect, is just another example of computers being too stupid to know what's right in front of them. Don't you see where we are, baker? Humanity has given birth to an entirely new form of intelligence, which has honored its creators with this gift – this plant."

The baker felt a glimmer of the excitement that he'd experienced on that spring morning, barefoot on the lawn. He was on the precipice of something magnificent. This was his chance to give the plant to the world again – not simply as a curiosity that could be turned into a profit, but as a gift from a sentient intelligence. "They did it to help us," he said. "They somehow knew that we could benefit from the eye plant. You should let people know about this – let them know that the computers created it, and that it still survives."

"What, and have them come and destroy it? Are you mad? You saw how people treated this plant. They exploited it, and when it got out of hand, we all ran to our computers for help handling it. They fixed it for us. They killed them all."

"But not the ones in this church. We have a second chance. People know that we lost something valuable. We can make it right."

"Do you really believe that? Do you believe that people ever learn anything?"

Charlie saw that there was no point in arguing, that Tidman would not be swayed. It was a shame, too, because the entire world was missing out. It wasn't just that the plant was beautiful and curious – it was a gateway to new medicines that could help people regain sight, recover from paralysis, grow new limbs. Better yet, it was a message from another intelligence – a higher intelligence, or a higher manifestation of our own intelligence. Losing the plants was tragic, but the greater tragedy was passing up the chance to bring them back. Charlie would not deny them their resurrection.

The computers wasted postage when they shipped the plant to the eccentric bum Tidman. Only after the plant arrived in Charlie's yard was its message relayed to all of humanity. Tidman may have figured out the plant's meaning, but he couldn't be trusted to convey it to the rest of the world. For that, the plant required someone who not only recognized its innate beauty, but who trusted humanity enough to deliver its message.

Charlie looked at the field before him. He considered the tragedy of the entire species winding up stuffed together in this room, when they could be growing freely – and saving lives. Humanity, contacted by another intelligence, was too self-absorbed to notice. In a moment of shameless self-importance, he dropped his mug onto the church's marble floor, where it shattered.

"I'm so sorry about that," he said, squatting down to clean the mug's shards from the floor. "Maybe I should go." He handed the remains to his host.

Tidman politely dismissed the infraction and saw Charlie to the door, not even noticing that the baker slipped an eye plant into his backpack during the commotion.

CHAPTER 31

Charlie set foot in the flower shop for the first time in a month, and it felt as foreign to him now as it had before he met Beatrice. Over the past year he grew familiar with its layout, down to the details of where the squeaky spots in the floor hid – yet he couldn't shake the distinct feeling that he no longer belonged within its walls. Shelves that just weeks ago overflowed with eye-rabidopsis plants now held an assortment of antique wares for the country home: tea pots, coffee grinders, watering cans, a complete set of Fishman China Company pie birds.

Beatrice, who was attending to a customer at the sales counter, hurried to greet her unexpected guest at the door. "Charlie," she said, her voice ringing a chord of surprise, disappointment, and maybe underneath it all, a hint of delight.

"Hi, Beatrice." He forced a smile. Everything he said to her now sounded contrite, despite his best efforts to be casual. They both understood that occupying the same small town would bring them into occasional contact, and they agreed that the death of their romance didn't force them to be hostile.

"You look well," she replied. It was one of those things that people say to people who don't look well at all; or, at least, who don't look as well as the person saying it. Beatrice, for her part, looked fantastic as ever. She wore a bright summer dress that agreed with her short hair and accentuated her girlish look.

"Thanks, so do you," he said, and he meant it. "How's business?"

"Slow. I have to refund a lot of pre-orders, and without eye-rabidopsis to draw customers in, sales of our other merchandise have tanked." She looked at him seriously. "The bills keep coming in, but there's hardly any revenue."

Charlie spotted the cat toy wedged between a couple of pots on a shelf. "Hey, where's Lulu?" he asked.

"Lulu? I don't know. Maybe she's in the back. Anyway, I'm glad you stopped by. Business isn't good, and I'm afraid I have to make a difficult decision…"

Charlie shook the stick on the cat toy, causing the bell to tinkle. "You know that shoe-less bum I told you about, who gave me the sober pills in the cemetery? Did you know he lives in that church on top of the hill?"

"That's great, Charlie. So I'm in this tough financial position…"

"You know what he's got in there?"

"Dead bodies? I don't care. Charlie, I'm trying to tell you something here." She seemed offended.

Odd, I thought I was the one who called this meeting. "Yes," he said, "difficult decision. Sorry. What is it?" He continued to twitch the toy off to the side, hoping to attract the cat to the ringing bell.

"I'm selling the bakery to Frank Chan. I need the capital to pay back the deposits." She motioned toward the customer sitting at the counter, who turned toward Charlie with a disinterested look. It was Frank himself.

"So you're just going to sell one of town's most beloved and long-standing institutions to someone who'll pick it apart? Why not let me buy it?" As Charlie said this, the cat crept along the wall, stalking the toy that he twitched. She stopped behind a ficus and watched the movement of the dope-filled blue bird.

"Because you can't afford it," Beatrice said, "and you're a terrible businessman."

"Yeah, that's true." Charlie could've been a decent businessman, had he cared a lick about business. It seemed like nothing but filling out spreadsheets and claiming your customers are getting a great deal while your vendors are robbing you. Where's the joy in that? "But Frank? You couldn't find a better buyer? And what the hell am I supposed to do when he turns the place into some godawful franchise?"

"I'm sure he'll give you a job. He might even let you design the menu for a whole chain of restaurants."

"Great. *Sell-Out Charlie's House of Eye-Plant Cakes.* I'm glad I came by here today. It's been a real pick-me-up."

Lulu pounced, setting the bird-on-a-string spinning. Charlie pulled the toy out of the cat's reach and placed it back on the shelf. The cat hardly noticed and seemed just as pleased to weave herself between Charlie's ankles.

"Why did you come in here, anyway?" asked Beatrice. She was somewhere between hurt and annoyed.

"I missed Lulu," he answered, scooping up the cat and cradling her in one arm.

"Oh, come on, Charlie."

"No, seriously. I kind of got to like that cat over time, and I missed her. You didn't think I missed you, did you? That'd be the day."

"Charlie, why do you have to be like this?"

"Like what?" he asked, feigning bewilderment. "I've been thinking of opening a cat café, and Lulu here's my inspiration."

"Charlie…"

"I know what you're thinking: *A cat café? Really?* Yes, really. It'd be better than selling my soul to Frank."

"Charlie…"

"*Beatrice…*"

"Why do you have to be such a jerk?"

"I'm not being a jerk," he said. But he was, and he knew it. He still hurt from losing her. Every night since their fight, he replayed the tape in his head, trying to figure out how things went from a simple disagreement to broken hearts. It was probably his fault, he knew. Seeing her now reminded him of how he dreamed things would have been, spoiling the reality of how they turned out. And it didn't help that she was doing so well. The least she could do was share in his discomfort.

"Listen," she said, "I'm sorry that your plant died. I know how much it meant to you."

"I'm sorry if I'm being rude," he said. "It's just that nobody seemed to care about this plant until they couldn't benefit from it. Snodgrass, Wigglesworth, ..."

"You," said Beatrice.

"Me?"

"Remember how we met? Your little video at the party we catered? You led the charge in exploiting this plant for selfish reasons. Don't forget that, Charlie Bishop."

Charlie tore open his backpack and pulled out a slightly disheveled eye plant in a cut-off plastic bottle. He thrust it at Beatrice. "This is what's in that church. Thousands of these. Look familiar? Maybe they'll help your business." Pointing to Frank, he said, "Maybe they'll help his son. They're sure as hell useless to me now."

<hr />

That evening, Ruthie sat on the counter in Fat BB's darkened store front, chewing her thumb nail and swinging her legs lazily. Charlie sat on the squeaky office chair near the empty display cases, one side of his face illuminated by the fluorescent light from the kitchen. Throughout the vacant store front echoed the sounds of the radio, which – according to the station's self-assessment – was cranking out the best hits of the last three decades. That particular radio had perched on the bakery's shelf for close to five decades and would beg to differ on which hits were *best*, but nobody ever asks the radio's opinion.

Fat BB's was closed for good. Frank paid cash for the place that afternoon in the flower shop, and he intended to strip it clean in the morning. Neither Charlie nor Ruthie mentioned this to the customers, preferring to work a normal shift and then never return – always leave 'em wanting more, as the saying goes. Ruthie claimed she'd cry if she said goodbye to the regulars, and Charlie suspected that he would, too. At the end of the day, they locked the door and shut off the lights as usual, but instead of preparing for the next day, they lingered in search of memories.

"I'm gonna miss this place," said Ruthie, eyeing the photos and newspaper clippings that lined the wall behind the counter. She took a swig from her own memory – a bottle of tequila that she stashed behind the sink months ago. Now seemed as good a time as any to polish it off.

"We made a lot of damn good cakes here," agreed Charlie. He was flipping through a binder of cake photographs. The early pages were filled with images of the traditional cakes that he baked when he first started working at Fat BB's. He'd already leafed past these and the more sophisticated variations on themes that marked his mid-career years. Now he was browsing photos of his most recent cakes – the custom orders that he created after winning best-in-state: *Ode to Soy*, *A Midsummer Light Cream*, *Meringue of La Mancha*. He turned the page and was greeted with a photo of himself, standing with Beatrice in front of the *Nataraja* cake he sculpted for Frank's party.

Ruthie saw him staring at the photo, stuck on it. She took a swig from her bottle. "I have a confession to make, Chuck."

"You're the one who's been leaving underwear in my mailbox?"

"What? Eeew! I'm serious here." She gnawed a bit of cuticle on her thumb. "I never got arrested for stealing turkeys. I made up the whole thing to get you and Bea together. I mean, I didn't make up the *whole* thing: The theremin part was true, and going to the farm for dinner and moonshine. And stealing turkeys." She spat a piece of nail onto the floor. "But we didn't get *caught*. We got away with the turkeys, but then stayed and chilled for the rest of the night. I just came up with the jail story because I figured that you'd cater that party with Bea, and maybe the two of you'd hit it off. I didn't mean to get your heart broken."

Charlie stood and walked to the counter where Ruthie sat. He splashed some tequila into his paper cup and swirled it gently. "Ruthie, you had no way of knowing that would happen. Besides, I should thank you for doing it. I had a blast." He raised the cup in a half-hearted toast and drank the shot. "I have a confession, too," he coughed. "I never wanted Soufflé Days – I just made it up to distract you. It was the day that I found the plant. I was going to show you a video of it, and then I had second thoughts, but you wouldn't leave me alone. I panicked and made up Soufflé Days to cover."

"You loser." She kicked him.

"I know, but you were really good at it...seriously." He smiled at her. "I guess we both lied with good intentions, but in the end we both lost out. Beatrice and I split up, and your soufflé days are over."

"The hell they are! I'm gonna sell 'em out at the farm. People love my soufflés out there." She finished the contents of the bottle and hopped off the counter. "If you decide to open your own place, let me know. I'll come work for you." She threw her arms around his neck and squeezed him in a way that jabbed some sharp corner of her earring into his jaw. To Charlie, Ruthie was yellow sheet cake. She was ordinary and uncannily comforting; unimpressive but constant. Life without her would be foreign and not nearly as sweet. Ruthie felt exactly the same way about Charlie. The moment was yellow sheet cake. Yellow sheet cake with a muddy sneaker in it. "Chuck," she said, "I know you're thinking about grabbing my ass."

He released her. "I'm gonna miss you, too." He pushed her toward the door and took a pink Fat BB's box from the counter.

CHAPTER 32

For the first night in weeks, Beatrice slept deeply, comfortably, her slumber filled with pleasant visions of prosperity and happiness. Upon waking, the fragments of her dreams drifted occasionally into her perception. There was the strong image of Frank lifting an enormous conch shell from her back, allowing her to float into the sky. In another vision, she recalled finding a hidden store-within-a-store, a wholly different Rose's, accessible by secret passageway and filled with baby blue pots of money. She awoke refreshed, and tackled the workday like a circus elephant charging an abusive ringmaster.

The previous day, she unloaded the burdensome bakery and initiated the revival of her eye-rabidopsis business. Financial ruin no longer loomed over her, thanks to Frank's influx of cash and Charlie's eye plant donation. In her slumber, she mapped out a path back to financial glory. She'd pay down what debt she could with the money from Frank and nurture the plant until it produced seeds. Once the next generation sprouted, she'd be back in business selling eye-rabidopsis – only this time, she wouldn't take pre-orders.

When she arrived at Rose's, she found a pink Fat BB's box sitting on the counter. On top of the box was taped a note:

> *Beatrice,*
> *Maybe we'll meet sometime on Porquerolles Island. Until*
> *then, build something wonderful.*
> *Love,*

Charlie

Making a mental note to get the shop's key back from Charlie, she lifted the top flap of the box and bent it back on the crease. Inside, where she expected to find another cake, sat an exquisitely golden-brown apple pie. Right in the center of that apple pie, looking up with puckered mouth, as if leaning in for a kiss, was a small token of appreciation that Mrs. Wigner had willed to Charlie: a red and yellow 1937 Johnstone pie bird.

Just as Beatrice was admiring the pie and its avian centerpiece, Phineas Snodgrass marched through the door and directly to the counter. "Frank tells me you have a viable *miltoni* specimen," he said. "I want to see it."

"Frank told you that?" Beatrice closed the box and placed it under the counter.

"I'm in a bit of a hurry, and my time is extremely valuable, so if you don't mind not making me repeat myself, it will help."

"It's just that he said he'd keep it secret."

"Clearly he didn't. I'm sure you'll get over it. Now, do you have the plant or not?"

"No." Beatrice hadn't spoken with Phineas since the failed negotiations in Charlie's yard the previous summer. She wasn't about to let him get away so easily now. Logan had a ton of money and stood to gain another ton from the plant.

"I highly doubt that. Although Frank may not respect you, he holds me in quite high regard. He said that just yesterday he saw one here with his own eyes. Why would he lie about that? I could use it to cure his son."

"George?"

"My company was on the verge of a breakthrough therapy when the *miltoni* suddenly vanished. They're impossible to get now. None of the reputable labs have any survivors, and anyone who claims to have one is a fraud." He eyed her suspiciously. "If Frank hadn't seen it himself, I wouldn't believe that you have one, either. I'm prepared to pay quite handsomely for a specimen in good health."

"Seven figures handsomely?" Beatrice asked.

Phineas's eyebrows hit his high hairline. "May I see the plant?"

She led him to the climate-controlled glass case where she stashed the plant the previous evening. Grabbing the soil-filled plastic bottle from the shelf, she gasped. The plant wore the color of ripe bananas. The leaves that were bursting with deep green vitality the previous day were now withered and yellow. Even its eye, which just last night sparkled in piercing blue, had dimmed.

"Clearly, this is some sort of sick joke," Phineas said, shifting his scowl from plant to florist and back again.

"No, no, no! It was alive yesterday!" Beatrice said, cradling a limp leaf on her fingertip.

"Mmm-hmm. You do know you have to provide them with a tolerable environment, right? Light, moisture, that sort of thing."

"I know how to keep plants alive," Beatrice snapped.

"The evidence indicates the contrary. Your negligence has sentenced a young man to a lifetime of anguish. I hope you're proud." the scientist headed toward the door.

Beatrice considered this statement. She had the chance to help George, and she failed him – just like she let down Charlie, and her customers, and her own bright future selling eye-rabidopsis. "Wait!" she called to Phineas, "I know where there are more!"

------------—∞◦◯◦∞—------------

The silver-haired scientist stood beside the florist at the doorway of the church, prepared to meet his student-turned-nemesis. After his abrupt departure from Logan Biotech, Tidman disappeared entirely for several years before returning to Milton in his current haggard form. He established a reputation for rummaging through trash cans and preaching discalced on the university quad – and for administering natural elixirs that suspiciously resembled the patented pharmaceuticals of Logan Biotech. Although Phineas remained on the lookout for his former student, he never actively sought him, until now. By Phineas's calculation, Tidman owed him untold piles of money for damages sustained from the distribution of counterfeit medication. Phineas was there to collect.

"If your story is true," he said to Beatrice, "then I expect we'll have no problem obtaining additional *miltoni* plants. The man you described as inhabiting this place is my former student. He's quite…eccentric, but I know how to talk to him." He rapped his knuckles on the heavy church door.

The door opened and Tidman's shaggy mug squinted out from the darkness within. "Phineas! What a surprise!"

The businessman looked Tidman up and down. "I've heard stories about your descent into filth and madness, but none of my imaginings fully prepared me for this moment. I finally get to view with my own eyes how absolutely astounding your transformation was."

Tidman looked at his bare feet, then proudly back at Phineas.

"Tell me," Phineas continued, "in the time since last we spoke, did you lose all capacity for logical reason, or just your sense of smell and your ability to function in society?"

"Time has dulled my wits no less than it has your tongue," offered Tidman, shaking a finger at his old mentor.

"Then perhaps your wits will serve to entertain you during your imminent incarceration."

"What crime have I committed, other than distribute salvation in a worthless pill?"

"As that worthless pill was not yours to dispense, your crime is theft."

"And yet I took nothing from you – and if nothing was taken, then no theft has occurred. Should you seek to press charges, look for those souls to whom I dispensed the pills. They're the ones who *took* it."

"Perhaps you *took* nothing from me, but you *mistook* something about me: That I am a fool who will suffer a greater fool speaking nonsense from a church."

"Then you admit I am greater than you! The student has surpassed his master!"

Beatrice heard enough. "Are you both insane?" she asked.

"Who knows?" said Tidman.

"No!" cried Phineas. "You may have deceived this town with your little charade, but I know for certain that you're no mad man."

Tidman seemed positively moved. "Thank you, Phineas," he said. "That's the nicest thing that anyone has said to me in a long time." He threw his arms around Phineas and latched onto the old man like a baby orangutan.

Phineas threw him off, "Knock it off, Tidman!"

"We have so much catching up to do! Would you like some coffee?"

"We're here for the plants."

"Plants? Ah...the baker. I should've known he wouldn't keep a lid on this. I can't blame him, really – he's very fond of the sweet things."

"Yes, the baker," said Beatrice. "He gave me an eye-rabidopsis that he said came from this place."

"Ah! Then *he's* the thief, right, Phineas?"

"I'm afraid he lifted an unhealthy specimen," said Phineas. "Either that, or the florist here can't care for a plant – which is entirely possible."

"It died, didn't it?" asked Tidman. "They all do, outside the church."

"What the hell are you talking about?"

"The plants can't survive outside the church. There's something about the place – lingering stench of incense, presence of an omniscient deity, what have you – something keeps them alive. As far as I know, this is the only place in the world where they can still live."

"That's preposterous."

"Is it? I welcome you to investigate for yourself; prove me wrong. It's been such a long time since I qualified to meet your academic standards for what a scientist is...maybe I've forgotten the difference between living and dead."

Although a cunning businessman and a prolific innovator, Phineas Snodgrass remained a scientist at heart. He had his hypothesis about how Tidman's stock remained unscathed, and he designed an experiment to test it. "Permit me to select a few specimens from your collection," he told Tidman, "and I'll prove you wrong."

"A welcome challenge," said Tidman. He led Phineas and Beatrice into the sea of eye-rabidopsis that blanketed the floor of his church.

———— ∽o⌘o∾ ————

"*Miltoni*," said Phineas. "Thousands of them. Tens of thousands, even." He was seated on a leather arm chair in Frank's lavish study, swirling a snifter of Cognac.

"The eye plants?" asked Frank. "In the church?"

"It's like a greenhouse in there."

"How did he keep them alive?"

"I have no idea," Phineas admitted. He sipped his drink. It wasn't the good stuff that Frank usually served, but it warmed the atmosphere.

Two days prior, at the church, Phineas selected four *miltoni* plants from Tidman's forest. He placed one behind some bushes along the building and another in the shrubs at the base of the church sign. He brought the other two plants to Logan Biotech.

The next morning, Phineas arrived at work to find his two *miltoni* plants looking as if they'd just been regurgitated by a sick dog, their half-dead eyes drooping lazily against their recycled plastic containers. He witnessed a similar scene beneath the church's sign, where the plant he left the previous day now wore the color of a fish won at a carnival, two days after the carnival. The plant he'd left beside the church wall was in perfect health and stared at him wide-eyed as a child on Christmas morning.

He placed one of the dog vomit-colored plants next to it and hid another along the church's back wall. He then went home and slept the peaceful sleep of those who just exposed priceless and critically endangered plants to the elements and curious passers-by.

In the morning, the plants next to the church looked happier than ever, their eyes bright as toddlers' during story time. The one under the church sign was dead.

It was clear to Phineas that Tidman spoke the truth, and the plants would only live inside the church, or just outside its walls. He already formed a few ideas about how the church protected the plants – a geographic or electromagnetic anomaly, or gas emanating from the sinking foundation. He never considered that the plants were kept alive by the signal from Tidman's Wi-Fi toaster, constantly pinging the ether for signs of a piece of sliced white bread that could benefit from a little crunch. But this didn't matter, in the end.

"This might be good news for your company," said Frank, tilting his glass toward Phineas. "Maybe it won't go the way of the bakery after all." His talk of going public with George's story seemed like a lot of noise to Phineas, at first. In the past, he made threats like this to stimulate productivity. The current situation was different because George gave Frank a personal stake in the game, and Phineas no longer possessed the key resource he needed for success: the plant. When Frank mercilessly shuttered one of town's oldest and most beloved establishments, Phineas recognized the true urgency of the situation.

"That's what brings me here tonight," said Phineas. "These plants will allow us to move forward with George's therapy." He chose his words carefully: Frank handled being misled just as poorly as he handled losing money.

"Great! Let's fix him up, Phin. The boy's miserable. He's constantly scratching his ass – shoving things up there. It's disgusting. We've tried medicating him, but he doesn't trust me."

"We'll do everything we can to quickly resolve the situation, but we want to make sure that we don't make things worse."

"Worse? The other day I found him rubbing the bottoms of his feet with a saw blade. He said it helped the itch. There was blood all over the goddamned work shop. Can't get much worse than that."

"The plants will only live inside the church. I have yet to figure out why. I've tried transferring them to the lab, and they just die – but there is some hope." He sipped his brandy. "We may be able to perform the procedure in the church, and keep George there until the eye has fully developed. I'm testing on mice right now. If we succeed, we'll try it on George."

"How long?"

"We'll know whether the procedure works in a few weeks. Then George may have to live at the church for a couple of months while his new eye grows. If everything works out, he'll not only get a working eye, but it'll cure him of any allergic reaction that he had to the last one."

As Phineas explained this, Frank's gaze wandered to the door of the study, which silently opened throughout the conversation. George stood in the shadows of the hallway, his feet in bandages. His hair partially obscured the scarlet hollow where his eye once dwelled. The look annoyed Frank to no end. He had repeatedly commanded his son to don an eye patch, but the boy refused – for no other reason, Frank suspected, than to rile his father.

"George!" said Frank, his voice ringing with saccharine for his disappointing child. "Come say hello to Dr. Snodgrass."

George lumbered sullenly into the study and stood before Phineas's chair. He flipped his head defiantly, exposing to Phineas the angry tissue of his mutilated eye socket. "I heard everything you said, asshole," he told Phineas.

Frank stood. "George! Manners!"

The adolescent cyclops held his position and stared at Phineas. His rage further reddened the empty socket. "A fucking *church*? You want me to live in a *fucking church*?"

Phineas said nothing. He understood the lad's passion and admired his spirit. In a way, George reminded him of himself when he was younger. That lack of tolerance for other people's crap might pay dividends in the future.

"George!" called Frank, rushing around the desk. "Enough! Apologize right now!"

George continued to stare at Phineas. "Sorry, asshole. Sorry that you let your own kid die, so now you have to fuck up someone else's."

Frank leapt to the spot where George was standing and swung his arm in a wide arc, laying his open palm across the boy's face. *Crack!* The blow knocked George off balance, and he stumbled into the stuffed bear, jarring the glass eye from its cheek. He righted himself and turned to face his father, hands balled into fists. Frank stood motionless in front of Phineas, teeth clenched, waiting for his son's retaliation.

"Fuck you!" shouted George. "Fuck you both!" He bolted from the study.

Frank straightened his clothes and walked calmly back to the desk. He poured himself another sifter of brandy. "Another splash?" he asked Phineas, who declined. "Well, then," said Frank, slumping into his chair, "a month in the church, you say? Oughta be good for the boy."

Beneath the church's clear glass ceiling, thousands of *miltoni* plants rested their eyes on a clear night, slumbering soundly in their warm nest. They dreamed the dreams that only plants can dream by the light of the stars and streetlights. On the other side of one of the stained-glass windows, a faint blue and orange light flickered in the blackness. It was too dim for the plants to notice, even if they'd been awake. The light became brighter, larger. From a dull bluish speck, it grew into an orange orb, then a bright and dancing yellow glow. It bobbed and grew larger, then paused.

In an instant, the number of bottles in the church increased by one. This new bottle was in mid-air, having just penetrated the church window from outside. Unlike the other bottles, it held not soil and a *miltoni* plant, but yellow liquid and a flaming rag.

The bottle crashed on the floor amid the wooden benches, breaking into shards and spewing orange flames across the church floor and up its walls. The blaze devoured the wooden benches, chewed the ornate antique woodwork and gnawed the colorful tapestries that hung for the entertainment of the *miltoni* field. In a minute, the church was swallowed into the belly of an inferno.

Outside, illuminated by the orange glow of the maelstrom, a slim figure walked briskly away from the conflagration, scratching his backside vigorously. Amid the shattering of glass and popping of wood in the church, the shade's voice filled the air with song: "And you! And you! And you! You're gonna love me!"

CHAPTER 33

Nearly a week into his trip, Charlie found himself at a small-town greasy spoon.

He was serious when he told Ruthie that he was taking time off, and he intended to use his vacation to decide whether he should start his own business or simply accept life as a producer of everyday cakes. He hit the road early in the morning, plotting only a rough southward course to the sea. He drove until he was tired and then stopped for the night at the first friendly-looking town he found. The next morning, he woke up, drove until he was tired again, and stayed in another small town. He repeated this pattern, stringing together small town motels with leisurely day-long drives.

The sign over the establishment where Charlie currently sat read "Jo's Diner," and in the window was taped a sheet of paper reading "Experienced Baker Wanted." The place was cozy as a cup of coffee held in wool mittens. Sitting at the counter, Charlie studied the daily specials written in pastel chalk on a blackboard near the front door.

A slim waitress approached like a ballerina crossing a stage. She placed a menu and a plastic cup filled with icy tap water in front of Charlie. "Good morning, sunshine!" she said. "Coffee?" She held a coffee pot in one hand and an empty mug in the other, waving them both temptingly before Charlie in a tiny dance.

"Please."

"Good choice. I gotta warn ya, though: We only have one kind of coffee here, so don't ask for any of that gourmet stuff." She looked him in the eye as she filled his cup, the hint of a cryptic smile on her face. He felt acutely visible, and loved it. She left Charlie to look over the menu and went back to doing her work behind the counter, humming as she did so. Charlie noticed the conversation coming from the booth behind him. He turned to see a group of white-haired men hunched over their coffee mugs.

"No, the Italian grocery," one man was saying, "it was at the Italian grocery. The one that the midget ran."

"That's not the Italian place," said another. "That was Goldstein's."

"Goldstein? Naw, it couldn't've been him. We never went to the Jewish grocery. Or the Polish one – well, sometimes we'd go to the Polish one. For the bread…"

"Their bread was good," said a third man. "Their rye bread."

"Goldstein wasn't a midget. He was just short."

"That's what a midget is. A short person. But now they like to be called something else…"

"'Little people.' That's the term."

"Little people. I thought that's what a midget was…"

Charlie smiled and turned back to face the counter. He was met by the waitress's soft eyes. "They're our regulars," she said, "and that group's a bunch of kids. There's a three-hundred-year-old Swedish man who comes in here for the coffee."

"He just got out of prison, right?" asked Charlie.

"You know about Gustav III?" asked the waitress, "I'm impressed. You ruined my story, but I'm impressed. I should've known. A guy comes in here wearing a shirt like that, he's got to be smart."

Charlie inspected his attire. He was wearing a blue Hawaiian-style shirt featuring colorful octopuses. It declared boldly to the world that its wearer was on vacation.

"Octopuses are the smartest of the cephalopods," said the waitress, "and cephalopods are pretty smart."

"Not squid," said Charlie, delighted that she didn't say *octopi*.

"Not when you compare them to octopuses and cuttlefish, but a squid can think circles around your average house fly. You know what you want?"

"Pancakes and eggs," said Charlie, "and can you tell me about the Help Wanted sign?"

———————⊸०ᘉᗒ००⊸———————

In a dusty corner of a city on one of the planet's other land masses, a disheveled foreigner meandered through an open-air market. The aroma of exotic spices colored the air, mixing with smoke and the stench of meat hanging on hooks. He wove his way around the vendors' tables, passing baskets of fish pulled from the local rivers and streams, and waving off offers of freshly harvested vegetables. He sought only one item. As he foraged, he tuned out the din of heavy chopping, the clanking of pans and the voices laughing and arguing in a foreign tongue.

Spying his quarry, the foreigner approached a booth and pointed to a jar. "How much for this one?"

"Fi' thousan'," answered the man at the table, pointing to the number written in black marker on a piece of cardboard.

The traveler reached into his bag and pulled out a brand-new argyle sock stuffed full with the local currency. He separated a few wrinkled bills and handed them to the man.

"Sock," said the vendor, pointing to the sock. "Pretty. Pretty sock."

"Thank you. It was a gift from a friend." The traveler took the jar of honey and disappeared into the crowded market. Later, he would feed a drop of this honey to the blue-winged queen bee that he carried in a tiny box around his neck. He wanted her to have a good local meal before he released her into the wild.

This behavior was all part of the traveler's natural repertoire. He was a member of a species that had a knack for moving other species vast distances across the planet, to lands they could otherwise see only by waiting eons for the continents to drift together. His species had been doing this for millennia, making things messy in accordance with scientific law.

Little did he know that the air around him and the ground beneath his bare feet was saturated with a new strain of yeast that contained within its DNA a Message in the form of the recipe for the world's most delicious apple cakes, stolen from the hard drive of the computer in a small town bakery.

www.ingramcontent.com/pod-product-compliance
Lightning Source LLC
Chambersburg PA
CBHW051948220626
47052CB00004B/851